PART THREE

Visions and Dreams

J.L.ROBB

"...On the earth, nations will be in anguish and perplexity at the roaring and tossing of the sea."

Luke 21:25

Cover art and design by: Erica Robb, Yoni Art and Design, www.yoniartanddesign.com

Editing by Jacqueline Poulton and Lynn Thomay

Energy Concepts Productions books may be ordered through booksellers or by contacting:

Energy Concepts Productions
A Division of Energy Concepts
1502 Howell Walk
Duluth, Georgia 30096
1-770-476-0887

ISBN: 978-1-6284-7482-4 (sc)
ISBN: 978-1-6284-7483-1 (hc)
ISBN: 978-1-6284-7481-7 (e)

Printed in the United States of America

Energy Concepts Productions rev. date: 10/01/2013

Note from the Author

THE END The Book series is a fictional account of the predicted apocalypse as outlined in the Bible. Several readers have asked me, "Is this book true?"

It is true that the Biblical end will happen, but I have written this series as a counter-weight to the apocalyptic fiction coming out of Hollywood, like *Armageddon* and *2012*, that fail to mention God and His role. Any similarities between things that are occurring now and things written in this series are purely coincidental. It would be impossible to write a "true" account of the Biblically described End Times.

I hope all readers will find this series thought provoking, as well as thrilling, and might make us think about some of the things we believe and why we believe them.

In Part Three: *Visions and Dreams,* Jeffrey Ross continues his journey of unbelief in a Divinity from one tragedy to another, disaster lurking just moments away. The current world events certainly reminded him of some of the preaching his Mom used to do about the end of the world that was sure to come, soon. She thought that her whole life, but it never happened. But now, he found himself beginning to wonder, and he worried about his dreams. They seemed to often come true, at least the bad ones.

Wars, rumors of *nuclear* wars, disease and plague, famine and drought, crime and violence, the severe storms and earthquakes and a world economy in a tailspin. Not to mention the abundance of meteorites colliding with Earth, unprecedented in human history. Could meteorites be the stars that fell from heaven to Earth that his Mom talked about from *Revelation*?

Glancing up in the night sky, looking at the Moon, now pink with rings, Jeff made a decision. He would dig out that mysterious Gideons Bible that kept appearing and would read *Revelation.* He started it once, but the story was just too unbelievable.

What would you do if you woke up one morning, turned on the news and found out the often-predicted end-of-the-world really *was* near? This time the story was true, and there was no escape. What would you do? Where would you hide? Could you somehow survive; and if so, what then?

I hope you enjoy reading *Visions and Dreams* as much as I enjoyed writing it for you, and for the glory of God, the father of Abraham.

J.L. Robb is an author and free-lance writer with a degree in Zoological Sciences from North Carolina State University. A U.S. Navy veteran and cancer survivor, he lives in the Bible-Belt with his two Great Danes and his kitty named "Glock."

Robb is a member of Civitan International and The American Legion.

WHAT'S HAPPENED SO FAR

PART ONE

Jeffrey Ross is Duluth, Georgia's most eligible bachelor, but not by choice. Retired Navy SEAL and successful entrepreneur, he had been married to Melissa almost 25 years; and he thought everything was hunky-dory. They had beautiful twin daughters and adopted daughter, Audry and a nice home in a country club community, nice cars and toys, what could be wrong.

Melissa asked for the divorce, begrudgingly. She loved Jeff, but he didn't believe in God, never had; but what was worse was his ridiculing of believers. Over the years, her faith grew stronger and she enjoyed her church community; but she and the daughters enjoyed it alone. No way was Jeff going to step foot in a church.

The divorce and Melissa's subsequent remarriage had taken its toll; and while Jeff wasn't a broken man, he remained in the dumps for the next four years. The most eligible bachelor wasn't available. He was hoping his wife would come back.

Jeff made new friends and maintained most of their old friendships too, as did Melissa, including The Admiral, Sheryl, Chadbo, Wild Willy and Abe the Bartender.

Nine-thousand miles away, along the border of Pakistan and Afghanistan, the Korengal Valley of Death festered with various jihadist groups, Muslims with a common cause: Kill the infidels. That would be everyone except them.

Jihad's Warriors, virtually unknown, unlike al Qaeda, had infiltrated the borders of Europe and the United States for years, decades. The U.S. border with Mexico was as porous as Swiss cheese; and jihadists had taken advantage with bribery and murder.

The Chechen jihadists from Eastern Europe looked, talked and acted as American as mom's apple pie. The Arab jihadists passed easily for Latino immigrant laborers, but these were not laborers.

The Divine Plan was to run America and Europe out of money. The warriors knew the West couldn't protect every single nursery school, church, synagogue, campground, shopping center, hospital and highway. It would be easy. Once economically destitute, the Islamic takeover of the world would finalize.

While Manhattan and Chicago remained the desired targets, security was tight. The Islamists would concentrate on the Bible Belt. More Christians that turn the other cheek rather than fight.

Jihad's Warriors were financed, not by Muslims so much as by a group of wealthy Japanese businessmen bent on revenge for the nuclear bombings of Nagasaki and Hiroshima during World War II. They were the grandsons and granddaughters of those burnt alive in December, 1945, the Baby Bombers. Money was no problem.

Jeffrey continues his pursuit of Melissa, now widowed, and can't help but notice all the people carrying *The End Is Near* signs. They seemed to be everywhere. Then there were the disappearing people, and Jeff remembered his mom's lectures.

"In the last days, sonny boy, people gonna be disappearin', yes they is. You start seeing folks vanishin' in thin air, you better find God. That's all I can say."

A creature of habit, Jeff had a routine that included the Dunwoody Starbucks every morning for coffee and the Atlanta newspaper. He was a news junkie. The Mayan Apocalypse was just around the corner, and people world-wide were preparing for *The End*. Ridiculous.

One warmer than usual Spring morning, record heat the words of the day, Jeff enjoys his latte and paper when suddenly his world changes… again.

The brown cargo van circling the small shopping center explodes with vigor as America's first suicide bomber begins a wave of terror like the nation has never seen. Two minutes later another explosion several blocks away blows up the Dunwoody Day Care Center. Forty-seven dead in a split second.

Jeff's Navy buddies, Chad Myers and The Admiral, work with the Goddard Space Flight Center in Maryland. Astronomy buffs, their primary concern was space objects on a collision course with planet Earth. Near-Earth objects, mostly small asteroids, had become more commonplace.

Unfortunately, news of the object most recently discovered would now have to be shared with the world as it made its way past Jupiter on a course that would hit Earth in less than a year. The object, still invisible to most telescopes, was dark, massive and unavoidable.

Sixty-five million years earlier, the dinosaurs and most living creatures had been wiped out by an asteroid only six miles in diameter. The Dark Comet was more than a hundred

As the world reacts to the coming devastation, many begin to believe that the end really is near this time, and there was nothing anyone could do about it. There was little panic.

When Jeff's friend Samarra receives a strange call, she returns home as instructed. She would follow the instructions as directed, or she would receive her son's head in a box instead of the finger she stared at in desperation. And she did.

Samarra's access to Atlanta's CDC biological disease labs made her job simple and soon the Spanish Flu, one of the great killers of all time, is loosed into an unsuspecting world. It was inevitable, millions would die.

In the Indian Ocean, a hijacked nuclear attack sub vanishes. The only remnants were an oil slick, clothing and assorted debris but not enough to indicate the submarine was at the bottom of the Marianas Trench.

As New Year's Eve approaches, Jeff and Melissa visit Grand Cayman Island to celebrate memories and await the coming comet. To most it seemed the Earth would end months before the predicted Mayan prophecy.

A few hundred miles east of Grand Cayman, on the island of Montserrat, the Soufriére Hills volcano erupts and is blown into the Caribbean Sea. The massive tsunami that is generated speeds across the ocean toward Puerto Rico, Jamaica and... Grand Cayman.

PART TWO

Jeff returns from Grand Cayman Island alone. He and Melissa tried to escape the giant wave but were washed off the 4-story roof of their beachfront hotel. Melissa's body was never found, and Jeff mourns his loss. He had prayed they would reconcile, his first prayer since a child; and it looked like it might happen.

The new year started off with a bang, literally, when the U.S. suffered its first nuclear strikes, one at the Diego Garcia island chain in the Indian Ocean that destroyed most of America's B-52 bomber force. The second destroyed the Buford Dam, Atlanta's fresh water supply.

The Dark Comet continued its journey toward Earth, two weeks until impact. Attempts to destroy the comet with the world's nuclear weapons supply failed to deter the coming tragedy.

The world became unified for the first time in history in their effort to stop the comet, and joyous applause erupted globally when the comet slammed into the Moon instead of Earth. Unfortunately, the resulting debris from the lunar collision meant waves of meteor showers for Earth, many of which made it through the atmosphere, destroying numerous communities, including the Three Gorges Dam in China.

Thankful that the world was still intact, Jeff flies to California to buy his million dollar dream car, a one of a kind 1954 Cadillac Pininfarina Cabriolet. Maybe that, he hoped, would occupy his mind a while. Shopping was great for depression.

Upon arrival at the La Jolla Jetport, Jeff's tragic misfortune continues as he is struck with the deadly and pervasive Spanish Flu. During his hospitalization, he begins to have a series of strange dreams, dreams of small white churches in fields of blooming daffodils. Dreams of a tiny Arizona town named Lukeville.

The European riots had become infectious, and America's cities did the same as gasoline reached $ 8.00 a gallon. The police forces, hampered by budget cuts and not enough employees, became brutal; and rioters were killed mercilessly.

The jihadists coordinated closely with a well-organized Christian militia under the philosophy of, *The enemy of my enemy is my friend.* Their common enemy was the U.S. government.

The Admiral's romance with Sheryl blossoms cautiously, at least until the kidnapping. That's when he discovered his real feelings, the ones he had sheltered for sixty years.

Recalling their private conversation, he wasn't really surprised that the President had sold out Israel; only, it wasn't Israel's God that was trying to kill everyone in America, it was Islam's God.

What was surprising, and shocking, was the rumor that there were thousands of infiltrators living and working in the nation's infrastructure: nuclear power plants, water treatment facilities, food distribution warehouses.

Vinny, aka Aboud, hasn't gotten any nicer as he continues to meet with his *deputies* at the concrete plant in Lukeville. The meetings, though brief, usually occurred on the Mexican side of the deep, underground tunnel connecting the concrete facility in Lukeville with the beer distributor on the other side of the border. Plans were made, plans of terror, death and destruction; and the stored weapons and nerve agents were the vehicles Allah would use.

Wild Willy continues his work with Mossad and Senator Jack Russell, Samarra's husband. The nanotech spybots were no longer experimental and looked like assorted bugs, but Will was especially fond of the dragon fly style. Looked just like the real thing.

Samarra's case goes to the U.S. Federal Court in Atlanta. The charges are numerous, including international homicide charges for the tens of thousands killed because of the Spanish Flu. During the trial, Samarra's senator husband is arrested in a San Francisco shower house with a young boy and charged with possession of child porn and sex with a minor. Senator Russell stated that he thought the boy was 12, the new legal age of consent in the United States.

After Jeff's recovery from the Spanish Flu, he continues to have the strange dreams about a couple named Missy T and Kipper T, reggae music and disco lights; and the room, the one with the dark door. Y*ou don't want to go through that door*. Missy T made the comment numerous times.

Jeff's life, a life that's never dull, continues to change suddenly and often. He finds himself having second thoughts about the whole religion thing, at least sometimes. He really couldn't explain how the Gideons Bible kept showing up.

One day Jeff gets a call from Samarra. Her trial was over quickly, temporary insanity; and her penalty was light. She asked if she could visit, they had been friends for many years.

During her visit to Jeff's Sugarloaf estate, yet another megacryometeorite storm hit North Atlanta. Jeff's home was spared, but a young girl in a Porsche was killed in his neighbor's driveway. The large ice bomb that hit the new Porsche Spyder was estimated to weigh 120 to 150 pounds, larger than a beach ball.

Samarra informs Jeff that she and Senator Russell are now divorced; and over the next few months, a new romance blossoms. There had always been *something* there.

The months passed swiftly, and soon Jeff plans a visit to his dive shop in Negril. Before going to Jamaica to check on the business, Jeff and Samarra become engaged, though a date is not set.

Jeff's journey to Jamaica is plagued with thoughts and confusion, not about his profound love for Samarra but about all the natural disasters going on. It was downright scary.

The Admiral told him about the large rock that appeared to be leaving the Moon's orbit, and he found himself hoping to God that it wouldn't. He fell asleep and dreamed, dreams of earthquakes and volcanos, roaring seas and asteroids, drought and poisoned waters… and *Melissa*. He prayed in his dream, a prayer that Melissa hadn't suffered in the tsunami, that she had been killed instantly in the fall.

"The world is a dangerous place to live; not because of the people who are evil, but because of the people who don't do anything about it."

Albert Einstein

List of Main Characters: Alphabetical by First Name

Abe the Bartender: Key character. General Manager and bartender at The Divide Disco & Café.

Aboud Rehza: a.k.a Vinny, a.k.a. Ricky, a.k.a. Jean Philippe. In charge of U.S. Operations for Jihad's Warriors and various other Islamic Jihadist groups. Twin brother of Mohammed Rehza.

Aludra Khalid: Muhammed's sister. Lives with Muhammed, leader of terrorist Jihad's Warriors, in the Korengal Valley, Afghanistan-Pakistan border.

Amber Michelle: Investigative reporter with al-Jazeera USA.

Betty Davis: Also known as Betty Davis Eyes. Bartender at American Legion Post 251 in Duluth, GA.

Bill "Wild Willy" Briggs: Master of Nanotechnology, Georgia Tech Nanotechnology Research Center, Atlanta. Ex-U.S. Navy, CIA and Homeland Security. Works closely with Israel's Mossad. His cover is high dollar repo man.

Chad "Chadbo" Myers: Assistant Director, Near Earth Object and Heliospheric Laboratory, Goddard Space Flight Center, Greenbelt, MD.

Chuck Hutz: a.k.a. Hutz the Putz. After accident, speaks fluent Hebrew and witnesses to others while in a trance.
CJ: Bartender at American Legion Post 251 in Duluth, GA. Helped capture terrorist wannabe that attacked the Post.
Condi Zimmerman: Independent news anchor/reporter and Atlanta contract correspondent with FOX News Network and OLNN.

Dan Brunson: Nuclear physicist and public speaker.

Dennis Duncan: Geophysics Professor and public speaker.

Dmitry Ustinov: Chechnyan-Russian arms dealer. Brokered the sale of 5 high-yield nuclear weapons and delivery systems from Pakistan to Iran. Arranged high jacking of Nerpa 155 nuclear submarine.

Dr. Joseph Rosenberg, PhD: Public Speaker and Professor of Apocalyptic Religions, Candler School of Theology, Emory University.

Edgar Allen Poe: Homeless veteran who discovers terrorist plot, and ends up working with Army Intelligence.

Erica P. Robbins: Freelance reporter and U.S. War Correspondent.

Farmer J. Kinsella: Owns large cotton farm in Clemson, S.C. He survived an assassination attempt, but terrorists stole his dust cropper plane for a planned chemical attack on Atlanta.

Gray and Andi Dorey: Close friends of Jeff and Melissa Ross, philanthropists and owners of Dine for Dollars, a restaurant for the homeless or just the hungry.

Jack Russell: United States Senator from Cumming, Georgia and ranking member on the Military Finance Committee. Married to Samarra Russell.

Jeffrey Ross: Main character. Ex-husband of Melissa Ross and father of three daughters; Jami and Jenni (twins) and Audry,his youngest. U.S. Navy SEAL until discharged with injury after the Vietnam conflict.

Jill Haskins: Wife of Leon "Bubba" Haskins and Melissa Russell's closest friend.

Judi Ellis: Director of Paleobiology, Emory Primate Research Center, Atlanta.

Judy Blanton: Lives in Lukeville, Arizona. Previous owner of J. Blanton concrete Company.

Kara Mulherin: Missionary to Haiti and future girlfriend of Scott Johnson.

Kari K. Vermi: News anchor with OLNN, Omega Letter Network News. Columnist with www.omegaletter.com

Kipper T and Missy T: Angels who appear to Jeff in dreams.

Kyoto Kushito: Founder and Director of The Foundation, a shadowy terror think tank, based in the Hiroshima, Japan area. The Foundation consists of disgruntled grandchildren of Japanese kinsmen killed by the U.S. nuclear attacks of World War II and funded the hijacking of the Nerpa nuclear submarine.

Leon "Bubba" Haskins: Owns the largest minority contracting firm in Georgia and a tourist submarine facility at Lake Lanier Islands, Georgia. Married to Jill Haskins.

Mehdi: Chief of Security and Jihad Planner for Muhammed Khalid. Lives in Korengal Valley along the Afghanistan-Pakistan border.

Melissa Ross: Also Melissa Ross-Jeremias. Divorced from Jeff Ross, mother of twins, Jami and Jenni, and adopted daughter, Audry. Recently married Robert Jeremias, later killed in a plane crash. Rumors are that he and the other missing were raptured.

Mohammed Rehza: Ruthless Islamist in charge of European operations for Jihad's Warriors. Twin brother of Aboud Rehza (a.k.a. Vinny and others)

Muhammed Khalid: Islamic Jihadist and founder of the extremely secretive Jihad's Warriors. Lives in Korengal Valley, Pakistan with his sister, Aludra.

Naomi: Old Jewish woman who carries a cross necklace. Helps Aludra escape Korengal Valley through Tajikistan.

Pam MacLott: Owner of *The Divide Disco & Café*, the South's only News Bar. The café becomes a meeting and planning place for those interested in combatting the Islamic takeover of America.

Richard "Rich" Badey: Investigative reporter.

Robert Jeremias: Missionary, philanthropist. Married Jeff's ex-wife, Melissa but was killed in a plane crash during a missionary trip.

Russ Ivies: Chief of Security, Centers for Disease Control and Prevention, Atlanta. Actor and producer. Suffered one of first Spanish Flu cases and later became Chief of Security for the Atlanta Veteran's Administration Hospital.

Samarra Russell: Director of Research of Communicable Diseases, Centers for Disease Control and Prevention, Atlanta. Married to Senator Jack Russell.

Scott Johnson: Assistant manager of *The Divide Disco & Café.*

Sheryl Lasseter: Director of the United States Public Relations Liaison. Works directly for the U.S. President.

Terry and Toni Fahey: Next door neighbors of Jeffrey Ross.
The Admiral: Justin P. McLemore. A graduate of the U.S. Naval Academy and retired four-star Admiral. Director of Near-Earth Object and Heliospheric Laboratory, Goddard Space Flight Center, Maryland.

Three Wild Women: Wanda, BJ and Beverly manage the American Legion Post 25. The three very attractive women are seen together often. Skilled in self-defense and sharp-shooting, they seem to attract encounters with street thugs and drunks.

Vinny: A truly evil man, his real name is Aboud Rehza, a product of wealthy Saudi parents. He and his twin brother, Mohammed, had been child prodigies; and both spoke several languages fluently. A man of many aliases. Vinny resides in the United States after infiltrating across the Mexican border. Aliases include Vinny, Ricky, Jean Philippe, and others.

PREFACE

"The vine is dried up, and the fig tree is withered; the pomegranate, the palm tree also, and the apple tree, even all the trees of the field, are withered: because joy is withered away from the sons of men."

Joel 1:1 830 B.C.

Pomegranate's Café
Jerusalem, 33 Anno Domini

"You denied me."

The statement wasn't what you might call *loud*, it was more like a loud whisper. It had come out of nowhere and seemed to resonate off the dingy limestone walls of the gloomy tea house. The approaching afternoon was another hot one in Israel. The four men stared at one another but said nothing.

"You blew it..."

This time the voice was a faint whisper, no resonating off walls; and it had an air of sadness to it, maybe disappointment. James looked around the room. The man at the front, he looked like a sheep herder, didn't seem to hear anything. The two Roman Guards, the ones who had just scared the pomegranate stew out of all of them, didn't take note.

John, Judas and Andrew said nothing, except John kept glancing at the ceiling. The voice seemed to have come from the ceiling, or *up there* somewhere.

"Did you hear that?" James whispered, but the three others said nothing.

Outside, the two guards continued their daily routine, walking the dusty streets of Jerusalem trying to keep the peace among the Jews. They were a testy bunch, them and their invisible god. Riots could happen anytime, but they were always met with brutal Roman street-judgment.

"What were you talking to those Jews about?" Romulus asked his friend and fellow guard. They had been soldiers and friends for ten years.

"Wanted to see if they were followers of the prophet pushed a beggar back to the edge of the dusty street.

"The man in the desert?"

"Yes Romulus, the man in the desert."

They walked in silence, and the men thought they were getting too old to be Roman Guards. The equipment was heavy and hot, especially today with the Sun beating down. Neither man could remember a time when it had been so hot. Naomi, a Jewish *prophetess* said the prophet in the desert was causing the heat.

"You think it's hot now?" Naomi would scream as she walked Jerusalem's dusty streets, "Just wait until the man in the desert arrives. The whole world will burn when you kill this man with your stones and crucifixions. It will be a sad day for Judah when that happens. She will be no more."

The two soldiers laughed at the woman as they headed for Herod's Temple.

"What did the Jews say?"

"The same thing they all say Romulus, they deny knowing him. Who would blame them? They're scared of the crazy rabbis, especially the Sadducees."

"The Sadducees are brutal in their judgments, I'll give them that," Romulus said and wiped more sweat from his face. The helmet was heavy and soggy. He needed a vacation, a respite away from this dusty, god-forsaken place. He hated his duty in Jerusalem.

"I saw him you know," Romulus said.

"Really? No, I didn't know; but I've seen him too."

Antonius seemed despondent, and Romulus thought it was the heat. The two guards paused at the corner of Mount of Olives Way and Pomegranate Street to stop a fight. Three Judahites were beating another, yelling that he was a blasphemer for believing the man in the desert. One of the three attackers picked up a rock about the size of a grapefruit and slammed it into the follower-of-the-prophet's head. Blood flowed heavily. The Roman soldiers separated the fighters.

"Clean up the street you fools! Stop killing each other. What's wrong with you?"

They would leave the arrest and judgment to the Jews, and the Pharisees would decide. They knew the Pharisees would decide on the side of the three attackers. They hated the desert preacher, and the jealousy showed with their constant whining and griping. The guards continued toward the Temple.

"What did you see Romulus? Did you see any of his so-called miracles? All the Jews, especially the Jews who follow him, are talking about this man. I heard one say there were too many miracles to count."

"I heard one say he was the *King of the Jews*. Just wait until Herod hears that," Antonius answered. *And maybe he is*, he thought silently. He had heard of the predictions among the Jews, that a savior with a great sword would come free them; but this desert dweller didn't even carry a sword or armor.

"I saw him feed ten thousand people with two fish and five loaves of bread," Romulus whispered in hidden amazement, "maybe more. There were four or five thousand men, and then there were their women and children. He has these special followers, disciples or something like that; they serve him. They brought the preacher the loaves and the fish, he held them up in the air and stared at the sky and then…"

Antonius didn't doubt Romulus; he had seen a grand miracle with his very eyes.

"And then?" Antonius asked.

"And then…," another pause, "and then they fed all the people, thousands of them. I've never seen anything like that in my life."

"That's amazing, Romulus. You actually saw it? With your own eyes?"

A fire brigade passed the two guards, and they stopped to watch. Smoke was rising from an industrial kiln.

"That's not the amazing part. Not only did the preacher feed thousands with a couple of fish and loaves of bread, when they all left for home, the preacher's disciples picked up the remaining scraps."

"There were scraps? How could that be possible?" Antonius asked, eyes wide. The Jewish fire brigade was passing buckets of water down the street to the fire, one bucket at a time. Fires were a problem.

"It's not possible my friend. That's why it's so amazing. Twelve baskets full. They collected twelve baskets of scraps when the fish and loaves hadn't even filled one basket to begin with!"

They continued their watch, and the Sun scorched their bare arms. The brass handles of their close-combat swords were hot as fire.

"Yes, not possible," repeated Antonius. "What I saw wasn't possible either. I had duty in one of the small villages, trying to protect Matthew the tax collector from the Jews. A man came running up and told Matthew that 'Y'shua,' that's what the Jews call the preacher, had just brought a young girl back to life, some ruler's daughter.

"Well, I didn't believe that one for even a second. The preacher raised a dead person? I didn't buy it. But then I saw him walking down the trail just outside the village, and all these Jews were following him, listening to every word. Some threw flower petals on him as he walked by.

"This village I was working in had two blind men, blind since they were born. The men looked like they might be in their late thirties. The two heard the crowd and started yelling like crazy."

"What did they yell?" Romulus asked.

"Have mercy on us, son of David. They kept calling him son of David instead of Y'shua, not sure why. Anyway, he asked the blind men if they really believed he could heal them, and they said 'yes.' He touched their eyelids with his thumbs; and faster than a heavy Roman sword can sever a head, the men could see."

"Really?"

"Really, Romulus. The two men were jubilant and dancing around, the Jews were dancing around. It was wild."

"I can imagine. Never seeing anything for thirty years and in an instant, you are cured. That's amazing too, Antonius. This preacher is not of this world."

"The Jews were asking each other, 'has anyone ever cured a blind man in our whole history?' Apparently the coming savior, the messiah if you will, was supposed to heal the blind. All the Jews are talking about it."

"I bet that makes Caiaphas happy, that snake. Those Sadducees are jealous of anyone who steals their attention, so they especially hate this preacher. I guess they must think the common man can't recognize this savior, only the priesthood."

"I will watch this man, Antonius. He has a power from his gods."

"That's the strange part," Antonius replied. "He only speaks of a single, invisible god, his 'father' in heaven. I would like to know this father in heaven."

The men continued their march around Jerusalem, and a storm was rising in the west. Rain began to pour outside the Pomegranate Café.

The four followers of Y'shua, still sitting at the table in Pomegranates Café were sullen and watched the rain fall outside the café, large drops dimpling the dirt. Soon the dusty streets would be muddy.

"I heard it James, a voice. Just as the two guards walked out the door. Who was it do you think?" John asked.

James and John were brothers, the sons of Zebedee. James was the level-headed son, and John was the mischievous one. They had followed Y'shua right from the start, the first time he called them. Now they had denied even knowing him. The day had been hot, but now the humidity rose. The four men were silent, contemplative.

"Do you think the guard really wanted to know more about the preacher? I think he did. We should have been a witness," John pouted.

Zebedee had raised his children to be honest, direct and as helpful to others as possible. Sons James and John had followed Jesus when he first called them, right after he had chosen Peter to be his first disciple; but John seemed to have formed a special relationship. The preacher had told him *things*.

"Does it bother you that the rabbis hate you?" John had asked Y'shua. "I don't know why they do, but they do? They've seen your works with their very own eyes."

"They are blinded by Satan," Y'shua had explained. "They believe the messiah is coming on a big white horse to rescue them, but the messiah doesn't even know who they are. They will not inherit eternal life, I tell you now. That is the gift, to live forever without sickness and death. This is what I offer.

"The one who rejects me and does not receive my words has a judge; the word that I have spoken will judge him on the last day."

John had memorized those words that day and often thought about what the preacher had said. *Was Y'shua saying he would be the final judge?*

"I think the Roman soldiers will believe in Y'shua before the arrogant rabbis do. They are always worried about their 'position'," John said to the others.

The rain continued; and the four apostles finally left the café, their toes squishing in the mud with each step. A fire burned in the distance.

Prologue

Jeff walked down the stairs toward the dark room, sweat beginning to bead on his covered arms. He enjoyed the beat of the Reggae. The air conditioning just couldn't keep up with the record temperatures, and he subconsciously slapped at another mosquito. By the time he was halfway down, he was perspiring profusely; and he subconsciously wiped his brow on the sleeve of his black, long-sleeved jersey.

Exiting the stairwell, he found himself in a vast room, dark but bathed in different colored lights and a mirror ball suspended over a mirrored dance floor. Ahhh, to be thirty again.

He spotted a familiar face but couldn't place the dark-skinned man. He started a conversation.

"The A/C must be broken." Jeff knew it wasn't broken, just inadequate for 106 degrees; or as his aunt might have said, "It's pretty daggone hot for a January mornin'," and it was.

"Pardon moi?" The familiar-looking man answered with a French accent. He was tall, maybe six-four with black hair and well-dressed in a dark suit, dark like his skin; and Jeff thought the man might be from the Caribbean. *Where have I seen this guy?*

"It's hot in here," Jeff said to the French-speaking man. "What's your name? You look familiar."

"It's always hot down here. You haven't been here before?"

The man ignored the question.

"No," Jeff answered, scanning the vast room and was awed by the ancient artwork that graced the walls. "I don't really even know where I am."

Jeff felt light-headed, and his eyes fluttered. The man had the darkest eyes he had ever seen, and there seemed to be a tint of red in the center of each pupil. He blinked twice and rubbed his eyes, not believing what he saw. Looking back in the man's eyes, there was no redness this time. He thought it must have been a reflection of one of the tiny red, rotating lights.

"Aren't you hot in that suit?" Jeff asked as he again wiped his brow and then rolled up his sleeves.

He didn't remember putting on the long-sleeved shirt and wondered why he had. The weather had been hot for months, maybe years; but this might be an oncoming fever. His head spun like a witch's brew in a large stir-pot, and thoughts of Spanish Flu frolicked briefly in his mind. *Where am I?*

Glancing around the room, Jeff spotted the bar in the middle, circular like the one in Park Place Café had been… before the explosion, with one exception. The only patrons sitting on the barstools were women, women with short skirts and long legs highlighted by the soft neon lighting circling the underside edge of the bar. They were all young and beautiful.

"Would you like to play pool?" the Frenchman asked.

"What?"

"Would you like to play a game of pool?" The man repeated.

"I guess. I haven't played for a while. I've never been to a bar where there were no men."

"This is a different type of place, monsieur. You are fortunate to have found it, it's like heaven mon ami."

The Frenchman nodded toward the electronic dart board in the corner. "See there are a couple of other men, playing darts over there."

"What's your name?" Jeff asked the man for the second time.

"Jamal. My friends call me Jamal the Jamaican, but I was born in Montserrat."

Jeff thought that made no sense, but neither did this whole scenario. Jamaicans and Montserratians didn't usually speak French, especially flawless French. English or Patois, a Creole flare added to English were the common languages.

The hair on the back of his neck bristled as he walked to the pool table, the 9-ball rack in a perfect diamond at one end of the black, felt tabletop. He chose a cue and chalked the tip. He hadn't played pool in years.

"You break, monsieur," Jamal said as he grabbed a cue of his own.

With a crack, the cue ball slammed into the bright orange 1-ball in front, a perfect break; and the 9-ball plowed into the corner pocket, game over.

"Wow, monsieur, you won that one quickly. Your break again." Jamal racked the balls again into a perfect diamond. "Would you like to make it interesting?"

Jeff never forgot a face and knew he had seen the man before. He vaguely recognized the French dialect as memories stirred in the depths of his mind, like a computer searching for a file, only faster. *Where have I seen him?*

"How interesting?"

"Maybe one thousand dollars, monsieur?"

Jeff reached in his pocket without thinking and pulled out a roll of hundred-dollar bills. He had no idea where the money came from, because he carried very little cash as a rule. The sweat continued to bead on his tanned forehead, and the hair on the back of his neck began to settle. He found the room warm, beautiful and quite comfortable. The reggae had morphed into soft mood music.

Jamal the Jamaican backed away from the table and waited for Jeff to break again. Jeff chalked the tip of his cue stick, leaned over the black felt tabletop and took aim. The cue ball again slammed into the 1-ball; and the yellow-striped nine made the journey to the right corner pocket, as before.

"Unbelievable, monsieur; two in a row. What can I say?"

Jamal handed Jeff ten crisp one hundred dollar bills and again racked for 9-ball.

Jeff's smile wound around his face, and he couldn't remember ever making the 9-ball on the break twice in a row. A crowd began to gather around the table, all beautiful women except one balding man with a pudgy red face and perspiring heavily.

Jeff aimed the cue ball once again, same result. After six breaks, six wins and six thousand dollars Jamal suggested they have a shot at darts and led Jeff over to the dart board in the corner. Jeff had never played darts and turned toward the bar for a drink when he nearly ran into the small brunette. She handed him a glass of Duckhorn, his favorite merlot. He felt *giddy*.

"You go first, my friend," Jamal repeated and smiled broadly, his white teeth nearly glowing.

Jeff picked up the small dart with the sharp steel tip, took aim and *Bingo!* Bull's eye. Three more throws resulted in three more bull's eyes. The crowd applauded as Jeff's head continued swimming, and the brunette rushed over and embraced him as her lips found his. Jeff felt faint and swayed to the music. *Did someone spike my drink?* He looked in the beauty's eyes and said, "I must've died and gone to heaven."

"But you don't believe in heaven, Mr. Ross."

Jeff was sure he hadn't mentioned his last name, nor had he mentioned his religious views.

"Care to try bowling?" Jamal asked.

"Sure why not? Does this bar have a bowling alley too?"

The brunette led the way as memories of Samarra passed subliminally through his spinning head and then faded. Jeff wrapped his arm tightly around the young woman's small waist. She reciprocated, molding her body into his and lightly kissed the back of his neck.

"You go first this time."

Jamal balanced the fifteen-pound navy blue bowling ball, took three steps forward and the ball began its journey to the back of the ally, knocking all the balls down except the two in the back corners. His second ball missed both pins. Jeff gulped the glass of wine, and this time a tall blonde handed him another Duckhorn.

"How did I find this place?" he asked out loud. The crowd laughed and celebrated Jeff's good fortune.

"You're a lucky man, Mr. Ross," and Jeff didn't remember telling Jamal his last name either; but what the hell, he was having a blast.

"How do you know my last name?" Jeff slurred, slightly.

"We met in New York a couple of years ago, Mr. Ross. You chartered my medical helicopter for a tour of New York City."

It all came back to him. The medical helicopter was sitting idle at the airfield in New Jersey, and Jeff had asked the dark-skinned man how he might charter the machine. Jamal turned out to be the owner. What a small world. *What a strange world?*

Jeff took the first ball, inserted his fingers and it was a perfect fit. The ball seemed to glow as it journeyed down the lane, edging closer and closer to the left gutter. Miraculously the spinning ball began a slow curve to the right and hit the lead pin just slightly left of center, a perfect strike.

The first strike was followed by more, and before he knew it he had bowled the first perfect game in his entire life. That perfect game was followed by another, and Jeff began to get bored. Winning every time was not fun.

"Let's get out of this place," the brunette cooed in Jeff's ear as she stood on her tiptoes. Jeff was a head taller.

"Alrighty then. Where too?" he asked, and the girl again found his lips. Making out in public would have normally embarrassed him; but he found himself enjoying it like never before. He felt like a thirty-year-old man.

Walking out the back door and into the night, the royal blue 1954 Cadillac Pininfarina waited by the curb, motor running. Jeff opened the door for the young lady and couldn't remember if he had asked for her name. He also couldn't remember starting the car, but who cared? The night was young and the Moon, full; and he had no concerns about driving.

Jeff looked into the night sky; and the thought suddenly hit him; the Moon was no longer pink and had no rings. *And where were the meteorites lighting the night sky as had become the norm?*

Exiting the parking lot Jeff turned left onto Lukeville Highway, and the Cadillac purred. Jeff's pride swelled at the magnificent one-of-a-kind machine.

"Where to?"

"My place, of course," she cooed and began to massage the back of his neck as he headed down the highway bordered by large fields of yellow daffodils on each side. The bright yellow flowers seemed to glow.

Six hours later, Jeff's eyes opened; and he tried to remember the night's events, something about 9-ball, and darts and bowling and… the beautiful brunette. He hadn't had this much fun in a long time, from what he could remember; but he suddenly felt guilt at the romantic encounter that just fell into his lap. Could he have died and gone to heaven? He had no idea where he was as he tried to recall the events.

He turned over and slid up against the woman's back, her long hair flowing across the satin pillow. He snuggled up to her closely like two spoons in his Mom's silverware drawer. Her scent was stimulating as he whispered in her ear, "This can't really be heaven. I haven't seen St. Peter."

The woman slowly turned over and said in a gravelly voice, "What makes you think you're not in hell?"

Jeff's eyes opened wide, and his heart stopped beating as he looked into the woman's face; but it wasn't the face of the woman from the night before. Saliva drooled from both corners of her mouth; and her beautiful white teeth were now rotted, with several missing. Her face cracked with deep wrinkles, wrinkles like he had never seen, even in National Geographic. She growled like a rabid coyote, and her eyes burned red.

The growling woman who had been a beautiful brunette just a few hours earlier pounced in an instant and started gnawing Jeff's face, biting hard and ripping off his right ear. He screamed in pain and rolled over, swinging his fists violently at the woman-monster and fell out of bed. As he hit hard on the ceramic-tiled floor, he heard a chirp in the distance but couldn't figure out where the sound was coming from.

Coyote-woman pounced out of the bed, landing on all fours as Jeff scrambled out the bedroom door and down the hallway; but the hallway went on-and-on with no end in sight. She bit at his heels as his fist slammed into her… *its* face; and the hideous woman was stunned for a moment, a moment long enough for Jeff to find a door. He slammed the door after him and headed across the kitchen, out the back door and into the driveway. This time there was no Cadillac waiting with the motor running.

Blood flowed down his neck as he felt for his ear; but there was no ear. There was only a hole where his right ear had once adorned his handsome face.

The coyote-woman bounded out the back door in a gallop, chasing Jeff's bloody body down the driveway and into the street. He never saw the large garbage truck barreling down the road until it slammed into his body and threw him under the truck, dragging him underneath and down the road.

He somehow heard the chirp again and suddenly the pain was gone, the truck was gone and the gnarling coyote beast was silent after one last comment, "This is not heaven, Jeffrey Ross."

Lying on the hard pavement in a foggy mist, Jeff's heart continued to beat rapidly and sweat poured from his clammy skin. Another chirp and his body jerked in pain.

"Jeff!."

Someone, or some *thing,* was shaking his body; and he tried to scream. His vocal chords didn't cooperate, and the scream was nothing more than a whimper.

"JEFF! WAKE UP!"

This time it was a shout. He opened his eyes as the pavement became the soft confines of a king-sized bed; and he recognized Samarra's face, a concerned look in her almond-shaped eyes.

"You're having a bad dream, honey? What were you dreaming? I've never seen you so frightened."

Sweat rolled off of Jeff's body in small rivulets. Samarra's words were soothing, and his heart rate slowed again toward normalcy.

"What were you dreaming, honey?" and Samarra began to cry as she held him close in her arms. "It's only a dream."

The smoke alarm chirped again, asking mercifully for a new battery.

CHAPTER ONE

"Dmitry, are we set my friend?"

The French air was stuffy and warm, too warm for early morning. A mist dripped from the gray clouds above, and Mohammed thought about brother *Vinny* and smiled at his American alias. He wondered if the weather was as strange in America as it was in Europe. The hailstorms had killed millions of animals and livestock in France and had wiped out several villages, pounding them into the ground.

The Russian arms purveyor had proven to be a friend indeed, at least for the enemies of the West. *The enemy of my enemy is my friend.* The café in Monaco was small and private, a single TV mounted to the cracked-plaster wall on the left.

"I hope so Mohammed. I have worked hard for you. It will be New Year's Eve tomorrow, and I hope your plan works out for you."

Dmitry referred to *The Preacher* by his Muslim name, which annoyed Mohammed greatly; but he made no comment.

"I hope in the coming year you will become a Muslim, Dmitry. You need Allah in your life." Mohammed laughed.

"I doubt it Mohammed. I don't believe in religion. You know that. I believe in money."

The Russian smiled and sipped his mocha-vodka. Mohammed remained silent, as another CNN newsbreak flashed across the television screen. The two men read the scrolling message along the bottom of the screen.

"The Mississippi River remains closed for shipping due to the continuing drought, the worst since records have been kept in the United States. The National Weather Service said there was an unusual shift in the jet stream and has issued a severe storm warning for numerous tornados and downdraft winds from the Midwest to the Northeast, and large hailstorms are again forecast along the Canadian-Minnesota border where several thousand cattle were killed yesterday from the large hailstones.

"The largest naval buildup since World War II continues in the South China Sea and the Pacific as world powers try to prevent war between China and Japan over disputed islands and the surrounding fishing rights as food is becoming more and more scarce, largely because of unprecedented red tides. Red tide algal blooms are highly toxic and often make the water look like blood.

"Yesterday a Russian destroyer fired four rounds over the bow of a Japanese ship as a warning, and the United States responded by sinking the Russian ship. Tensions are high, and World War III is the fear throughout the world as sabers continue to rattle to the north of Israel. Israel's military remains on high-alert.

"Meteor showers have been forecast for eastern areas of Europe..."

It was early in the day, and the café was nearly empty as the two men sat in the window booth, watching the few tourists go by, most wearing surgical facemasks. Dmitry pondered the coming events but with no guilt in his soul. Smuggling the fifteen thermonuclear weapons into Europe and Russia from Iran and Pakistan had proven easier than he thought, but

Pakistan's Taliban militants had made it simple. All it took was dinar, and Dmitry had lots of dinars.

"So what's the plan?" the Russian asked.

The Preacher knew the arms dealer well, had become good friends over the past few years; but he had learned to never trust anyone with details, especially an infidel. *The enemy of my enemy is my friend.*

"We have plans, my friend. That's all I can say."

"They're big ones," Dimitry commented concerning the nuclear weapons, "much larger than the ones used on the Japs. Be sure and show them respect. One of these bad boys, from the right altitude, can flatten a city. Every man, woman and child within 5 miles will be vapor.

"You know, if you be patient the Russians and the Chicoms will take care of the United States and Europe for you."

The Preacher wasn't worried. He would surely sacrifice his life for Allah and Paradise, and the seventy-two virgins. Mohammed wished Vinny had been able to obtain one of the large-yield weapons, but his dear brother would have to make do with the numerous briefcase nukes. The Islamic Chechen Brotherhood had three of the large nukes, and St. Petersburg and Moscow would soon be no more. The new year would bring the beginning of a new world, Insha'Allah.

"What do you mean, Dmitry?"

"The Chinese and Russians are talking about taking the U.S. out, a joint venture if you will. They believe that the U.S. sent most, if not all their nuclear weapons to destroy the Dark Comet. They also know that half the U.S. submarine fleet is grounded because of the flu."

"And this from Chili: The ALMA observatory has reported two asteroids that appear on a close-encounter with Earth. It is

believed these asteroids are relatively small, less than a half-mile wide and came from the Kuiper Belt, well beyond our solar system.

"Dr. Chad Myers at Goddard Space Flight Center in Maryland said in an interview yesterday with Kari Vermi of OLNN that activity departing the Kuiper Belt was 'disturbing' and probably caused by gravitational tugs from planetary alignments. Stay tuned for updates and have a nice day. I'm Condi Zimmerman."

"These are big-ass balloons, Vinny."

Vinny laughed because they were. Nearly three feet in diameter, the flat-black balloons seemed huge when compared to the normal balloons one sees in parades, except Macy's.

Vinny thought about Allah and the gifts of knowledge that Allah had bestowed upon him. It was Macy's after all that gave him this idea. He reminisced and entered the world of his childhood when, as a young boy his parents took him to the Macy's Christmas Parade.

He had fallen in love with the parade and dug into its history and how so many balloons became a part. He had been at the previous year's Thanksgiving Day Parade, and he wondered why the stupid Americans changed the name from Christmas Parade to Thanksgiving Parade? *Why would they shun Jesus?* But once an infidel, always an infidel.

Vinny looked out the floor-to-ceiling glass windows of the luxurious penthouse suite and could see the new building in the distance.

The Grand Opening of New York City's "newest office tower" would be tonight, New Year's Eve; and the planned celebration would be "one of a kind" according to Condi Zimmerman the news-babe. She would certainly be right about that, Vinny thought out loud.

"What did you say, Vinny?"

"Nothing. Just talking to yourself."

"Myself."

"What?"

"Never mind, Vinny. You just messed up the saying," and the three men in the suite laughed loudly; because Vinny always messed up the sayings. This would be a day to rejoice, praise Allah. Several of the Great Satan's major cities would not likely forget this New Year's Eve fireworks show.

As the Sun crawled westward toward the horizon, New York City became the city of lights; and the festivities could be heard on the streets below. New York City continued to "move on" after the tragedy of the *9/11 Event* as it was now known. Just six more hours, Vinny thought, until the midnight hour.

This would be the night that the world's Christians would know the feared Tribulation had begun, at least as far as he was concerned.

Vinny scanned the large living room, dimly lit with window coverings closed, annoyed by the loud hiss of the helium tanks as the balloons filled to maximum capacity. Only a few of the large balloons would be needed. He had researched the helium lift effect and discovered it would take hundreds of regular-sized helium balloons to lift a sixty-pound bomb, the weight of the two briefcase nukes. It would only take sixteen of the large black, Mylar balloons. He smiled and was proud that he had researched thoroughly, had "done his schoolwork."

Vinny turned on the Weather Channel to check wind speed and direction; but he had planned well and had all bases covered, no matter what the wind direction.

What was happening in the penthouse suite of the new eighty-story *5th Avenue Tower One* was happening in three more penthouse suites surrounding Manhattan. No matter what direction the wind blew, one nuclear weapons package would surely explode in the night sky, possibly all eight, a quarter-mile above the New Year's Eve celebrations.

With the sixteenth balloon finally inflated, the room was filled with large round, black objects, enough to carry the two briefcase nukes to the appropriate height, based on the current barometric pressure and wind speeds.

The packages were secured, the bombs wired to explode simultaneously at midnight unless the balloons reached an altitude in excess of 1,800 feet. The detonators would activate based on altitude. If the balloons gained too much altitude, the eight bombs would explode as programmed, regardless of the time. With an explosive force of sixteen thousand tons of dynamite raining down terror, debris and despair on the infidels below, there would be no Times Square or New York Stock Exchange opening tomorrow.

Vinny knew there was no assurance that all eight nukes would explode properly. Some of the trigger mechanisms may have reached the end of their shelf life, but only one would need to work. A single 2K nuke over Times Square and Wall Street would damage or destroy the bridges, and Manhattan would be a ghost town. Thousands would be dead. Vinny loved explosions and smiled, but he would not be around to see this one. Allah had other plans for him.

"Are we set?" Vinny asked.

"We're set, Vinny. All we have to do is get the packages to the balcony."

"The balloons will be no trouble. The French doors are two meters wide. Keep all the lights off. You know what to do. May Allah bless you Jamal, and your brothers."

Vinny finished the final instructions to his fellow warriors, left the room and took the elevator to Parking Level Three. Exiting the elevator, he glanced around the parking garage. No one in sight. He remotely unlocked the rental car's doors; but before he could reach the car, he heard the sound.

Mohammed sent the email from Viva Café, a favorite coffee shop just outside Naples. The brown vans, all painted to look like delivery trucks, were parked and ready.

"You need to get those things in the air," the Russian had instructed Mohammed; but that had been impossible with the large thermonuclear weapons, now armed.

The multi-megaton bombs weighed far too much to lift by balloons or small aircraft, and they had no missile delivery systems. If the nukes could be a couple of thousand feet high when they exploded, the effect would be more devastating; but it wouldn't matter. A 5-megaton bomb exploding on the top deck of a large parking garage in downtown St. Petersburg would still blow the Russian city to China. Like brother Vinny, Mohammed loved explosions. He continued to type.

Is the chicken prepared? Mohammed waited.

It's finger lickin' good, came the response.

Mohammed repeated the procedure until confirmations came in from all outposts. *This has been too easy*, Mohammed thought and smiled. Allah was willing.

Leaving the late-night coffee shop, the only other customer recognized him.

"Preacher!" the lady shouted in French.

Mohammed stopped and turned to face the lady. He liked being called *The Preacher*.

"Buon giorno, signora!" The Preacher answered in near-perfect Italian and gave the lady a warm smile, but he had little time to spare and explained that he was on his way for a children's New Year's benefit. It was already January 1 in Italy.

Mohammed apologized and hurried out the door of the dank coffee shop, the TV still spewing news about meteor showers in Indonesia. Approaching his bicycle, the ground suddenly but gently shook beneath his feet. In the distance a plume of smoke rose from the top of Mt. Vesuvius.

Mohammed wasn't worried, because the volcano had been dormant since 1944; but still… he recalled what Vesuvius had done to the Roman cities of Pompeii and Herculaneum in 79 A.D. Sixteen thousand dead in a flash. The city was buried under thick ash until 1748 when explorers rediscovered the ancient metropolis. The ash flow had happened so quickly, buildings and skeletons remained intact underneath, some in the fetal position.

Just three hours until midnight in New York and the beginning of one of Paris' biggest shopping days.

Vinny knew the sound all too well as a shell slammed into the chamber of the shotgun.

"Gimme the keys, a-hole."

The two olive-skinned men approached Vinny, their pants nearly dragging the ground; and they reminded him of Atlanta's infamous Pants-on-the-Ground Gang. He didn't try to stifle his laugh.

"Perdóneme?" Vinny answered in Spanish. "Hey man, what's with your pants. They look so stupid dragging the ground."

Vinny laughed out loud.

"Pardon *this* kemosabe. Gimme the keys." The assailant's partner stayed in the shadows as kemosabe-man raised the shotgun. In a flash, Vinny disarmed the young man and slammed the gun into his skull three times, hard. The kid hit with a sickening thud and blood poured from his ear. Vinny took the stiletto out of his holster, slammed it through the man's neck and repeated, "Kemosabe this."

The assailant's friend disappeared into the darkness of the garage, and Vinny decided not to pursue. He entered the non-descript automobile and drove the white Hyundai out of the garage, turned left and headed for the southbound freeway. He would be well on his way to Atlanta before the nukes exploded in New York City, Charleston, Miami and San Diego.

Six hours until midnight.

Vinny began to sing out loud the Wilson Picket tune… *I'm gonna wait 'til the midnight hour*. He merged onto the freeway, aimed the small car south and sang like a rock star.

The young mother, tall and thin in stature and dressed in a blue running suit was anxious with anticipation and held her daughter's hand tightly. Like mother-like daughter, they were blessed with the same hair, brown with golden highlights and lots of curls and ringlets. She wished so much her husband could be with them for the night's celebration; but he was one of New York's finest, and the Port Authority would be busy tonight. In less than a minute the large crystal ball would begin its descent in Times Square and the din of the New Year's Eve crowd nearly drowned out the approaching sirens.

"Look at all the balloons, Momma?"

The small girl, maybe eight, tugged on her mother's sweatshirt adorned with Notre Dame across the front. The weather was almost muggy for New Year's Eve in the Big Apple.

"They're everywhere, honey!"

"No, Momma, I mean *those* balloons. Way up there!"

The small girl pointed skyward toward the new office tower. The mother looked up but saw nothing, when suddenly one of the streaming search lights briefly lit several large, dark balloons floating high above the vibrant crowd. She was amused at the large size but thought nothing of it.

"There're more over there, Momma," shouted the small girl, again pointing skyward but in the opposite direction. Momma looked up and counted two more, at least it looked like two; and then the balloons disappeared as they ascended into the night sky. The sirens grew louder, approaching from every direction.

"Three…Two… One..." The noisy crowd was the largest in history, and they jubilantly shouted the countdown. At the strike of twelve, the crystal ball began to move.

Goddard Space Flight Center
Greenbelt, Maryland

The gray walled laboratory wasn't stifling but close as the Maryland temperature had hit yet another record high, eighty-seven degrees on a windy New Year's Eve. The winds were blowing at a constant forty to forty-five miles per hour because of the unusual dip in the jet stream.

The two large windows in the laboratory let the darkness stream in, fought off by the numerous LED lighting fixtures recessed in the white-tiled ceiling. To Chad Myers, the night's darkness wasn't so dark, highlighted by the dark blue but transparent colors of the jet stream high above. Sometimes his ability to see the wind was more burden than gift from God.

Wall-mounted monitors surrounded the space, tracking several newly-discovered near-Earth objects approaching from the Kuiper Belt beyond the solar system. Chad and The Admiral stared at the NEO data, mesmerized by the dismal analysis; but both knew the immediate problem was the large rock heading their way from the Moon.

When and if the large, lunar space rock hit the Ross Ice Shelf as predicted, the Antarctic would never be the same; and all indications were it would be a direct hit in less than five days.

"I'm glad it's a small one," The Admiral whispered, mostly to himself. He was surprised this asteroid hadn't generated all the hype that the Dark Comet had; but then, they just discovered this space rock two days earlier. Not much warning. "At least we have all the base personnel evacuated, thanks to calmer-than-usual weather in the southern hemisphere."

"It ain't that small, Boss," Chadbo said matter-of-factly. "Nearly a hundred meters. That's a football field, a lot of mass."

"Well," The Admiral continued and glanced at the large flatscreen on the wall that monitored the Moon and her evolving set of rings. "I'm just glad Antarctica is uninhabited."

"How many ships are in the Pacific?" Chad asked. "The news says it's the largest naval buildup since World War II. Looks like China's gonna get even with the Japs."

The animosity between Japan and China wasn't new news. It had been going on since the end of the Second World War.

"A bunch, why? Four aircraft carrier groups in the Pacific and South China Sea."

Chadbo Myers had always been a little on the wild side, especially for his age and was known to occasionally imbibe in illegal smokable substances and vodka tonics; but he was a brilliant scientist and specialist in the world of near-Earth objects, those large and larger rocks floating through space, potential disasters for Earth and her moon. Most of the NEOs came from the asteroid belt, a cloud of various-sized orbiting rocks between Mars and Jupiter, but nearly all of the newly-discovered objects were coming from well beyond Jupiter, a long way from Earth.

The Admiral and Chad had been friends for many years and were both old enough to get senior discounts at the grocery store on Wednesdays. Everyone who knew Chadbo knew he was about as laid back as laid back could be. Today however, he looked worried, his ever balding head amiss with a few gray hair sprigs aiming for the facility's tiled ceiling. He was restudying the data when the power went off again. The UPS backups kept the electronics going until the generators cranked up.

"That's becoming an everyday event, Justin."

Chad never called The Admiral by his first name unless he was distressed, and Justin made note.

"And we're gonna have a hell of a disaster when and if."

"At least no casualties, Chadbo. McMurdo Station is empty, so there's no one left. What are you getting at?"

"The wave. If this asteroid hits the Ross Ice Shelf, it could possibly collapse. That would mean almost four hundred miles of solid ice falling into the sea, ker-plunk. The tsunami will be enormous, you can bet on that. It will not be a good day for the beach."

The lights flickered, and the winds tried to find an opening into the lab.

"I hadn't even thought about that," The Admiral said, rubbing his chin; and lightning flashed outside the window, in the distance. "You don't think it will just penetrate the ice shelf, like a straw can go through a potato if it hits fast enough?"

"Oh, it will definitely penetrate the ice; but remember, ninety percent of the ice is under water. The part we see is the ten percent above water. It's the largest ice mass in the world. If it collapses, there could be a tsunami of..."

Chad's voice faded in thought.

"How big?" The Admiral asked.

"Oh, I don't know, Justin; maybe a mile?"

"What? You're kidding."

"Afraid not. The massive displacement of water would send a gigantic wave from Antarctica through the Pacific, South China Sea and Indian Ocean. Hell, it could theoretically cause tsunamis all over the world. Hawaii will be completely swamped except for the mountains, as well as Japan, Taiwan, the Philippines, any island community. You wouldn't want to be vacationing in Bora Bora."

"Should we be evacuating the islands? Has Hawaii been warned?"

"Are you kidding? How would we evacuate the Hawaiian island chain in time; and what if it goes straight through the ice and there is no tsunami. This is one of those 'damned if you do; damned if you don't' kinda things I guess, know what I mean?"

"But if the Ross Ice Shelf does collapse, a lot of people will die."

"Yeah Admiral, you're right. And every ship in those oceans will sink, even the aircraft carriers. They will sink or wash inland, possibly for miles."

CHAPTER TWO

<u>One Year Earlier</u>

"This message is not for the United States but for the world. Your waters will be poisoned, your streams defiled. A big war is looming just over the horizon; and when the Day of God's Wrath comes, there will be no unbelievers."

Chuck Hutz

Jeffrey Ross drove the new, blue Cadillac south on Peachtree Industrial Boulevard toward Atlanta, dodging one of several potholes and admiring the Caddy's throaty exhaust sound. It wasn't quite as throaty as the Nissan GT-R he once owned; but then, the Cadillac wasn't really new. She was a beauty though.

The 1954 Cadillac Cabriolet Pininfarina was royal blue, a real head-turner; and he liked that, always had. He reminisced about the Caddy, the only one of its kind ever produced, well worth the million he paid for it. He knew he had to have it when he learned about it on a *History Channel* special two years earlier.

As Peachtree Industrial became Peachtree Street, the traffic was noticeably light, the streets almost desolate. The top was down, and the air was pungent. Homeless people lined the sidewalks outside the boarded up stores in what once was some of Atlanta's finest shopping districts along Peachtree Street.

It wasn't a perfect morning. Mornings were never perfect anymore, with record heat in most parts of the world, and the other parts suffering through record cold and blizzards; and then there were the plague and the meteors. *I believe I have a plague in my mind* he would often think.

At 9:00 A.M. on a perfect February morning it wouldn't have been eighty-seven degrees. With the convertible top down, the attention-seeking Cadillac's air conditioning was working full-force. Jeff's smile grew in spite of the stench. On the right, in a small parking lot behind Dunkin Donuts, a gang of kids dressed in black were kicking something… or someone.

Looking to the left after hearing a ruckus, he was startled at what he saw, a man's body lying in the gutter with three men and a woman going through his pockets. The dead man's swollen, dark face was covered with boils; and blood spilled from his gaping mouth. This must be from the mutated virus Samarra told him about, some kind of strange derivative of the Spanish Flu, as though the non-mutated version hadn't been sufficient. That version had only killed an estimated one million U.S. citizens, and now a more virulent form had apparently paid a visit. The four thugs would soon have dark boils on their faces, and the beat goes on.

"The mutated version seems to have characteristics of the 1918 Spanish Flu and black pox," and Jeff recalled Samarra's warning… and her guilt.

Seeing two UPS trucks and a couple of cars, Jeff was relieved to finally see other traffic once he entered Buckhead. He turned right onto Peachtree Battle and into the neighborhood where the "Old Money" lived, as well as Samarra. He couldn't wait to see her and felt his heart skip a beat. He tried to convince himself it was possible that she was just as beautiful on the inside as the outside. He wasn't sure of that possibility, because she was *BF*; and he laughed at the memory from his Navy days, *Blemish Free*.

Listening to Bob Marley on the radio, Jeff was in a good mood today for some reason, maybe the new ride or maybe the new fiancée; maybe all of the above. Life suddenly seemed to be "good" for a change, but he did remember what Abe had told him.

"Things are changing, Jeff. The *Bible* talked about a lot of this stuff, these plagues and hailstorms and droughts; the wars in the Middle East. For the unbeliever, things are going to get really bad. They don't believe a final war was foretold to happen in Israel. They haven't read the Book."

Jeff had a lot of respect for his good friend Abe the Bartender but still found it odd that Abe was both a Jew and a Christian. Abe certainly seemed like a pretty smart guy, but who could possibly believe all those biblical stories? Jeff had taken note of some of Abe's comments but still found the "one God" teachings of the Jews, Christians and Muslims to be mostly mythology. Any belief in gods was mythology he reassured himself, but he was perplexed that his feelings seemed to be changing a little. *What if the stories are true?* He erased the thought.

The previous two years since Melissa's death had been difficult, but now… He still missed his ex-wife, and her death would always haunt him as he remembered watching Melissa wash over the side of the hotel roof on Grand Cayman Island the day of the Great Wave.

He slowed the Caddy to take the turn onto Tuxedo Drive, and the hair on the back of Jeff's stiffened as he saw the white car pull out of Samarra's driveway. He had seen the car before, or one awfully similar. Only briefly did he think of following the car as he rushed down the quarter-mile driveway and screeched to a halt in front of the main entrance.

Starting up the stairs of the palatial Southern home, listed in "Atlanta's Most Historical Homes" magazine, Jeff first noticed that the double-front doors were both open. *Is that blood on the wall?* He knew it was though, and his bright mood suddenly dimmed.

Where is Harley he asked himself, realizing that his Great Dane would most likely be outside if the doors were open. Samarra usually kept the dog with her, ever since the hate mail started coming in. The adrenaline pumped through his body, and the retired Navy SEAL removed the Glock from his back holster.

Three steps from the top, Jeff's heart stopped. Harley the Great Dane was now Harley the deceased Great Dane as he lay in a gray heap at the base of the doorway, a fresh pool of blood still flowing heavily from his bullet-riddled body.

Chapter Three

Goddard Space Flight Center
Greenbelt, Maryland

"What the hell is that?"

The Admiral spoke quietly, but few were around. Most of the staff were either quarantined at home with the flu or were already dead. He turned away from the image on the screen and rubbed his unshaved chin, a habit. This was the second time in less than a year that he had seen the strange phenomenon.

Could stars really just disappear? In a few short months? Were they burning out? He perspired more than normal, the air conditioning barely keeping up with yet another record heat wave. The early January temperature was a muggy 88 degrees, and it was still morning.

"What's *what*?" Chad asked, walking into the small gray cubicle in the near-Earth object lab with an image of his own. He wiped the perspiration from his forehead on the flowered sleeve of his loud, Hawaiian shirt.

"Look at this, Chad; and tell me what you think."

Chad Myers was an NEO expert, one of his many areas of expertise. Ex-Navy himself, Chad, The Admiral and a select group of other senior citizens in their clique watched the world situation closely. The world had suddenly gone from the wrath of terrorists on Earth to the wrath of Mother Nature in outer space. Chad scratched his balding head, sipped his lemonade and spoke.

"Stars have disappeared before Admiral. Maybe due to the age of the universe, maybe they're going supernova on us. Many astronomers believe the Star of Bethlehem in the Jesus story was a supernova, at least the ones that still believe in God. That number seems to be dwindling, wouldn't you say?"

Chadbo knew that most scientists didn't believe the Star of Bethlehem existed at all, even though there was evidence.

"The most pressing agenda I see at the moment is the solar activity. We've passed the eleven-year solar max, yet the Sun's acting like an alien in an outhouse. There are twenty-seven viewable sunspots, highly unusual."

"What is that?"

"What?" Chad asked.

"What the heck is an 'alien in an outhouse' Chad? Where do you come up with these things?"

"Never mind. Just pass the vodka."

The Admiral thought an alien probably would be confused in an outhouse; but he was more perplexed about, and continued to question, the disappearing stars. He had never seen stars disappear.

"These aren't stars disappearing as supernovae, Chadbo. A supernova is one of the most energetic explosive events known to mankind. You can often see them during the day. These are just disappearing. They grow fainter and then they're gone."

"You're correct," Chad responded. "When a star's nuclear fuel is consumed and the core collapses, the light intensity is enormous. And we haven't detected any extreme light sources, not even Jeff's 'blip'."

"Don't think it's a supernova, Chadbo. The last one observed happened in 1604, Kepler's star. This seems entirely different. Wasn't there a reference in the *Bible* about stars disappearing?"

"I don't have a clue," Chad answered.

"I thought you believed the *Bible*."

"I do believe the *Bible*, but I don't have it memorized. Geez, give me a break. Do you?" The Admiral thought Chadbo seemed a little testy this morning but said nothing.

"You must be out of pot," The Admiral said with a laugh, but Chad let the insinuation pass without comment.

"Maybe they're getting farther away, Mr. Admiral, Sir."

"Maybe so, but they would have to be moving awfully fast to be going from faint to gone in such a short period."

"So maybe they are going awfully fast, away from us. They would eventually disappear. If it weren't for the Hubble and other space telescopes, these stars would have never been seen in the first place.

"The Sun is our most immediate concern, other than all the meteorites falling on us," Chad continued. "Even though Solar Maximum has passed, the Sun's surface temperature is increasing at a rate previously unseen, except in other star systems. That's not good."

Chad had become almost obsessed with solar activity over the last couple of years, at least The Admiral seemed to think so.

"Global warming is not being caused by man," Chad continued. "Now, I'm not sayin' that man doesn't contribute, only that man's contribution is negligible. It's being caused by something natural or something supernatural. Volcanos are erupting all over the world, unprecedented eruption activity I might add. Then there are the deep sea hydrothermal vents spewing out seven-hundred degree water."

"And the Sun is getting hotter!" The Admiral interjected.

"Yep," Chad said, "but based on the Sun's age, it should not be warming up this dramatically this quickly. Used to be that the hottest place on earth would be 120 degrees or so. Iran just recorded the hottest midday temperature, ever; at least in the time we have been keeping records."

"Really? Hadn't heard. How hot?" The Admiral asked.

"One hundred forty-six degrees."

The interior office lights flickered as yet another brownout occurred, and the backup generators sounded in the distance. The air conditioning did not restart. Chad wiped his head with a wet hand towel, walked over to the tinted window and looked up at the Moon.

"And then there're those large rocks orbiting the Moon."

"The ones you said may be coming out of lunar orbit?"

"That's right, Admiral. If that happens, and it looks like it will, these monsters could wreak great havoc, depending on where they might crash. These rocks won't be world-ending; because they won't be traveling at the same rates of speed as an asteroid from Kuiper or the asteroid belt, but you don't want to be near when and if one hits."

"I need a Bloody Mary," The Admiral said and ran his hand through his thick, gray hair. "Think I'll call Sheryl and see if she wants to meet."

"Is she back in Washington?"

"Yep. We're keeping the Warner Robins Air Force Base as a temporary White House Ops Center, but for the most part the flu problem in D.C. is over. The new vaccine seems to be working."

"You mean the vaccine that Jeff's new honey developed?"

"That's right, Chad. Samarra has been a great help."

"Yeah, right. If it hadn't been for her, we wouldn't need a vaccine!"

"Chad, don't be so judgmental. You have no children, so objectivity isn't in your corner. Samarra went home to find her son's finger cut off and stuffed in a box of what looked like Valentine's candy with a note saying the kid's head would be in the next box. You don't know what you would do in that situation. It's easy to Monday morning quarterback, but I know that a mother will do anything to protect her kids. Lionesses, hyenas and baboons do the same thing."

"Yeah, maybe; and I'm not being judgmental. Would you have done it?" Chad asked.

The Admiral didn't answer and picked up the laboratory phone to call Sheryl. The dial tone suddenly went dead as light flashed outside, and a small meteor slammed into the roof of an adjacent office building. The explosion was deafening, and the suspended ceiling in the laboratory collapsed.

Mohammed Rheza enjoyed the freedoms of Europe in a way but found himself envious of brother Vinny. He had wanted to go back to the United States since his last visit years earlier. He hated cold weather, and Europe was having unprecedented cold spells all of a sudden.

Europe's record heat had been replaced with the coldest weather in decades, and Paris was blanketed with twelve inches of snow. Mohammed knew for a fact that Allah didn't approve of the near-naked women and porno shop districts; but he could feel the allure in his body, especially his loins. It almost made the cold worth it. Still, the United States was warmer; and there were even more porno shops there.

He smiled and felt guilty about the previous night. He had been a bad boy he knew, but he smiled again at the memories of the Ritz Carlton luxury suite and the two women. He couldn't do *that* in Saudi. Maybe the record cold was Allah's punishment for his recent decadence. He would have to pray for forgiveness; and Allah was very forgiving to the followers of Muhammad, may peace be upon him.

Mohammed operated out of an Islamic safe-house in Paris, once a small, non-denominational church with a white cross on the small steeple and stone walls. The computer setup in the hidden basement of the church was elaborate, and French security was scant in the Christian neighborhood. Muslim neighborhoods kept the police plenty busy.

Mohammed, like brother Vinny, had several aliases and was known in the area as Pierre LaFonte, though most referred to him as *The Preacher*. What Vinny was to the United States, Mohammed was the same for Europe.

The Preacher had been hard at work for the last couple of years and had single-handedly engineered the bombings of the Eiffel Tower, as well as the bombings of the London Bridge and Big Ben. The London Bridge was a special gift for Mohammed because it had been built by the pagan Romans just thirteen years after Jesus was hung on and nailed to the cross.

Sliding the leather-swivel office chair to his computer desk, *The Preacher* studied the graphics display on the twenty-seven inch monitor. A computer whiz and cyber-attack expert, he was in the system and had been for a week. His associate pastor, a Chechnyan Muslim, was hard at work in Germany; and the Brokdorf nuclear plant, Germany's largest, would soon have an "accident."

France's Civaux reactors were located in the small French community of Civaux, population less than a thousand. The reactors, some of the largest nuclear power plants in the entire world, provided electricity for a large swath of France. The two reactors would soon cease to produce a large part of the 76% of France's nuclear-created electricity; but the meltdown and subsequent radiation, depending on the winds, would cripple Paris even worse than the snowstorm had.

Mohammed pondered the movie he had so often enjoyed, *The China Syndrome* and like the movie, he thought it might be possible for a nuclear core to get so hot it melted through the Earth. He hoped Tel Aviv was on the other side. The winds were perfect, praise Allah.

When the clock strikes 2:00 P.M., Greenwich Mean Time, the coordinated attacks on some of the world's largest nuclear reactors would begin. The intrusion would be so subtle, the damage would be complete before even the slightest warning signs.

"Fantastic," *The Preacher* said to himself. There was no one else around to hear.

The cooling tower temperatures slowly began to rise, unbeknownst to technicians and engineers at the facilities. The cyber-hackers had dismantled the cooling tower alarm systems and placed the water temperature indicators in safe-mode. The Emergency Cooling Bypass Valves were frozen in place with a little help from Allah and *Liquid Nail*. The shutdown power switches were disabled, and everything appeared stable to the reactor staff.

Vinny was busy; and the early morning Arizona air was stifling, as was now the norm. Today was a big day; because today would start a new reign of terror, not just in America but Europe and Russia too. Brother Mohammed was hard at work in Paris. Vinny pulled the white Impala into the Lukeville *Stop Shop* to buy a soda and pick up a girlie magazine.

"Jean Philippe!" Vinny heard his alias and glanced across the newly-striped parking lot.

Oh great, he thought. He liked the previous owner of his concrete company and found Judy Blanton to be disarmingly attractive. Blonde, petite and shaped like a goddess, Vinny had thought about her a lot, though his preference was younger women, under fifteen. However, he remained focused on the mission. What he didn't realize was how attracted Judy found him to be.

"Mademoiselle Judith." He smiled as she approached. The timing could've been better. "Good morning to a very lovely lady."

Judy loved the French accent and planned to ask Jean to dinner. A gourmet cook, Judy was known around the small town of Lukeville, Arizona as the *Martha Stewart of Lukeville*. She had been attracted to Jean Philippe since she first met him a couple of years before during negotiations for her family's concrete business, but he traveled a lot.

The new managers at J. Blanton Concrete were nice enough but aloof; and they appeared to all be Mexican. They would never tell her Jean's whereabouts, and the secrecy worried her. She would've been worried more had she known that *none* of the men were Mexican but were of Middle Eastern descent.

Vinny had often considered the similarities between the olive-skinned Mexicans and the Semitic Arabs, like himself; and he considered it Allah's blessing. The Mexican border had been a piece of cookie, he knew *that* and laughed at the stupid

American sayings. Most of the so-called homegrown terrorists looked just like Mexican laborers. The disguise was perfect.

Vinny was proud of his Semite ancestry. The Semites were descendants of the prophet Abraham's sexual union with his servant girl, Hagar; and then with his wife, Sarah. He revulsed at the thought of the Hebrews being a part of his family tree, but that's the way it was. After Ismael was born to the slave girl, Abraham's wife finally got pregnant... and that was the trouble with the world today. Sarah's son, Isaac.

Isaac became the father of Judaism, and Ismael became the father if Islam. Even though they were half-brothers, Vinny and most Arabs refused to acknowledge their genetic relationship with present-day Jews. The Israelites had stolen their birthright, just like Jacob stole Esau's. That was the way the Hebrew scum operated; theft and manipulation. Ismael was the first-born son, and Abraham's inheritance should have been passed to *his* descendants.

"Jean Philippe," Judy loved to say his name, "where have you been? I've been meaning to ask you to dinner, but you've been traveling. Did you go to France without taking me?"

She tilted her head and smiled, her blond hair blown by the warm breeze.

"No, my dear, I have not been to France. I have been in Sacramento negotiating contracts," he lied.

Vinny couldn't help but notice Judy's short dress and knew her attire would never be allowed in his own country. The modesty police would have stoned her. She had nice legs he thought but controlled his desires. He wished she was thirteen instead of thirty-something. He had always been attracted to young girls; but he was in good company since Muhammad the Prophet had a six-year-old wife, his favorite of all.

Vinny dared not tell Judy he had been in Charleston, Savannah and other key cities of the Bible-Belt. He also wouldn't mention the scouting trips through the Chesapeake Bay Bridge Tunnel, nor his tour of the Vogtle Nuclear Plant in gnatty Waynesboro, Georgia. Waynesboro would soon be without power, as well as much of Georgia; and Vinny wished death to all the obnoxious gnats and other pests that vacationed in the South. He also declined to mention his stakeout of Samarra Russell's Buckhead estate in Atlanta. Samarra seemed to be spending more time at the Sugarloaf home of Mr. Dine-for-Dollars than at her own. Vinny would not venture back to Jeffrey Ross' home though, the Great Dane no longer a puppy. His first encounter with the dog had been fearsome.

"And I would love to come to dinner, any place, anywhere, any hour." He loved that line and had picked it up in a John Wayne western. Vinny was a fan of American movies, at least the old westerns.

"Great! Saturday night, six-thirtyish?"

Judy felt like a school girl, though high school graduation had been almost twenty years earlier. She hoped she wasn't coming on too strong.

"I will bring a bottle of fine wine for you, pretty lady," and he bent forward to kiss the back of her hand.

A few minutes later, Vinny was back in Mexico just a mile away, crossing under the border through the deep tunnel from the J. Blanton Concrete plant to the beer distributorship in Mexico at the other end, nearly a half mile away. The workers at the beer distributor looked Hispanic too, but none were. They were all Middle Eastern, proficient in English and Spanish and excellent shooters. Most had AK-47s in their possession.

Vinny's computer setup was more elaborate than his brother's was in France, because Vinny wasn't confined to the small space of a country church. The Plant Vogtle cooling and containment systems were laid out in hi-def graphics on the thirty-two inch plasma display; and temperatures flashed in a neon-blue light, indicating everything was within limits. The blue neon indicators would soon change to red, though the displays at the plants would not.

"Are we in?" Vinny asked.

"We're in, Vinny. Alarms are deactivated, temperature displays are constant on the plant computers, and..."

"Wait, did you say 'constant'? Does that mean the temperature display will remain at one setting? Won't that look suspicious?" Vinny asked Ahmed but knew that he was the premier hacker for *Jihad's Warriors*, probably as talented as the Christian hackers that froze all the stoplights on green a couple of years earlier.

Ahmed lived up to his name and was always smiling. Vinny grinned as he thought of the death and destruction of *that* day and how simple it had been to hack into the Department of Transportation computers. He also thought about Hutz the Putz, the man who survived the severe crash caused by the stoplight malfunction, only to die and then come back to life. Vinny doubted that story, though some of the aspects were puzzling, like how did Chuck Hutz learn to speak Hebrew so fluently after his near death experience? He had to be a Jew, even though he denied such a connection, Vinny knew that for sure.

"The temperature indicators at the plants are programmed to vary slightly. They won't notice, Vinny; and if they do, it will already be too late. The emergency cooling valves are locked in place. Ten minutes 'til GO."

Vinny was pleased with the progress, and the warriors had been unleashed. Soon, this very year, the Great Satan would be brought down, a victim of the wrath of Allah, with a little help from the failing economy and Spanish Flu. He was *not* pleased with the results of the Spanish Flu, a virus he personally installed in the HVAC systems of Atlanta's International airport terminal. There were plenty of deaths, but the virus didn't seem to be as contagious as the original Spanish Flu of 1918. And now that woman, Samarra, had developed a vaccine.

I should have killed the woman and the kid. He would have a chance soon; and Samarra Russell would be no more, nor would her young son Thomas. Then again, he would have his way with her before killing her. He had never raped a Jewish woman and knew this was not allowed by the Quran; but he remembered her olive skin and dark hair, and her body. Satan had made her beautiful.

Vinny thought about the night at CDC in Atlanta, it seemed so long ago now and smiled as he remembered the gasoline transport truck explosion, the "diversion." He loved explosions.

The Russell woman had done just as instructed, perfectly. A mother will do anything to protect her child, especially when she finds her young son's finger in a candy box; but she fooled him.

The vials she stole from her laboratory and left in the rooftop mechanical room for him to pick up, turned out to be a *less potent* version of the virus. Now Samarra had developed a vaccine with KKD Labs, and the plague was less than he had hoped. She had fooled him twice, but his greatest pleasure of the year so far was bombing the KKD Labs facility. He thought Samarra would be at the lab, but this had not been the case. Later he would take care of her.

"Ten… nine… eight…" Ahmed began the countdown.

Outside Paris in a small, country church, Vinny's twin began his own countdown. Three… Two… One…

Mohammed and brother Vinny hit *send* at precisely the same time, and the signals weaved their way through the myriad of shadow links and ghost sites that *Jihad's Warriors* had built to maintain secrecy. By the time the coded messages reached their destinations, the encryptions would evolve into nonsensical gibberish about *Kentucky Fried Chicken and finger lickin' good.*

Chapter Four

"People will faint from terror, apprehensive of what is coming on the world, for the heavenly bodies will be shaken."

Luke 21:26

Now on high-alert, Jeff had a foreboding feeling as he left the front stoop and his now deceased Great Dane and headed around the back of the palatial home. He would use the storm cellar entrance. There was no "fight or flight" consideration for Jeff, never was. He would always fight.

Why is this happening, God? Jeff asked himself as he ran to the back. He knew God had nothing to do with it, but there sure seemed to be a lot of *coincidences*. Or God-incidences as Melissa would have said. He tried not to think of Melissa. She had been a wonderful wife, giving, nurturing, *Godly*.

"Why are you asking God, Jeff? You don't believe in God."

Melissa's voice echoed in his mind, as though spoken from a faraway place, like a ghost might sound if ghosts existed.

Who said that? He asked the question silently but knew whose voice it was. Looking around, scanning for any hiding places, Jeff saw nothing and no one. There were no sounds from upstairs, and there was no ghost of Melissa to be seen. His thoughts drifted back to his fiancée; and a great, weighty fear descended upon his soul.

The storm cellar in the rear of Samarra's home was accessible from outside or from three separate rooms. Two rooms had hidden entries located beneath carpet runners, but the master suite actually had a doored entrance.

Jeff opened one of the massive outside doors using the security code for access. The space was dimly lit by LED nightlights, and his eyes adjusted quickly to the darkness. He would try the master bedroom first, but he found himself dreading what he might find. Suddenly life *wasn't* good, and Jeff scanned again for movement while wiping perspiration from his face. The muggy air was heavy.

God, please. Have you taken Samarra too? His heartbeat was in overdrive.

Stealthily, Jeff made his way through the storm cellar, noting the well-stocked bar and separate gym. The eastern-most hallway ended in a small staircase. Jeff climbed the twelve steps and quietly tried the door that would exit into Samarra's large walk-in closet. It was unlocked. That was good news, but he wondered why Samarra had left it unlocked. She was cautious.

The door opened without a sound, partially blocked by rows and rows of dresses, blouses and other feminine apparel. He was surprised to see a row of men's clothing but recognized several of Jack's suits. He guessed Jack, Samarra's ex-hubby and one-time U.S. Senator didn't need the clothing now that his abode was the federal pen in Butner, North Carolina where a special section for pedophiles was filled to the max.

Entering the master suite, he was startled by the sound of Samarra's home phone as it began to shout for attention. Looking across the bedroom, the queen-sized Victorian bed was rumpled and not made, also unusual. He looked for blood but found none and breathed a sigh of relief.

The foyer of the home was massive with dual, circular, white oak staircases and a large crystal chandelier centered above the marble-tiled floor below. Jeff approached the stairs and scanned the entryway thinking again about his beloved dog Harley, dead on the front stoop below. Blood was everywhere, on the walls, all over the floor. One wall was painted in red letters, only it wasn't paint:

Allahu Akbar, God is great, and the lone word inked in blood on the marble floor in capital letters: INFIDEL.

"Be confident," the young man said quietly as he headed for the front entrance of the Atlanta Veterans Administration Medical Center. Aaron pushed the Medline wheelchair, using it as a walker, through the front entrance of the crowded VA Hospital, no security in sight.

The man's name wasn't really Aaron, but he liked the moniker given to him by Vinny, his mentor and personal hero. As a Bosnian Muslim, "Aaron" was European and had acclimated easily to American life. He looked as American as mom's apple pie, with blond hair and blue eyes.

One of five siblings, Aaron was born and given his father's name, Abdulah. His parents and siblings had moved to the United States via Canada, where Aaron became a "born again" Shi'a Muslim, possibly out of rebellion to his parents who converted to Catholicism, a religion of the anti-Christ in Aaron's twenty-three-year-old mind. He would have nothing to do with bowing down to graven images or splashing himself with "holy water." Muslims recognized the second commandment of Allah, and he knew what Allah thought about man-made images.

Dressed in heavily starched United States Army fatigues, Aaron's wheelchair contained an Army duffle bag full of C4 plastic explosives, easily detectable through most screening processes. There were no screening or metal detectors to worry about at the VA Hospital, as the military budget cuts meant lax security for the men and women who risked everything. He would not be a suicide bomber on this day, because the slack security made it unnecessary. Aaron spotted the cameras mounted in the hallways, but paid no attention. He would easily escape.

Passing through the tiled-floor hallways, Aaron-Abdulah reached the emergency room and estimated quickly. There were at least two hundred soldiers and ex-soldiers, U.S. Navy Sailors and Marines mostly. Many infidels would die this day, as the acts in *this* play were taking place in several cities across the U.S.; and Aaron-Abdulah was pleased that Allah was blessing his efforts of destruction.

He pushed the duffle bag-laden wheelchair, fake-limping as he went, into the heart of the emergency room and placed the duffle bag on the floor. He then took a seat in the chair, continuing his ruse as a wounded vet. In eight minutes, all hell would break loose. He spoke to the young, black sailor-girl sitting next to his chair, chit-chatting for a couple of minutes.

"Wouldya watch my stuff while I go to the head?" he asked in perfect Southern-style English. He had to admit that he liked the way Southerners spoke, making one word out of two or three.

"Of course; be glad to," the young girl replied as she continued to read *The Military Times* newsletter.

"I shouldn't be very long," Aaron continued. "I just had breakfast and got the runs."

"That's a little too much information, dontcha think?" the young girl stated while continuing her read and told Aaron not to rush; she would keep a close eye on his belongings.

Aaron left the Emergency Room and limped toward the men's room. Out of sight of sailor-girl, he walked briskly past the restroom and toward the back entrance, past the cafeteria, down the stairs and exited by the Radiation Therapy Department. He had six minutes to escape, and he did.

Aaron-Abdulah was unaware that he had a compatriot mimicking his actions, now one floor above; but the other jihadist actually sat in the wheelchair as he rolled his way into the crowded hospital cafeteria, a large, leather-bound catalog sample-case sitting on his lap. The case was adorned with a decal that read, "The Few, the Proud, the Marines."

The wheelchair-bound jihadist rolled through the line, ordering scrambled eggs and sausage. The sausage would not be eaten, as Muslims abhorred pork about as much as they abhorred homosexuals and other infidels. He paid the cashier, smiled warmly and said, "God bless" to the lady working the cash register.

He worked his way to a remote part of the cafeteria, set his sample case in the seat by the table adjacent to his wheelchair and waited for his opportunity. He would be a martyr if necessary to carry this event off, but that was not his desire. Looking around the cafeteria, no one was paying attention to him. Most of the vets seemed to be in their own worlds. He saw no security cameras.

The wars in the Middle East had not been kind to the American soldiers, as amputee after amputee made their way stoically through the cafeteria lines. Thinking his activities went unnoticed, the young jihadist stood up slowly and walked away, faking a conversation on his smart phone. The sample case, also loaded with C4 explosives, would offer plenty of bang-for-the-buck; and the warrior smiled at the silly American saying that made no sense.

۞

Jeff held the Glock firmly in both hands, still no sounds or signs of anyone, including Samarra; and he hurried to the kitchen, his heart racing. Blood was on the floors, walls and even the ten-foot high ceiling as he rounded the corner.

With his mind in overdrive, a million things flashed through his head. Married to Melissa for twenty-five years, he never thought he would get over the breakup six years earlier when she divorced him and married the missionary. Then the missionary was killed in a plane crash off Puerto Rico. He hadn't rejoiced about Robert Jeremias' death, but he hadn't mourned either. Robert's death, or rapture as some of the ignorant claimed, might've opened the door to reconciliation with Melissa; and it almost had.

Many "church people" believed that Robert and the other missionaries had been raptured straight to heaven, escaping death. There were numerous reports of global disappearances, and they questioned why they were left behind. Jeff's strengthening curiosity led him to do some research on the rapturic belief and knew the term wasn't even in the *Bible*, just another myth. But still, there had been the disappearing people, here one minute and gone the next.

Jeff and Melissa's last vacation together in Grand Cayman with close friends had been grand indeed, and the romance seemed to be budding anew. Then the Cayman Tsunami came out of nowhere, and that event ended everything. In the years since Melissa's death, Jeff had found it easier to cope with her demise than with the divorce.

Then, two years later, the stunning CDC epidemiologist Samarra Russell, a fellow Mensa member and longtime friend of both he and Melissa, divorced Jack the pedophile U.S. Senator and again entered Jeff's world, no longer as a friend but as his future wife.

Now they were engaged, and he feared that Samara had also been taken from him. He wiped the thought from his mind, not wanting to face the tragedy of another death. *God, why are you doing this to me?* his mind screamed; but the God that Jeff had so long denied did not answer his question and remained silent as God seemed to always do.

Turning right, into the kitchen, his heart stopped as did his breathing when he saw his bride to be splayed out on the kitchen floor. Her pink skirt was pushed up to her waist and her blouse ripped open. The corpse was headless, and Jeff had not seen so much blood since he had been in Vietnam.

"Noooooooo, noooooo, noooo," Jeff wailed; and thoughts of suicide briefly entered his mind as he sobbed uncontrollably. In the distance someone called his name; but it was as though he was in a huge container, and the voice came from elsewhere, like an echo in an empty warehouse.

"JEFF!"

Where was the voice coming from? He searched.

"JEFF!! Wake up Jeff, you're having another nightmare."

Jeff tried to stand up, and anger writhed throughout his body. He again remembered the white Chevrolet Impal…

"Jeff! Wake up honey. Wake up. You're only dreaming."

Someone was slapping him in the face. His eyes suddenly opened; and he was in a cold sweat, his heart racing at a million miles per hour.

Samarra was standing beside the bed, shaking him and crying. His face was pale and his skin clammy. Samarra recognized the symptoms and realized that Jeff was almost in shock. She wondered what he could have been dreaming to cause such a reaction.

Gradually, Jeff became aware that the nightmare was just a nightmare; and while he should have been relieved, he began to weep openly.

Samarra held him tightly in her arms, tears pooling in her eyes; and she worried about Jeff's recurring dreams. They started right after he discovered that Melissa was still alive and living in Jamaica, rescued from the giant wave by Jamaican fishermen. She wondered if he would try to reconcile his marriage. She would know soon.

Chapter Five

"You have lost your blessings America. You have lost your blessings Europe. And you are losing your blessings again Israel, chosen by Yahweh as His very own. Don't you know your history? Don't you know, my brothers and sisters in Israel, that Yahweh's discipline is severe? How many times must you fall? Why do you always backslide and rebel against the ways of Yahweh, your God. He abandoned you after the death of Y'shua on the cross, like He abandoned Adam and Eve in the Garden. But after two thousand years, He gathered you again and gave you your land. You were obedient then, but now you have drifted away again and worship at the Altar of Decadence. Will you ever learn that your God is not playing games?"

Chuck Hutz

Jeffrey Ross, tall, gray hair and "distinguished looking," was Duluth's most eligible bachelor, only now to the dismay of a few… several thousand Jeff would say…. he was engaged.

Sitting in his gated community at Sugarloaf Country Club, the January morning Sun beat down with a vengeance. He watched the TV rant by Hutz the Putz while awaiting his daughters' visit, dreading in a sense what he had to tell them, though there was a certain joy to the coming conversation, joy that their Mom wasn't dead after all. There was also sadness at the sudden turn of events.

"Jeff, I can't imagine how it would be to lose your wife and then find out two years later that she's still alive. You must do what you have to do."

Samarra's encouragement had been altruistic enough, but she was absolutely correct. The joy of *that* news was masked with pain and confusion.

"You have made pedophiles into petty-philes, like it's no big thing to Yahweh, your God. He had rules about sex. You better pay attention and stay alert, because the day is coming when..."

At first Jeff thought Chuck Hutz was a dim light in a large forest but found himself beginning to like the guy. Right or wrong, Chuck told it like it was. At least, as it was in *his* mind. And he was intrigued with the name Yahweh, a name he had never heard, pre-Chuck. So he researched.

YHWH, the Tetragrammaton with vowels added for pronunciation. The Tetragrammaton had been a new one too, something even his Mensa friends never mentioned; but most of them didn't believe in gods either. He had to admit, Chuck Hutz was the best preacher he had ever heard, and he wasn't even a preacher. Of course, he hadn't heard many sermons in his life that he really liked and hadn't stepped inside a church in decades, other than setting up a church SCUBA outing or two.

The troubled visit to Jamaica over Christmas, intended as a brief trip to check out his remaining SCUBA business, had brought a strange twist of fate; and then there were the dreams that had not abated. He thought about the last two and found them troubling. Had he gone through the dark door? Or was that just another dream too? Missy T had warned him about the *Dark Door*.

The dreams, or "visions" as the imaginary Missy T had called them, were persistent; and Jeff often wondered if Missy T and Kipper T might be real but in another dimension of some kind. Since his recovery from the Spanish Flu, he had not dropped into the world of Missy and Kipper very often, not like he had when he was dead.

"Jeffrey, you will someday see Melissa again, that's a promise."

"How do you know that, Kipper T? You and Missy keep saying that, but I can't wait for a visit to the heavens."

"Oh, you won't see her in Heaven, Jeffrey, since you don't believe in it; and especially on the pathway *you're* living. Heaven is where God lives."

"I have no clue what you're talking about," Jeff said.

"Well then, just let me continue, Mr. Flawless. First, you have to stop thinking you're so smart. Ever since you became a Mensa member, your smartness went straight to your head. And you know what, Mr. Ross? You really aren't all that smart."

Jeff listened to Missy T's insult and did not interrupt. He had already discerned that interrupting Missy T would get him nowhere. These were after all, just dreams; but her tendency to get ticked off seemed real enough.

"What does she mean by that, Kipper T?"

Kipper's wife was suddenly gone, as though she had been an apparition; and he answered.

"Don't take it personally, Jeff. You know how women are. They never forget anything. Don't worry, be happy; we think you're plenty smart."

Kipper was so diplomatic compared to Missy T.

"No, he isn't!" Missy T commented matter-of-factly. "You're not even smart about some rather simple things!"

How did she *do that* he wondered? Gone one minute and back the next.

"I'm an angel." Missy T said.

"What?" Jeff asked. "What are you talking about, Missy?" He scratched his gray head that was beginning to ache.

"Missy T. The name's Missy T. You were wondering how I could disappear and reappear, so that's how. I'm an angel. Anymore questions?"

"Yeah, actually. When you said 'you're not so smart,' what were you referring to?"

Jeff noticed the small speck of blood that appeared through his blue and white seer-sucker pants. He paid little attention and scratched the spot on his knee, now itching. Too many mosquitos; too little spray.

"Oh, like when Melissa asked you what SCUBA meant? Do you remember that? Do you remember what you told her?"

As the owner of two dive shops, at least it had been two before the *Wave* hit, Jeff knew exactly what SCUBA meant and blurted the answer like he was answering a question on *Jeopardy*. He knew it in his sleep.

"Self-Contained Underwater Breathing Apparatus." He smiled but wondered how in the world Missy T knew that to begin with. How did she know about that question? Things were getting stranger by the minute.

"Well Congrats! You got it right this time, but you told Melissa it stood for Self-Contained Underwater *Buoyancy* Apparatus. Now Jeffrey, that was just plain goofy, don't you think, Sir Mensa???"

Missy T was a beautiful woman, almost glowed; but she had a certain bluntness about her. He looked at Kipper T who just rolled his eyes in one of those "what can I say" looks, as he always did.

"And what about that *King of Persia* bit you spouted off to Audry that time? Misinforming your young and impressionable daughter. You told her Nebuchadnezzar was King of Persia, didn't you?"

"He is!" Jeff retorted.

"No he isn't, JR. Audry tried to tell you, but she was so respectful you didn't get it. I need to teach that kid to learn to speak bluntly!"

"But Abe told me that, I didn't make it up." Jeff was always a little confused where Missy T was taking the conversation.

"You shoulda checked it out, 'cause he told you wrong. Be careful what you report as fact. Nebuchadnezzar was King of Babylon and was an *enemy* of Persia. He's the Babylonian king that invaded Israel, hauled off the booty and destroyed the first Temple. That would be *Solomon's* Temple, the ones the Israelis still pray at every day, except now it's a wall. And by the way, Melissa discovered you were wrong about the SCUBA thing but never mentioned it. She knew you were *always* right. She knew a lot Jeffrey, things you don't know."

Jeff ventured back into the present, leaving the daydream behind. Melissa *had* been the love of his life for decades, and the divorce had been a heart-breaker; but then things changed drastically.

After two years as a widower, convinced that Melissa had been killed in the tsunami, he now found himself engaged to Samarra. After Melissa divorced him, Jeff never lost his love for her and constantly obsessed that she would eventually get her head straight and come back; and she almost had.

Throughout the aftermath of his divorce… Melissa's quick marriage to Robert Jeremias, Robert's death on a missionary trip, the near reconciliation and then Melissa's death… he and Samarra had remained friends, even through her federal trial on conspiracy to commit terrorist acts. He really doubted that Samarra would ever get over that, or the guilt. And now it turned out he wasn't a widower at all. Confusion gave birth to angst, and his mind reeled.

Jeff turned the TV volume to level eight and prepared to take a dip in his expansive pool. The Georgia weather was unusually tropical, warm and muggy for January; and he hoped there would be no hailstorms. The late-morning temperature climbed to the low nineties; and he dove in the pool, swam two laps, dried off and plopped the heavy bath towel in a seat at the bamboo hi-top table closest to the big screen.

"Man, that's a big-ass television, Mr. Ross. You thinkin' that thang big enuff for you ta see?"

Jeff smiled as he remembered what his gardener said the day it was installed. The new Samsung 96 Ultra was the best eight-foot screen on the market; and the LED technology made it clear as a bell, even in bright sunlight. A little pricey but worth it.

He grabbed a fresh cup of *Chocolate Perks Jamaica Me Crazy* and watched the interview, enjoying the fragrance of the chocolate-flavored coffee.

Chuck Hutz interviews always got his attention even though he was sure *Hutz the Putz* was just a little on the *Nutz* side, maybe a lot. After all, daughter Audry was his Hebrew translator, a strange thing in itself.

Pre-teen Audry, as precocious as ever, was also getting a little moody; and Jeff had difficulty accepting that she was becoming more of a little lady than a little girl. Kids seemed to mature much sooner than in his day. Raising a young daughter wasn't easy for a man his age.

Chuck was on another rant, speaking Hebrew as though he invented the language; but for some reason, a few people could understand him, even though they didn't know a lick of Hebrew. Jeff and Audry were two who did.

"There you have it folks, the latest from Mr. Chuck Hutz, recorded two days ago in San Francisco, just before the earthquake. There will be more to come I am sure. Now to our guest.

"Dr. Rosenberg, you're a public speaker and well versed in many areas, not just Bible prophecy. You are a renowned public speaker and Professor of Apocalyptic Religions at Candler School of Theology. Your Ph.D. is in ancient Middle Eastern languages; and I know the project you and Rod Smith are working on, the analysis of the alleged discovery of Noah's Ark, has kept you in the spotlight the last year.

"What do you think of this Chuck Hutz fellow, and how could he be so fluent in Hebrew? Apparently, before his accident in Raleigh, he knew no Hebrew and wasn't even a religious man. What happened?" Condi asked.

Condi Zimmerman paused and sipped a glass of iced tea. The studio was normally hot because of all the lights; but the day's heat wave took its toll, and all the ice had melted.

"Condi, I've followed the story of Chuck Hutz; and it's amazing, to say the least. I've met with him many times..."

"You're writing a book about him, aren't you?" Condi interrupted.

"Yes, it's now at the publisher and should be available in about a month. There have been several cases in the past of someone having a stroke or NDE and recovering to find out they can speak another language. Not just speak another language,

but speak it fluently, write it fluently and spell it fluently. My book examines this phenomenon in detail."

"NDE? What's that stand for, Dr. Rosenberg?"

"Near-death experience. These are cases where someone actually dies, usually in a hospital surgical suite or emergency room. After a time, usually a few minutes to as long as thirty, the person regains blood pressure, heart rate and breathing, like it never happened. They died and came back to..."

An intrusion alarm notified Jeff that someone was entering the driveway, and his heart raced in anxiety. How was he going to explain the news about Melissa to the girls? Heading to his bedroom to slip on a clean pair of shorts, a news alert flashed across the screen, interrupting Condi's interview; and Jeff turned the volume higher. Was he getting hard of hearing?

"This just in, pardon the interruption, Dr. Rosenberg. Leon "Bubba" Haskins, once touted as a leading entrepreneur in Atlanta, has been transferred to the new Federal Terrorist Center in Arizona. He was originally charged with conspiring to blow up the Buford Dam, just north of Atlanta; but new charges are pending. Allegedly, Mr. Haskins was also involved in the release of the Spanish Flu virus at Hartsfield-Jackson International Airport. The new Federal Terrorist Center has replaced the secure compound at Guantanamo Bay, Cuba. The Center is deemed to be 'impregnable,' though most would agree that Guantanamo was pretty impregnable too."

The twins parked their Volkswagen by the pool entrance. Jami and Jenni had grown closer to their father since their mom's death and his bout with the Spanish Flu but were disappointed in Jeff's engagement to Samarra. It was too soon the twenty-eight year old twins thought, though Audry seemed okay with it.

They liked Samarra; that wasn't it. She and Jack had been friends with their family for more than a decade. They were all sickened when they heard about Jack's penchant for porn… and little boys. Still, they had never quite gotten over the tragedy that stole their mother from their lives. Plus, they were almost as old as Samarra.

The two girls walked through the side entrance to the pool. Jeff's maid had the table prepared, and the girls sat down with their father for a late breakfast of oatmeal and fresh fruit with yogurt.

"I was hoping Audry would be here," Jeff said after receiving the news that she would be staying in Raleigh. The twins seemed to get more beautiful each day, and he wondered why neither had a boyfriend. But that was fine with him.

"That was the plan, Dad but you know how enthralled she is with this Chuck Hutz fellow. She loves being the interpreter. I asked her if she was planning on just moving to Raleigh and living with Bennett and Sheri. At least Sheri is home schooling her. You know Dad, Audry is so unbelievably smart. Sheri said she was competing with high school seniors in math and science. She asked Bennett if he knew about erectile dysfunction."

"Say what???"

"Yeah Dad, like she asked you what it was one time after she saw that ad on TV. Remember? You told her to ask Mom."

The laughter was good and broke the ice, at least Jeff felt a little more relaxed. His mind raced.

After a few minutes of small talk, Jami could stand it no longer and asked, "So what is it you wanted to talk to us about?"

Jami and Jenni were sure it was something about Samarra, because their father seemed almost obsessed with the woman.

He had a one-track mind! Audry obviously got her obsessive personality from the family gene pool.

"I have some good news and, in some sense, bad news."

The twins had noted Jeff's demeanor since returning from his trip to Jamaica. He seemed to be melancholy in a strange way, not as happy as a newly engaged man should be after a week in sunny Jamaica.

"So what's the good news?" Jenni asked.

"Girls, I don't want to shock you but see no other way than just telling it like it is. When I was in Negril, the maid who usually cleans rooms at Charela Inn asked if she could discuss something with me. She proceeded to tell me, well…"

He hesitated.

"What?" the twins asked in unison.

"It appears that Melissa is alive in Jamaica, just outside Kingston. Apparently she was rescued after the tsunami and taken to Kingston. A fishing boat crew spotted her floating off the coast of Jamaica, about thirty miles off shore."

"What?" the twins screamed, incredulous. "Are you sure, Dad? Why hasn't she contacted us?" The twins eyes were wide open, as were their mouths.

"Well, that's the bad news. It seems she has amnesia and remembers nothing about her past life. The Jamaicans call her de Lady du Mer."

"What's that mean?" Jami asked.

"The Lady of the Sea. They consider her to be some sort of goddess."

The girls were excited, but worried, and sat in a moment of silence.

"Did you see her?" they asked.

"I saw a photograph. Rosalie risked her life taking the picture; but she did anyway. It's a little grainy but looks like Melissa."

"Why didn't you go get her?" Their eyes remained wide with excitement.

"Well, that's complicated. The maid said anyone who tried to rescue her would be killed; and besides, she doesn't remember me or anything else about what happened before the tsunami. The people who are guarding her, because they think she's a goddess of some kind, are not about to let her go. The only thing she seems to remember is the Gospel, which she's teaching them daily. You know, many Jamaicans believe in voodoo, black magic, that kid of stuff."

"What are we going to do?" the girls asked, anxious about this disturbing news. "Do you think she remembers us?"

"I'm afraid she does not; but then, it may not even be Melissa. The men protecting her have asked her many questions about her life, according to Rosalie, like where she's from. She doesn't seem to have a clue."

It had been excruciatingly difficult for Jeff to leave Jamaica without her; but Rosalie made it plain that his life would be in grave danger. Kingsport was not a safe place, especially for white people, she had explained. Since the world's near economic collapse, exports had slowed to all the islands of the Caribbean; and the natives were restless.

"So what are we gonna do?" Jami repeated, squirming in her seat.

"Samarra has insisted that we put the marriage off until I can get to the bottom of this. She's well aware of the strong feelings I still have for your mom. If we can get clearance for Samarra to leave the country, we will be going back in a couple of weeks. Wild Willy will join us to engineer a rescue and escape plan. If anyone can contrive a plan, it's Will."

"Can we go?"

"I hate to say no; but I need you to keep a long-distance eye on Audry and hold things down here. The world has gotten crazy. It's doubtful that we'll even make contact this time, but I have notified the Jamaican Prime Minister. He used to own Charela Inn and has been a friend for many years, so we will see. He can make things happen."

Jeff felt guilty. He had spent little time with his youngest daughter since the Cayman tsunami, how long had that been? Audry was growing into a young lady right before his eyes, but he seemed to have missed it. Her blond hair was beginning to change to Auburn, and she would soon be reaching puberty. He didn't even want to think about that.

Jeff thought about Audry's biological parents, supposing that at least one had red hair, a recessive genetic trait. He knew it had to be. Thunder in the distance interrupted the conversation, and the twins were noticeably nervous.

"Are we going to have another hailstorm, Dad?"

"I hope the hell not, but let's move inside."

The recent hailstorms had killed many people, livestock, pets and plants during the past few months; and hailstones the size of softballs were now the norm rather than the exception. A flock of birds scattered from the nearby trees, and Jeff saw the neighbor's cats running for cover. Animals seemed to have a keen sense of approaching climatic disaster. Duluth's storm sirens began to wail in the morning sky.

CHAPTER SIX

"Listen, I tell you a mystery: We will not all sleep, but we will all be changed in a flash, in the twinkling of an eye, at the last trumpet. For the trumpet will sound, the dead will be raised imperishable, and we will be changed."

1 Corinthians 15:51-52

"Do you believe in the rapture, Abe?"

Abe wiped down the bamboo bar top and handed Jeff another lemonade. It was mid-afternoon, and *The Divide Disco & Café* was nearly empty. Only a few locals could be seen lingering around the Towne Green. It was just too hot to be outside.

"Do you mean the *Biblical* rapture?"

"Yeah. That's the one."

Abe gathered his thoughts.

"I do believe in the rapture. There are some Christians who don't believe it because it's never mentioned in the *Bible*, at least not by that name. Why do you ask?"

Abe was surprised by Jeff's question and wondered how he even *knew* about the rapture. They had talked about God and why Jeff didn't believe, but Jeff was a stubborn sort. *I don't believe in mythology or man-made gods* was his usual response, but lately he seemed more interested and continued to ask Abe what he knew about this or that, picking his brain when the opportunity arose; at least when they were alone. Abe thought Jeff must be embarrassed that someone, maybe one of his

Mensa buddies, might hear and disapprove. Approval was important to Jeff.

"I was just wondering if Messianic Jews believed that aspect of Christianity. So you really believe that one day Christians will just disappear; zap, gone in an instant? Gone up in the clouds to meet Jesus?"

"I do. As a matter of fact, people are already disappearing, or at least they were. By the way, Messianic Jews believe most aspects of Christianity, at least early Christianity."

Abe recalled the disappearances, all the Messianic Jews that simply vanished in Israel a couple of years back. Some thought the IDF might have helped them out of Israel, but they hadn't turned up anywhere else. The Israelis weren't real fond of Messianics.

Heading south on Peachtree Street, Jeff couldn't get the conversation with Abe out of his head; and it had been nearly a week. *You have a one-track mind, Jeffrey!* His mother's voice echoed through his head, and he knew she had always been right about that. However, the rapture-concept… the possibility that one might disappear in thin air defied the laws of physics. He found the thought comforting nonetheless.

Atlanta had once been the Pearl of the South, a beacon of light in the Bible-Belt. That was until Buford Dam, thirty miles north of the city, was blown up in the first nuclear attack on United States soil. Recovery had been slow since Atlanta lost most of her fresh water supply, and western portions of the great city were still flooded after the waters of the Chattahoochee burst from Lake Lanier. With the local economies on the verge of collapse, the jihadist assault had slowed but not ceased. Jeff found that puzzling. Maybe the jihadists had the flu.

As a veteran and ex-Navy SEAL, if there was such a thing as an *ex*-SEAL, Jeff's new routine would take him to the VA Hospital where he would visit some of the patients in the Burn Clinic. This had become a weekly trend during the past year, as well as his activities at *Dine for Dollars* where he served the homeless warm meals and coffee alongside the founders and his good friends, Gray and Andi.

Atlanta's Veterans Administration Hospital on Clairmont Road was always the scene of activity. As the wars in Iraq and Afghanistan became a thing of the past, a new war-to-be was in progress to the north of Israel where the new Islamic Federation of States was stockpiling weapons and troops. Most of the citizens of Damascus had evacuated Syria completely since the Israelis flew over and dropped warning flyers everywhere telling the people, "Get Out! You Have Been Warned!" The fleeing civilians were quickly replaced with weapons and Islamic fighters, eager to take the war to the Israeli pigs.

The hospital had become even busier than in years past, thanks to military budget cuts that had closed ten other VA Hospitals around the country; and long lines always awaited the patients.

Driving down Clairmont, the pink and white crepe myrtles along the street were in full bloom. With the continuing hot weather, the flowers seemed to bloom more than not. He recalled his mom telling him, preaching to him, "When the end comes Jeffrey Ross, the seasons will be confused. You won't be able to tell one season from another. Says so in the Bible if you would just read it. You think you're so smart, but you ain't."

Glancing to the right, he saw the Gideons Bible lying in the floor board. He didn't remember moving the Bible from his bedroom to the car and was sure he hadn't. Another mystery.

His thoughts drifted back to the earlier conversation with Abe and the coming rapture.

"Then why didn't *you* disappear, Abe? Didn't a lot of other Messianic Jews disappear in Israel? Why didn't Melissa disappear? I've never known anyone more 'Christian' than Melissa. We used to argue about all the time she dedicated to church."

And argue they had. As a child, Jeff's mom had preached and tried to pound God into his head; but he had rebelled when he reached his teens. When he met Melissa, love at first sight, she hadn't been overly religious. As they grew older together, she seemed to change.

"I can't answer that, Jeff," Abe responded, "I've thought about it, ever since Chuck Hutz proclaimed that the rapture had begun. Maybe I haven't been judged worthy. God knows, I've certainly done my share of sinning. Or maybe Hutz is wrong…."

Abe had always been under the impression that the rapture, if it did happen, would begin and end in an instant. In "the twinkling of an eye" was how the New Testament described it, but last week an entire monastery disappeared and the monks with it. *Could the rapture be an on-going event?* Another thought to ponder.

"Do you think it's possible that some believers are left behind to help others find God? Melissa told me once that just because some people claimed to be Christian, many really weren't. I have another question," Jeff continued, now on a roll.

"Shoot."

"If this rapture event really is happening, do you think it pertains only to Christians and no one else? Do you think it's a one-time event?"

"Good questions, Mr. Ross. Have you been studying that Gideons Bible you found?" Abe poked Jeff in the arm and served up another lemonade.

"According to how I've interpreted the Bible, it's supposed to happen quickly, in the 'twinkling of an eye.' At least that's what Paul said."

"Who?"

"Paul, in the New Testament. Paul was a Roman citizen and a Jew and hated the new Christian movement. To him, any Jew who followed Jesus was committing blasphemy against God. He made it his mission to track them down and kill them. Haven't you heard of the Road to Damascus?" Abe would get into more detail later and explain who Paul was if Jeff was interested. His interest seemed to come in spurts.

"How long is a 'twinkling of an eye'?" Jeff asked.

Abe poured a bucket of ice in the cooler. The outside temperatures made it almost impossible for the ice machines to keep up.

"I would say it's something that happens fast, in an instant," Abe answered.

"But what is an 'instant' in God's eyes?" Jeff persisted. "Didn't Genesis or Exodus or one of those first books say that a day is like a thousand years to God, and a thousand years is like day?"

"How do you *know* that? You *have* been studying!"

Abe chuckled. Maybe his coaching had finally done some good, and he experienced a moment of brief pride. They had discussed a CliffsNotes-type Bible study before, but it had never happened. Apparently Jeff was doing some self-study.

"Dreaming mostly, not studying. Have I told you about my dreams, or visions… or *something*?" Jeff wasn't sure what they were, but he knew one thing for sure; it wasn't normal. But then, neither was that bright light he kept seeing in the night sky, the one no one else seemed to see.

"Back to the question. What do you think it meant, 'a day is like a thousand years?' Does that mean a day is a thousand years to God?"

Abe contemplated.

"Jeff, the Bible is full of mysteries, the greatest mystery book I've ever read. It's like, at least sometimes, God's playing with us, trying to see if we can figure some of the mysteries out. But here's what I think; and no, I don't think God meant a day is a thousand years necessarily. I think he is saying that a day to him could be a thousand years, or ten thousand years… or a week, whatever he wants it to be. I think he was only saying that time in his world is different than time in ours. God is infinite, not finite; and infinite is never-ending. That's a long time. The hundred years or so we get a shot at, if we're lucky, are nothing in the whole scheme of things."

"Then that's the point. Could this rapture, if it's real, occur over a long period of time, at least long in human terms? Could a 'twinkling of an eye' be a thousand years, or ten years?" Jeff asked.

"Or seven maybe," Abe said softly.

The Tribulation, the time of woes, was supposed to be seven years if the interpretations of Daniel the Prophet were correct; but Daniel seemed especially mysterious. He would reread the book tonight.

"You know, Jeff, I've never thought about that possibility. That's what I mean. Even Einstein asked why God played dice with the world. Let me think on it. There's one thing I've learned over the years since I started believing the Bible story."

Jeff sat silently, doing his own contemplating. Could Melissa still be here, assuming this rapture really had started, because she was some sort of guide for others who didn't believe? Could Abe still be here, just to help him?

"And what's that? What's the one thing you've learned my friend, Mr. Abe the Bartender turned preacher?" He chugged the last of his lemonade.

"I've learned that my-way-or-the-highway never works, and if you ever get to the point that you think you have the Bible all figured out; you don't. No one does except the arrogant, like the Pharisees and Sadducees used to be long ago in ancient Israel."

"Tell me about ancient Israel. I started reading a little of the Josephus book, the one about the history of the Jews; but you tell the story better," and Jeff did think Abe was a great storyteller. He made it interesting.

The two men's thoughts were suddenly interrupted by the man in black sitting on the other side of the bar. He had been there before, they both remembered, one afternoon long ago. That time he appeared out of nowhere, kind of like now. He made a profound statement of some kind... *what was it?* Then he disappeared, Abe remembered. Well, he hadn't exactly disappeared right before his eyes; but it had been sudden. He had turned to get a napkin; and when he turned back around the man was gone. Wasn't his name Michael?

"Israel was; then it wasn't; now it is. It was all foretold long ago by those who knew the future. This generation of Israelites will truly see remarkable things, *fearful* things. They await the Messiah, and he will be here soon; but the Children of Israel will be dismayed and in anguish by what they see."

Jeff and Abe stared at the man, his voice hypnotic; and his dark eyes seemed to draw their souls right out into the open.

"Isn't your name Michael?" Jeff asked. "I think you stopped by once before."

"Enoch. My name is Enoch; and I've stopped by many times, my friend. Michael is my brother."

"I'm here a lot but don't recall seeing you, except that one time." Jeff leaned over to pick up the napkin that he dropped on the floor.

"That's because sometimes I'm invisible."

Jeff wadded the napkin in his palm and looked across the bar, eyes wide. The man was gone, his glass of beer was gone; it was as though he had been an apparition. Jeff and Abe stared at each other and said the same thing simultaneously.

"Did that just happen?"

Abe was good and did stimulate his interest, Jeff thought, snapping back into the moment and realizing he had thought more about God the past year, really since the night of the Wave at Grand Cayman, than he had in his whole life. *Don't rule anything out* a voice seemed to keep telling him.

The light turned green, and Jeff started through the intersection when he saw a sudden blast or flash of light, followed a couple of seconds later by the first explosion. His car rocked from the shock wave.

۞

Russ Ivies and Jason Brach parked their white company cars in the VA Hospital parking deck at about the same time, planning on having breakfast in the cafeteria before reporting for work. Both men had once been employed in security at Atlanta's Center for Disease Control and Prevention; but after the Spanish Flu theft from CDC, they looked elsewhere for work. Russ had nearly succumbed from the flu, and his recovery had been slow and painful. After years of rehab, he was as good as new, almost. Exiting the elevator on the first level deck, Russ saw Jason and noted the puzzled look on his face.

"What's up?" he asked. The men shook hands.

"Not sure," Jason replied. "I just saw a guy run out the entrance by Radiation Therapy. He jumped on a pocket-rocket and screamed out of here like a banshee; almost ran over a nurse. Something just didn't look right. I guess I'm still paranoid.

Russ could hear the motorcycle in the distance, the sound of the Italian engine a signature in itself. They headed across Level One Parking and toward the cafeteria. He felt good about his new job. It was nice to be in a place where no one would be stealing exotic and deadly viruses. He felt secure.

Dr. Webbs, Head of Dermatology, exited the men's room and spotted the camouflage-clad soldier hurrying down the hall, almost running. It wouldn't have been unusual to see such a thing except… except ten minutes earlier he had seen the soldier in the emergency room, sitting in a wheelchair. He felt the worry-hair on the back of his neck bristle. He was both puzzled and concerned as he walked past Radiation Therapy and was positive it was the man he had seen earlier. He concentrated.

"Hey Tony. Whatcha lookin' at?" Dr. Hersshatter asked.

"Good morning, doc; not sure. I just have an uneasy feeling about a guy I saw a few minutes ago. I could've sworn he was in a wheelchair, but then I saw him running toward the exit."

"Let's take a look."

Both men hurried toward the stairwell to the downstairs exit and clambered down the steps. Rushing out the door, they were nearly mowed down by the black motorcycle before the rider clipped a nurse and headed the bike toward Clairmont Road.

Aaron-Abduluh banked the Ducati hard right, entered Clairmont and was out of sight in a flash. The light-weight bike was relatively quiet for Italian-made but had a top speed of one-sixty. The bike's braking ability was unsurpassed, allowing the bike to take sharp, hairpin curves at remarkable speeds. As a street bike, there was none so fast and agile. That was the reason Aaron had stolen the bike after seeing it advertised on the Internet, and he wondered if the young man's body had been found yet. He hadn't really intended to kill that day, but he did.

After leaving his *package* in the emergency room with the young lady keeping watch, Aaron exited the hospital quickly, as quickly as he could without drawing attention. His escape had been well-planned, and he made a left at the top of the hill.

Aaron finally heard the large explosion as twenty-five pounds of the plastic C4 ignited in a waltz of conflagration and horror. He smiled and gunned the motorcycle.

Racing through a neighborhood of modest homes and condos, Aaron again turned left as he applied moderate braking to slow the bike. He probably didn't see the large white oak tree as he slammed directly into the middle of the tree trunk, hitting the tree at what the police report would later describe as "a high rate of speed." The trauma paid no attention to the young man's hi-tech racing helmet, and Aaron's front teeth slammed through his skull, penetrating his brain. He would be dead on arrival by the time he got to Emory's emergency room, not as close as the VA emergency room except *that* emergency room was no more.

Russ and Jason noted the two doctors running from the hospital in hot pursuit of something, but the camouflaged soldier was long-gone. As the first bomb went off, Russ, Jason and the two doctors instinctively hit the deck. *Where did that come from?* Russ asked himself. It had to be near the front of the hospital.

The two security officers had a bead on another man in khaki pants and a light blue *Go Navy* sweatshirt, now hurrying across the deck toward the elevator that would take him to the main circular roadway below. The man evoked interest when he didn't dive for cover like everyone else but just kept running as though nothing unusual was happening, catastrophic explosions an everyday event.

Spotting Russ, Jason and the two doctors rushing his way, the man didn't wait for the elevator and leaped over the wall to the grass fifteen feet below. Uninjured, he was surprised when Russ and Jason came over the wall after him; and Russ landed squarely on top of the olive-skinned man.

A fight ensued. Russ, though rehabilitated after months of therapy, was out of breath from the fall. Jason proceeded to pummel the olive-skinned man into submission, as Russ pulled two nylon hand-ties from the pocket of his security uniform.

"You got some splainin' to do," Jason said to the perp as the two doctors rounded the corner of the deck.

Before the ties could be applied, the jihadist popped something into his mouth and was dead within fifteen seconds, frothing at the mouth and twitching uncontrollably. The cyanide tablet did its job. There would be no interrogation.

Doctors Hersshatter and Webbs studied the man and the froth spewing from the man's mouth. Dr. Hersshatter knew exactly what happened. He had seen it years before when he was the attending physician at a state prison in Arizona for the very last gas chamber execution. The executed German, Walter LeGrande, spasmed violently; and froth spewed from the man's mouth, almost as a mist. The almond smell of cyanide had permeated the air then like it permeated the air today.

Two blocks east of the Atlanta VA Hospital, the hijacked ambulance waited in a Chevron station parking lot. The bodies of the driver and paramedic assistant were in the back, covered by the same sheets that covered the one-thousand pound ANFO diesel-fertilizer bomb. The bomb was only a fifth as large as the Timothy McVeigh bomb that destroyed the Federal Building in Oklahoma City but would certainly be adequate.

The driver was comforted when he heard the second explosion, anxious to go. He hated the American soldier with a passion and had volunteered for this assignment. The first two bombs were small, killing a few hundred maybe. The ambulance bomb was much more destructive. The driver turned on the siren and flashing lights and headed to the scene. There would be a large crowd of rescuers by now, insha'Allah. He would gladly give his life to kill a thousand soldiers.

Chapter Seven

Jeff's dark gray boy-toy, the Nissan GT-R now with several dents from the recent hailstorms, headed south on Peachtree Industrial. *I need a new car*, he said out loud and thought about the 1954 Cadillac Pininfarina that had almost been his.

"Weather," he said, and the GT-R voice recognition system changed the satellite station obediently. There was another Weather Alert.

"...tropical storm should hit hurricane strength today. If so, Hurricane Abigail will be the earliest named Atlantic hurricane since records have been kept. There has never been a January hurricane. Residents in coastal Florida and Georgia are keeping a wary eye on the storm, the Atlantic coasts already devastated by the tidal surges and storms of last year. No evacuations have been ordered as the storm slowly moves to the northeast at three miles per hour. The Hurricane Center states the storm should cause no danger to the U.S. coast.

"Another hailstorm has hit Nebraska and thousands of livestock..."

"OLNN," Jeff said after the weather update; and the radio obeyed, tuning to the news station.

"... reports from across the nation that several Veterans Administration hospitals have been bombed, including the Atlanta VA Medical Center off Clairmont Road where two explosions have rocked the area. Many are reported dead."

Not believing what he was hearing, Jeff hit the accelerator, and the GT-R performed as designed. He maneuvered through the traffic and into the VA parking lot. Then he heard the next explosion.

۞

Kinsella Farms
<u>Clemson, S.C.</u>

"What's up?"

"Hey Boss. Just checkin' out the spreaders. This baby runs great! I never knew a biplane could go so doggone fast. You know why they call it a biplane don'tcha?" The grin already covered Buddy's broad face, shadowed by the full-brimmed, Indiana Jones hat.

"Nope, and I don't wanna know Buddy. But tell me just the same." The farmer laughed. "My wannabe comedian ranch hand."

He also knew from years of jokes that there was just no telling what might come out of his mouth. Buddy was a great man, and the farmer felt blessed that God had sent him. The twenty-five hundred acre farm was a lot to handle, especially for an old man like him. Buddy kept everybody squared away, yes he did.

Just north of Clemson University, the single airstrip stood alone in the vast field except for the small, modified double-winged crop duster parked to the side. The South Carolina landscape rolled with green hills and small mountains, working their geological way toward the Appalachians. Many of the rolling hills were covered with constantly blooming wildflowers, thanks to nature's hot flashes.

A large, three-story wooden-framed farmhouse stood nearby, painted white with white shutters and columns on the front porch, reminiscent of the home in Margaret Mitchell's *Gone With the Wind.* The five-bedroom home had been built in the late eighteen hundreds and had a feel that only a home so old could have. Even the smell was *Southern*, at least that's what Buddy always said. Surrounded by cotton fields, Kinsella Farms was one of the world's great cotton producers.

"How fast will she go?"

Buddy loved Ol' Man Kinsella. He wished the old man's wife hadn't up-and-decided to make a sudden visit to Jesus; but that's the way life was sometimes, a real challenge. They had been married for fifty-some years and were buddies, big time. He knew that's what it took if you wanted a good marriage; best-friendship, and humor. The farmer always told him, "Bud, when you get married someday, if you can find somebody to marry your sorry butt that is, just remember this. If you want to stay married and be happy, your wife needs to be your best friend. Lotsa folk stay married but miss out on the happy part."

The 1941 vintage biplane was a beauty and resembled the crop duster that chased Cary Grant in the classic movie, *North X Northwest*, only a lot faster. Buddy had the one thousand horsepower plane in almost new condition.

Powered by Daimler-Benz, the Italian Fiat CR42B engine was tuned like Elton John's Steinway; and cotton season was now year-round, thanks to global warming.

Many farmers, especially in the South, benefitted from the twelve-month growing season, a silver lining in the otherwise abysmal cloud of weather patterns, except for the severe hailstorms that seemed to occur more often to destroy crops and livestock. The last cotton crop had matured to a record harvest until the hail destroyed nearly a thousand acres and only God knows how many animals, smashed into the dirt by what looked like large mothballs, perfectly round pieces of ice. It was weird, Buddy thought.

"Keep her tuned, Buddy. We need to begin spraying in two weeks. It's gonna be a hot spring, hotter than last year's; and the pests will have a field day."

The farmer swatted a mosquito on his forehead, a bloody imprint left behind on the palm of his weathered hand. Mosquitos seemed larger this year for some reason.

"She's tuned, Boss. I'm gonna take her on a test flight t'night and see how the new sprayer does. Those three lights we added should make night sprayin' a breeze, and they pop off easy when we race her." Buddy's hand stroked the royal blue and yellow flying machine as though the biplane was his pet. "And you know what, Boss? We'll definitely win the county air show this year. She's so shiny, she can't lose!"

Buddy had worked for the farmer for six years and was a superb mechanic and pilot. The Italian biplane, the fastest biplane in history, was known for its top speed of 323 miles per hour. With Buddy's expertise, fine tuning and reinforced wings this plane could easily reach 400 miles per hour with an attainable ceiling of almost 30,000 feet.

Farmer Kinsella was a great boss; and since Mama Boss had died, the old farmer had nothing special to spend his fortune on. *Why not a two-million dollar crop duster?*

Buddy slapped at the annoying horsefly and knocked his Indiana Jones hat to the ground. That left an open gateway to Buddy's balding head, and the horsefly dive-bombed the front with well-practiced accuracy. It was a perfect hit and escape for the fly.

"Owie zowie," Buddy yelped as the obsessed bug came back for more. A quick slap later and the pest was dead; what all good horseflies should be.

"Survival of the fittest, my friend," Buddy commented to no one but himself and the fly, "but you lost this time, butthead."

The old farmer looked over the fields, the creamy-yellow flowers beginning to appear on the latest cotton seed planting. Night spraying was an art but dangerous. The pests would descend to the depths of the blooms during the hot afternoons but would migrate to the tops in the cooler evenings, though not nearly as cool as the evenings used to be.

The organic pesticides of today might do the trick, though the farmer remembered the days when DDT was the pesticide-of-choice and wished it hadn't been banned. DDT was much more effective; but thanks to Rachel Carson and her concern for the thinning bird eggshells, DDT was now used only in third-world countries, places which apparently have no birds. Miss Carson's *Silent Spring* might have saved some bird eggs but at a great cost to farmers and malaria victims. Food prices had been going up since, in addition to the mosquito population.

"Where's all the help, Buddy?"

"I don't know, Boss. They went to Clemson last night for a pre-Super Bowl party and musta got drunk. It's early. They'll be here soon. What do ya think of the extra fuel tank I welded on yesterday? This baby'll be able to fly for several hours before refueling. We can cover a lot of acreage."

The old farmer removed his Clemson Tigers baseball cap and ran his hand through the thick white hair, a look of concern crossing his wrinkled face. It was unusual for the migrant help to be late, and he thought the *new* crew might be a bad influence on his regulars.

"The extra fuel'll be a good thing, Boss; but this-here increased sprayin' capacity; that's the blessin'. We lost most of the crop last year to hail and boll weevils, so we need to git sprayin'."

Chapter Eight

"The death toll from the fourteen VA Hospital bombings has now reached 1492 dead and thousands injured. Two security guards at Atlanta's VA Hospital spotted one of the terrorists leaving before the explosions yesterday. They chased the suspect over the wall of the first floor parking deck; but before they could get the man handcuffed, he died on the spot, an apparent victim of a cyanide tablet..."

"Dad, Jenni just got six comp tickets to the Super Bowl. Do you want to go with us?" Jami interrupted the news as she ran for the phone.

"Hurricane Abigail now has sustained winds of 117 miles per hour and is spinning well off the Georgia coast, but high surf and rip tides have claimed the lives of three more surfers. The storm, the earliest Atlantic hurricane in recorded history, is stationary. Due to the record-high ocean temperatures, the hurricane is predicted to reach category 4 by tomorrow morning. The National Hurricane Center says the storm should be no threat to the United States, but Bermuda is under a Hurricane Watch.

"And finally some good news. There are no meteor showers predicted for this week anywhere in the continental United States. Alaska and western parts of Canada remain under a meteor storm watch. Scientists at Goddard Space Flight Center and Johnson Propulsion Labs are keeping a wary eye on several large chunks of the Moon that broke off, the largest yet

observed. The International Space Station is no more after being hit...”

“Six tickets. Wow, how’d she do that?”

“Dad, it’s Jenni! She’s always getting guys to give her free stuff. Wanna go?” She disappeared into the kitchen and caught the phone on the third ring.

Any other time Jeff would’ve jumped at the chance to go to the Super Bowl, but he and Samarra would be in Jamaica. That is, unless the meteor showers grounded all aircraft again. This was the new norm since Dark Comet crashed into the Moon and knocked it *silly* as Audry liked to say.

The trip to Jamaica wouldn’t be a vacation but an attempt to communicate with Melissa. *What if it’s not her?* But Rosalie was sure, seemed sure. *Will she remember the kids if she doesn’t remember me?*

“Samarra and I won’t be here. Now that the Spanish Flu vaccine’s been approved by the FDA, she can leave the country.”

He wiped the sweat from his face and slapped at the mosquitos, an unfortunate consequence of the humidity and record heat. Dengue fever was the disease du jour, and he constantly worried about Audry, a mosquito magnet.

Super Bowls are scheduled well ahead of time, but this year an exception was made, agreeable to all parties. Atlanta had suffered greatly from the Buford Dam explosion. Losing its largest water source was bad; but the irradiated fish, fowl and the oysters at Apalachicola that glowed at night, at least it was rumored, had everyone scared. The nuclear explosion had been small, but the effects lingered.

Of course, the people camping in the area of the dam were killed instantly that night; and the bodies, though impossible to identify, were easily removed by sweeping the remaining ashes into small, environmentally approved plastic bags with a Homeland Security logo on each one.

The dead animals and fish had been a different problem, and the Chattahoochee remained polluted. The area within three miles of the dam-that-used-to-be was off limits to the public, but who would want to go there? The smell was breath-taking; the "death stench" was what the locals called it.

With the Spanish Flu ravaging the Northeast, the powers-that-be decided that the Super Bowl in Atlanta's new open-air stadium would be great for the area's economy and safer for the fans. The largest obstacle would be water and how to get enough for the restrooms.

The flu hadn't affected the South like it had other areas of the country for some reason; and that was the topic of the latest *Dateline* report, *Why the South was Spared.*

"That's one of the things I can't figure out," Samarra told Jeff one night by the pool. "It's odd since the flu spread from here. The infection rate in the South is ten percent of other area rates in the U.S. That's totally mind-blowing."

"Maybe the Bible-Belt has a guardian angel."

"Jeff, you don't believe in angels, silly boy. You told me many times." Samarra leaned over and kissed him softly on the lips.

"I do now. You're *my* angel."

Jeff smiled at the memory of that night. Maybe she was an angel.

The NFL considered cancelling the Super Bowl because of the flu, but Atlanta became a nice fit. New stadium, lots of seats, Southern hospitality and cooking and lots of pretty people. What's not to love? The Game would go on!

"Jami, listen to me. I would *really* prefer that you and Jenni not go. I have a bad feeling about it."

When Jeff had bad feelings, he had an uncanny way of being right, especially if the worry came from a dream. A lot of his dreams seemed to come true, or at least close to true. He was especially worried about Samarra after the dream… and he cleared the thoughts from his head.

"Daddy, Audry will have a conniption-fit if we don't go. She's already invited Chuck!"

Jeff looked into Jami's beautiful blue eyes and wondered where the time went. The twins were almost thirty and little Audry was getting a figure. It was flying by, he knew that for sure; and age was creeping in, an unwanted tenant.

"Audry's invited Hutz the Putz? And what exactly *is* a conniption-fit?"

Jeff chased the questions with a sip of his favorite chocolate-flavored coffee, after a mid-air toast. Jami laughed, as she often did when her dad cracked her up; and he did, often.

"Dad, he does *not* like to be called that, just sayin'. Be nice."

"I hope he's not some kind of child molester! You never know about those goody-goody guys, especially when they speak Hebrew and never had a Hebrew lesson. Plus, I thought I read he was Presbyterian, went to some church on Hillsboro Street."

"I'm sure you and Uncle Willy have had Chuck thoroughly checked out; I mean, really. It's like I grew up at CIA Headquarters. Microscopic spybots? Puhlease."

Jeff wasn't really worried, and Jami was correct. Wild Willy's background check had been thorough. It turned out that Hutz had quite a history but no sexual perversions had turned up. He was enamored with Barbra Streisand, which seemed kind of odd for a used car salesman. Chuck had liked his booze though and occasionally made small purchases of cocaine, not enough to support an addiction, according to Will. Referred to by many of his neighbors as “Up Chuck,” especially by an older lady named Helen who was quite vocal about it, Chuck Hutz had been far from Godly. On the other hand, he had no criminal history, paid his taxes on time; and now he spoke Hebrew fluently since the accident.

Audry had a keen since of perception and intuition for a pre-teen; and Hutz appeared to be a different man than he had once been. Jeff’s greatest concern was the nut-cases who Chuck offended in his rants. They might try to kill him again, like last year in Raleigh.

“What an ordeal that had been,” he said softly.

“What ordeal? What are you talking about, Dad? Are you okay? You’ve been talking to yourself a lot, Dad. You know what they say about that.”

Jami worried about her father. He hadn’t been the same since he got back from Jamaica. She still wondered why he hadn’t rescued her mom while he was there, but she knew her dad well and knew he was planning. He was *always* planning.

“The assassination attempt last year, when those guys tried to kill Hutz while he was speaking in one of his trances. Wasn’t that in Raleigh?”

Jeff remembered that event like it was yesterday. It had been a miracle certainly, it had to be. He really never believed in miracles until that day, but what else could it have been? Plus he had seen it with his own eyes as it happened, right on the new seventy inch big screen at *The Divide*. Two men, high-powered automatic weapons and ammo clips that held far more rounds than the five that were now legal to have, not to mention the "illegal" automatic weapons. Investigators eventually found more than three hundred rounds were fired that day in the park. It was fortunate that only fourteen were injured; but the miraculous part was that Chuck and Audry weren't hit. They were in the direct line of fire but suffered not a scratch.

"That was so weird! How did they miss? It was absolutely a miracle, Dad!"

"It was a coincidence," he replied.

"No. It was a *Godincidence*. You need to read that Gideons Bible, Dad! You know. The one that falls out of suitcases and the sky."

Jami saw the News Alert and turned up the TV, trained by her father, the newsaholic.

"...hurricane. This is the earliest named Atlantic storm in history, though it seems we've said that the past couple of years. The low pressure system formed off the coast of North Carolina and is predicted to continue east-northeast and then out to sea. Though the coasts of Florida, Georgia and South Carolina are in the high-surf range, no evacuations have been ordered for the Category 4 storm. It continues to move northeast toward Bermuda at the whopping speed of one mile per hour. Top winds now exceed 150, with gusts to 180.

"Now to the Middle East. The Islamic Federation of States has formed a unified and unprecedented coalition against the Israeli government, and troops are amassing to the north. Evangelicals are proclaiming this to be the coming war of Gog and Magog... did I pronounce that right?... and Israel is back on highest alert."

Condi had heard the term before but really had no clue what "Gog and Magog" meant. She didn't think it could be good and continued.

"A meteor shower has killed several people and thousands of livestock in famine-ridden South Africa, and scientists say large concentrations of arsenic have been detected in local water sources. They are not sure where the arsenic came from, but there is some speculation that it has something to do with the Dark Comet that collided with the Moon."

"Dad, do you ever think about why all this bad stuff is happening everywhere?"

Jeff concentrated on the last news item, arsenic in the water. He remembered his mom's constant warnings. "Water will turn as bitter as wormwood and everything will be poisoned. Says so in God's Book." He would dig out Gideons tonight and try to find the verse.

"Not really, Jami," he lied. Of course he wondered.

"You mean you don't think it's odd that Mom disappeared in a Caribbean tsunami? When was the last time the Caribbean even had a tsunami? And now we find out she's alive?"

"Actually, there have been several tsunamis," Jeff paused in reflection, "… almost a hundred since 1498. There have been almost five thousand deaths, at least until the latest."

"Forty-foot tsunamis, Dad?" Jami asked, voice rising an octave at the end. "Dad, there were twenty thousand killed in the Cayman tsunami. You don't think it's odd that Mom turned up after we all thought she was in heaven?"

Jami began to cry, and her thoughts that her mom might not even remember her were devastating; or that it might not even be Mom. Jeff held her close as she sobbed. Jenni returned from the bathroom and joined her twin, now identical sobbers.

"No, there haven't been any forty-foot tsunamis reported," Jeff admitted. "Just *that* one."

The day was even warmer than usual; and mosquitos swarmed in the morning air, thick with humidity. Samarra would be over soon, and Jeff lit the mosquito fogger.

"Dad, do you ever think about why all this bad stuff is happening everywhere?"

Jeff considered the question. There had been the strange disappearances, though they seemed to have stopped. The terrorist attacks in the South were unusual since most attacks were in New York, Chicago or Los Angeles. However, it was nature's shenanigans that were especially worrisome. All the things his mom used to tell him about, the things of the *last days*, especially the strange weather.

Then there were the volcanos, earthquakes and hailstorms; the pink moon, now with rings; power losses from unprecedented solar activity; Spanish Flu, smallpox and HIV pandemics; droughts and floods; tsunamis and super-hurricanes like the one forming in the east.

"Did you hear about the cat attack in Canada, Dad?"

"Nope, can't say that I did."

"You mean I saw something news worthy before you? Glory Halleluiah! There is a God!"

Jeff put the flyer about real estate in Panama on the table and asked, "What kind of cats?"

"Regular cats. Feral cats, actually. Happened yesterday at Crystal Beach, close to Buffalo. This nanny was pushing a baby in a stroller along Lake Erie, because the weather was so warm. It was almost dark, and all these cats ran out of the woods and attacked. By the time some men heard her screams and got to her, she was almost dead and so was the baby. The authorities said the cats probably had rabies but didn't know for sure since they got away. Weird, huh?"

It *was* weird, Jeff thought, like so many other things.

"It's in the Bible, you know." Jenni said.

"What's in the Bible?" Jeff asked.

"Wild animals attacking people in the last days. Mom read it to us. God put a fear of man in the animals after the flood so they wouldn't attack people, did you know that? But in the last days, God's gonna remove the fear, so the animals will start attacking, just the wild animals though, not Harley. You know, like bears and coyotes. Scary huh?"

"And feral cats?" Jeff asked. "Where does it say that?"

"It's somewhere in Revelation, Dad. You can look it up in your mysterious Gideons Bible. I think it's Chapter 6.

Though the morning sky was perfectly blue and cloudless, loud thunder sounded to the east; and large chunks of ice began falling from the sky, sporadic as usual. Jeff and the twins ran for the newly- installed underground shelter out of reflex and fear. Jeff hoped his reinforced slate roof would withstand the storm. Megacryometeorites, that's what they called them; but Jeff had a better name. Megapaininthebutts, that's what they were.

Herding the twins to safety, thankful that these storms were always brief, Jeff found himself again thinking about the rapture, all the disappearing people; and he wrestled with the possibility. *What if it was true?* The thought was brief. Obviously, had the rapture already happened, if there was such a thing, Melissa would surely have been a participant. And why wouldn't Jami, Jenni and Audry have disappeared? They were good Christians.

For the first time, Jeff's heart felt heavy with the thoughts and possibilities. *What if he was wrong?* Melissa had always asked him that question. Now Samarra had asked the same, "What if you're wrong Jeff?"

While Jeff and the girls sought shelter, four-hundred miles to the north a bus sized, iron-laden meteorite slammed into Kerr Lake, one of the largest Army Corps of Engineers reservoirs, straddling the North Carolina and Virginia border. Kimball Point was the crown-jewel of camping sites and extended out into the pristine lake as a slender peninsula.

Unfortunately, in a flash the extravagant RV campground ceased to exist; and the surrounding lake homes were no more. The reservoir's large dam was weakened, though the cracks remained under water, unseen. The ground shuddered for thirty seconds, and the death toll rose. Nature had far outdone the jihadists when it came to terror, destruction and death.

Two miles away, a farmer tilling a distant field heard a whooshing sound and looked up into the morning sky, toward the lake; and he was sure, just for an instant, he saw a large, black horse in the rising smoke and clouds. Then it was gone, and the farmer was killed instantly when a large boulder fell from the sky and onto his tractor. He would never be able to tell his wife about the black horse.

"You know Admiral, I'm beginning to get stressed."

The Admiral had noticed the change in Chad's demeanor but thought the new haircut might have something to do with his personality shift. He was a proud man and was especially proud of his long locks. He was not pleased that he had been told to get a haircut by the new boss.

"I can understand that!" The Admiral said, and he could. The last three years *had* been stressful. "What's going on now?"

Chad was beginning to feel his age, and he figured the stress of his job had something to do with that; and now this.

"Oh, not much. Just a few thousand disappearing stars, which is a little weird. Meteorites are destroying dams and poisoning water sources all over the world. Come look at this."

The Admiral, Chad and the new lab tech gathered around the large display, a 108-inch LED flatscreen mounted to the wall of the lab, like several other flatscreens. Chad thought the new tech was pretty hot, and fantasies of a romantic dinner danced through his head even though she was a mere child in her thirties. He liked younger women.

"These images were provided by SOHO, and the information is semi-classified. Look at these coronal temperature graphs."

They studied the digital images from the *Solar and Heliospheric Observatory* spacecraft. Launched in 1995, the spacecraft monitored solar activity. In the process, SOHO had discovered thousands of roaming comets, many of which crashed into the Sun; and occasionally, other planets. Decades later, SOHO was still working like a charm.

"The surface temperatures have increased significantly," The Admiral commented. Chad glanced at the thirty-something woman and wondered what she might look like with her hair down. She smiled at him.

"Pay attention, Chad; your tongue is hanging out." The Admiral winked at the tech, now blushing.

"The temperatures are increasing," Chad responded, "but this is even more troubling. Data suggests there is a major Coronal Mass Ejection working its way up from deep below the surface. You can see suspect images here, and here." Chad pointed the laser to an adjacent wall monitor and was concerned that the CME might come to fruition while facing Earth.

"That would explain the coronal temperature increase. But why an increase in surface temp?" The technician quickly analyzed the data on the large screen. "Uh oh," she said, after a pause.

"Uh oh, is right," Chad repeated. "The data is consistent."

The tech was a graduate student from MIT specializing in the field of Solar Science and Technology. Even as a little girl, she had always been intrigued with the Sun. Her curiosity grew as she aged, and she marveled at what drove the solar engine with so much consistency over so many billions of years. She always thought it odd that the interior of the Sun was twenty-five million degrees, but the surface was only ten thousand. Just above the surface, the corona was a cloud of plasma gas a million degrees hotter than the surface below.

Her first solar eclipse at the age of six, looking through the dark, smoked glass had revealed the corona, flaring out from the Sun's surface. It was beautiful and looked like a cosmic engagement ring. She had been hooked on the Sun ever since.

"Look at this," she blurted. "The solar surface temp is consistent, except for the area in the left, upper quadrant. That definitely looks like a CME forming. It could be larger than the Carrington Event."

"The Carrington Event?" The Admiral murmured.

"Yes," she continued. "On September 1, 1859, Richard Carrington, a British astronomer, observed the largest-ever CME heading directly toward Earth. It reached Earth in seventeen hours, which was highly unusual. The journey normally takes about four days.

"The ejection was massive, and aurorae could be seen as far south as the Caribbean Islands. The Northern Lights were so bright over the Rockies that gold miners thought it was daybreak and started preparing breakfast. The lights lasted a couple of days.

"Though there were no recorded deaths, several workers on telegraph lines suffered severe electrical shocks; and some telegraph offices actually caught on fire."

The Admiral and Chad stared at the perky little tech with a new-found respect. Chad looked her straight in the eye and asked, "Do you want to get married? I have a ring."

The technician laughed out loud when The Admiral reminded Chad that he had two engagement rings in his home safe. She liked these guys already, they made her laugh.

CHAPTER NINE

Jean Luc, Senior Plant Manager at the Civaux Nuclear facility, was not a patient man. Like many Frenchmen, he had a tendency to show his emotions, and Jean Luc was definitely emotional.

"G'morning, Jean. Looks like another hot one," the programmer said. "Just made it to the parking garage before the hail started."

The programmer's car was already full of dents and the front windshield had been replaced twice in the last month. Almost all cars were dented from the unprecedented hailstorms.

"Good morning."

Jean Luc smiled as best he could and looked over the young programmer's shoulder to check the graphics on the screen. The indicators were all green or blue, no red; and that was a good thing. The first sign of red at a nuclear facility was never good. The bad weather continued unabated, but the heavy protective dome shrouded the sounds of the hailstones hitting the facility.

"Monsieur Jean Luc?" the programmer asked. "Can we talk a minute?" The man looked around nervously but remained calm.

"Sure Remy, what's up?"

"Can we talk in private?" Remy asked.

Jean Luc examined the monitor, and everything was well within limits, still no red. That wasn't the norm, but it was good news. There was always at least one red warning indicator. Jean

Luc had another headache and pressed the left side of his head as they walked into the Plant Manager's office. Jean Luc noted the troubled expression on Remy's face. Maybe it had something to do with the pregnant wife.

"What do you want to discuss, Remy?" Jean Luc closed the heavy metal door.

"Jean Luc, you know of my wife's pregnancy and all the trouble she has had."

"I've heard some," and Jean Luc had heard bits-and-pieces. "Is she doing better?"

"No sir, she is not. It is our second child, and you know," Remy wiped his eyes, "After the first baby died, she hasn't been the same. They are placing her in premature labor today. I must go to be with her, Jean Luc."

Jean Luc quickly analyzed the situation. Remy hadn't been with the French nuclear plant for long, less than a year. It had been rough he was sure, with the death of a child and then a complicated pregnancy. He would find someone to take over.

"Yes Remy, you go be with her. We'll handle it. Clock out; and Remy, I will pray for you."

Remy was thankful for Jean Luc's kind heart, and he felt a little guilt about lying; but not much. He needed to get as far away as possible, because he knew that danger lurked inside the nuclear core.

Gathering the personal items from his locker, Remy tossed the tube of Liquid Nail in the trash can and threw some paper towels on top, used the toilet and headed to the exit. The Liquid Nail was a wonderful thing, and the shut-off valves to the emergency water supply for the cooling towers were now sealed tightly. They would not be opened, at least not in time.

Remy made the short walk to the parking garage and started the twenty year old dented, dark green Citroen and was surprised at the pungent smell, an aroma of death permeating from the locked storage container in the trunk. He would dispose of his wife's body as soon as he was out of sight of the plant. She had given the ultimate sacrifice, only she had not volunteered. Remy smiled. Allahu Akbar.

A few miles to the north, *The Preacher* completed his manipulation of the French nuclear plants. He no longer needed his computers but knew they couldn't remain in the small church basement. They would eventually be found by French security. Packing and moving the electronics wasn't feasible in a short period of time, plus neighbors might think the sudden departure suspicious. Fortunately, he had planned.

Mohammed set the timer for thirty minutes, knowing that the white-phosphor bomb would take care of the computer equipment, melting it into an incongruous mass of plastic and glass. The barbeque grill had been stored in an adjacent room, along with twenty propane tanks. Once the heat reached the propane tanks, the small church would be no more. Security would question why there were so many tanks stored for the small grill, but the church was known for cookouts for the poor people in the area.

Mohammed moved the body of the slain man into the sanctuary, small statured like Mohammed with a similarly trimmed beard, as though that would matter. He picked up his smart phone and texted the planned message to the local police department.

"recved another threat msg. bro'hood has promised to kill me. somethin spicious. the preacher."

Mohammed sent the text after making sure the night sky was dark, the Moon obscured by thick clouds. He mounted his bicycle and pedaled into the distance, down a small trail and behind a storage facility where Remy waited in the dented Citroen.

"Smells good, Remy. Is there a dead body in the trunk?"

"There was. It deteriorated in the heat a lot faster than I thought. I threw the body in the river. The pieces are so small, they will never know if it's a man or woman, if they even find it. The fish are hungry."

The oversight and smell of death irked Mohammed to no end, and the careless mistake would surely be Remy's last.

Chapter Ten

"Good mornin' Dr. B! Visitin' your mom?"

The Physical Plant Engineer at Plant Vogtle was always jovial, and he had a special fondness for Dr. Brunson, mostly because of the way he treated his mom. Dr. B's mom had lived in Waynesboro her whole life, a good Christian woman if there ever was one.

"Good mornin'. Yeah, I'm visiting my mom; yesterday was her ninetieth." Dan picked a gnat out of his hair.

Over the years Dan Brunson maintained a certain fondness for Waynesboro but thought they needed to change the Georgia town's motto from The Birddog Capital of the World to the Gnat Capital of the World. They were always bad, but this year was like none he had seen.

"Dr. B, I think we have a problem. About thirty minutes ago I marked the cooling pool. It seemed to be losing water very slowly. I was headed to the control lab to check the temps."

"Is it in alarm status?" Dan asked.

"No, that's the goofy part. It's like an ultraslow leak, but the auto-backup should keep the cooling pool consistent."

"How much is it down?"

"Not much, almost negligible." The engineer knew that the loss wouldn't cause damage, but where was the coolant going? "The alarms shoulda picked it up."

Dan and Rich Robilliard became friends at their first meeting, and Rich had earned his respect as a plant engineer.

Several times during visits to his mother, he and Rich would have breakfast at the only remaining breakfast restaurant in Waynesboro, just across from Piggly Wiggly. He had no reason to doubt Rich's concern, and he didn't.

A Georgia Tech graduate with a Ph.D. in nuclear physics and a minor in nanotechnology applications, Dan had worked with some of the world's most sophisticated military weapons systems. Though nuclear power plants weren't his particular field, he did know there should be no loss of coolant in a nuclear reactor, just like in the radiator of an automobile.

۞

"Seas're gettin' a little rough, mate."

The captain was a weather-freak and knew Hurricane Abby was supposed to be well north of the luxury submarine. The seas that had been mildly turbulent were now seven feet and growing, murky and fearful.

"Weather Channel said the Gulf Stream was outta whack. Looks like the windstorm's making a u-turn." The Australian captain remained calm, cool and collected. That's why they paid him so much.

The Seattle 1000 submarine yacht was 118 feet long and could take the seas with no problem, except the sea sickness. The captain knew the water would be calm three hundred feet down, and clearer. He had piloted a lot of tourist subs; but man, this was a helluva machine. The see-through hull and bright underwater lights made maneuvering simple, with a little help from the sonar system that was "the best of its kind" according to ship specs.

"I'd say they're rough." The Japanese man answered the captain, curt as always.

The tourist was used to rough seas, including his tumultuous marriage, and had been on plenty of deep-sea excursions; this, the first with his wife. She was deathly ill, not just from the rough seas, but no one knew that except him. His opportunity might be lost if they submerged. He knew he must act fast and prayed to his gods for good fortune, though he thought the hurricane had missed them. It was supposed to head north with the Gulf Stream.

"We need to submerge," the captain yelled over the howling wind.

The captain's encounter with the Japanese charter group was a first, and one he was likely to never forget. He studied the weather images, updates changing rapidly, as everyone in the group stayed in their staterooms, or more likely, the head; except the Japanese businessman who remained cool as a cucumber.

The captain empathized with the group, as even two of his three-man crew were sick. A sudden wind-gust rocked the ship and it leaned hard to port. Several wine glasses toppled inside, unheard by most.

"In a second. My wife is almost delirious, and I'm concerned about pressurization. We're not sinking are we?"

The man didn't wait for an answer and entered the lounge of the luxury yacht, passing by the mahogany bar inlaid with small crustaceans under a clear acrylic top along with other tiny sea creatures. He must hurry.

The *tourist* was a member of a subversive and secretive group of Japanese businessmen and women, *very* wealthy men and women, known secretly as "the baby bombers" and by a privileged few, as the *Select.* No one really knew they existed, except for the *Select.*

The group was intent on destroying the United States with the same kind of destruction that hit Hiroshima and Nagasaki when they were still in the womb, at least some of them. Some of the small but politically powerful group were young but knew the stories of their grandfathers and uncles, mothers and sisters, vaporized in a flash as though they hadn't even been there, all because of America's nuclear bomb on August 6, 1945. They would not forget that date, and they had big plans.

The *Select* had financed the successfully-hijacked Indian nuclear sub. While the mission had not been a failure exactly, it was far from a success.

The mission had destroyed America's large bomber-base on Diego Garcia. No B-52's would be launched from that base for years to come.

The story about the nuked air base had almost no news coverage, unlike the successful attack on the Panama Canal. Though the Panama Canal wasn't destroyed, the Pedro Miguel Locks were. The canal would be closed for months or years to come. Even if workmen could repair the disaster, the radiation should keep them away for a while. However, New York and Tel Aviv were still standing, as was the Suez Canal; so the *Select* considered the mission less than a success.

They didn't really hate the Jews like their Muslim partners in terror, but the Jews were friends with the Americans which made them the enemy.

The Japanese tourist's thoughts journeyed back to the present and his uncontrollable wife's ongoing threat to expose the secretive operation. She only threatened when drunk, but she was drunk a lot lately.

The wife remained on her knees in the bathroom, almost leaning completely into the toilet. This was not the typical head you might see in a submarine, with granite countertops, a marble tub, bidet and private shower with champagne bar. He fingered the small vial and handkerchief in his pocket, fishing it out as he heard his wife making friends with the toilet, one more time.

The Florida Keys weren't everything they were touted to be, at least after the wave; but still, they had recovered for the most part. The sand was white, the water was clear and the temperatures were cooler than Atlanta, a mild 78 degrees with a warm westerly breeze, a perfect January morning.

The Soufriére Tsunami, one of the names the wave was now called, had not totally wiped out the Keys but had accomplished some architectural cleansing. Most of the historical sites, including Hemmingway's home, remained; though some remained damaged. The shanty town areas were now gone as were most of the iconic feral cats, washed away in an instant by the series of five-foot waves.

Taci left the small, Caribbean themed bed-n-breakfast in her now packed Volkswagen Beetle; and the small red car with red wheel-covers headed northeast, leaving Key West in her rearview mirror. The skies were sunny, the seas calm; and her relaxing vacation had come at a good time.

She turned the radio up to listen to the latest weather as clouds rolled in from the north, and wind began to gnaw at her Beetle.

Taci was refreshed and healed thoroughly from her tragic accident a couple years earlier in L.A. She still didn't remember much about the meteorite that destroyed the van she was driving, but at least she was alive and well. The small car swayed in the wind.

Taci's recovery had been a long and painful journey. The burns were surgically repaired and healed as best severe burns could heal; and the two-month vacation at Key West, thanks to the generosity of one Mr. Jeffrey Ross, had been the icing on the proverbial but painful cake. She was looking forward to meeting Mr. Ross again. It would be her second meeting, her first when he was the passenger in the Jetvan she was driving when the meteorite hit.

With the station settled on *The Weather Channel* and the latest commercial for one of JL Robb's upcoming novels fading in the background, the news of Hurricane Abigail was back on. Taci figured that's all that would be on the station until the unusual storm was over.

"... 87 for today, and a high of 91 tomorrow in Miami with heavy rain and winds.

"In the plains, there will be thunderstorms to the north and meteor showers to the south. The meteor showers will be lighter than yesterday, and most will burn up in the atmosphere."

"Oh mannn...," she said out loud though no one was in the red Beetle except her and God. "God, help us all; I mean, meteor showers? Really? On the weather report?"

She longed for the good old days when big rocks and huge chunks of ice weren't falling from the sky.

"It's like the Earth's in a shooting gallery."

That was the last thing she remembered Jeff telling her before she lost consciousness that afternoon in La Jolla, the day her whole world changed in a split second. She had since learned that split-second, earth-shaking changes in one's life had become fairly common.

"Hurricane Abby is making a U-turn it seems after gaining respect as a Category 4 storm."

The weather girl had a lisp, and Taci thought of her scarred body. Most of her skin escaped the burns; and her youth helped in the healing process, at least the physical healing. The mental healing would take longer, she was sure. Her arms healed well, but her left leg would forever be blemished. She didn't feel insecure and thanked God for not letting it be worse. *Thanks for my guardian angels, Lord. They're always there when I need them,* she prayed silently in gratitude. The wind continued to gust, sometimes blowing the small Volkswagen into the oncoming lane.

"Abby was headed east toward Bermuda when the free-spirited storm suddenly veered southward at a slow rate of speed, but winds are strengthening rapidly. There still appears to be no threat for Atlantic coastal areas as prevailing winds should steer the storm back toward open-ocean within twenty-four hours. The Gulf Stream is showing a strong northward current. The path at this point is contradictory to all computer models, including the European model known for its accuracy.

"Hurricane Abby is noteworthy, not just for being the earliest hurricane in the Atlantic but for the rapid drop in barometric pressure. The pressure has dropped from 1007 to 960 millibars in less than twelve hours, unprecedented."

The commentator sneezed.

"I'm sorry; must be getting a cold," and the young woman hoped it wasn't the new Spanish Flu variant CDC was talking about. "*Let's go to Dr. Dennis Duncan on assignment with The Weather Channel."*

Taci adjusted the mirror and checked her hair; lipstick was perfect. She slipped her beach sandals off and proceeded northward, barefooted. The Diet Coke was gone, so she would stop soon. Her throat was dry, probably the salt air.

"Dr. Duncan. What can you tell us about this sudden drop in pressure?"

The young weather girl wiped her nose with a small tissue and appeared uneasy to those watching on television. She flexed her fingers together, intertwining and untwining nervously.

"It certainly doesn't bode well for shipping traffic in the mid-Atlantic; and at this rate it could make Category 5 by tomorrow morning. That would be..."

Taci, tired of the news, turned the radio to a Reggae station, playing the steering wheel like a steel drum with her fingertips. Her thoughts were suddenly in Jamaica and the Land of Negril, and she hoped one day to make a visit.

The skies to the east of Miami were darkening; and had Taci listened to more weather and less Bob Marley, she would have heard the *Weather Alert*. Then she would have known that the storm had turned further south toward Florida, and the forward motion had increased "considerably."

Driving north on U.S. 1, she passed the Cheeca Lodge Resort in Islamorada and thought she might have to stay there on her next trip to the Keys. It was beautiful and very tropical with a blue-tiled roof. With large date palms lining the entry and the tiny white lights wrapped around the trunks, Cheeca Lodge looked like paradise.

A sudden gust shoved the Beetle off the road and onto the small shoulder, and Taci fought for control. Two of the date palms fell, one crushing a black Mercedes convertible; but that scene was lost to Taci as she continued northward.

Driving over the numerous bridges just a few feet above the water had been fun on the way down, when the seas were calm; but now water splashed on the roadway, some waves beginning to break the railings. The sea had been calm in Key West; but now just an hour later, the world suddenly seemed darker and foreboding. Lightening flashed in the east, and a dark funnel cloud was born but hidden from view by the surrounding rings of rain.

Jeff's flight to Jamaica was uneventful, a nice change, no space rocks knocking planes out of the sky. Glancing out the window, the Moon faintly appeared off to the left in the morning sky. The pink rings were barely visible as the plane flew at 30,000 feet, and the sky was a dark blue. He couldn't see much to the north as he pressed against the portal, but the sky was gray, almost green. He ordered a latté but was asleep by the time the young stewardess brought the steamy cup, overflowing with a creamy froth. The next thing he remembered was the announcement.

"Please secure all seatbelts and store any loose items."

Jeff opened his eyes, squinted as the sunlight shown in and then closed them again in reflex more than voluntary response. Surely they couldn't already be landing. How long had he slept?

"Mr. Ross, you need to secure yourself for the landing."

Her voice was soothing. He opened his eyes again to focus, and the Sun's bright glow silhouetted the attendant. He saw nothing but a dark, feminine form. Montego Bay appeared below, and the plane adjusted for final approach.

The stewardess leaned over and checked his seatbelt, then took a seat beside him. Putting her hands together she appeared to be praying, lips moving silently while she spoke with God, or whoever her god might be. There seemed to be enough for everyone, he thought.

Seeing the stewardess ardently praying as the plane prepared to land was a little unnerving. He checked his window and the sky was still clear, like the Caribbean below.

Jeff felt no guilt for leaving his fiancée to come to Jamaica to visit his ex-wife who was dead but was now alive. He hoped Wild Willy had some good news and would be on time for a change. What a year this had been, and it was beginning to look like this one would be even weirder. Jeff felt the landing gear descend and lock. Glancing out the portal, he was shocked to see all the seagulls on the beach and circling below the descending jet.

Driving down Peachtree Street, azaleas and dogwoods were in full bloom. Samarra knew the strange weather-events were signs from God. Dogwoods and azaleas did not bloom in January.

She chose to stay at her home in Buckhead of her own accord. Jeff encouraged her to move in with him, but she could tell his heart wasn't in it. She knew it was because of his daughters, and she understood.

The engagement now on hold, Samarra had decided to let Jeffrey handle his first meeting with Melissa on his own. She knew how much he had loved her, even when she remarried; and Samarra wasn't sure she would ever be secure in Jeff's feelings for her. She loved Melissa but didn't want to be a "replacement." She had already experienced one husband with *other* interests, and once was enough.

Samarra turned off tree-lined Peachtree Battle and drove her Mercedes into the quarter-mile driveway. She was suddenly lonely. Her Buckhead home was on the market, whose wasn't;

but there had been no serious inquiries. At an asking price of twelve million, her market was dwindling as the world economy continued its downward spiral. Gas was nearly ten dollars a gallon, and her electric bills had gone through the roof since the "alternative energy" law had been implemented. Crime was epidemic, though not in this area of Atlanta; but it was imminent. She kept a close watch.

She stopped the dark sedan at the front entry, by the three-tiered, marble fountain. She was often amused at why two small statues of young boys standing at each end of the fountain peed recirculated water toward each other, and why that was ever cool to begin with. She found it disgusting. Now she wondered if her imprisoned ex-husband had the fountain designed like that intentionally. The defamed U.S. Senator had surely liked little boys it seemed.

Suddenly her mood dimmed, and she probably would've cried had she not seen the man dressed in camouflage leaving the back deck by the gardens. Had he seen her?

Samarra's hand slid into her purse and confirmed the presence of her *Bond Ranger II* Derringer, a gift from Jeff. She slowly eased her car door open, planning her escape and wished she had her Glock instead. Changing her mind, she decided to leave and call police when safely away.

As she hit the electronic *start* button, the twelve-cylinder engine came back to life; but there would be no escaping this day as the man attacked and pulled Samarra from the car, placing a chloroform-soaked rag over her mouth.

Her body now limp, Vinny carried the small woman into her home. It would be a nice night, he thought to himself; and then he would kill her, Insha'Allah. But first he would have to see her naked, and the corners of his mouth turned upward.

Vinny was the personification of evil; but in his mind, he was the personification of Godliness, ridding the world of the infidel for Allah, and this miserable Eve of a woman.

Chapter Eleven

Plant Vogtle Nuclear Plant
Waynesboro, Georgia

"Any HH?" Dan asked the facility engineer.

The afternoon Sun had Waynesboro at a steamy eighty-six degrees, and it was only January. The gnats in the past had been stymied by a few cold, winter days; but that hadn't happened in years it seemed to Dan, and he would know.

"No sir," Rich answered.

The facility's software kept precise data on any attempted unauthorized intrusions in a Hack-History file. Rich had examined the HH file as soon as he noticed, or at least thought he did, a slight loss of reactor coolant.

"They would have to be exceptional to break through all the layers of security we have, Dr. B."

Dan knew "they" *were* exceptional. The Chinese were probably the world's leading experts at invading the networks of other countries, especially the United States. However, a U.S.-based Christian militia had compromised several Department of Transportation networks and at least two water treatment plants. There were reports yesterday from Europe of a similar problem with nuclear plants in France and Germany, only the leaks were apparently worse.

"Rich, have you ever heard of al Quds?"

"Sounds familiar, Dr. B."

"Al Quds is Arabic, and it's the Muslim name for Jerusalem. It means "Holy."

"Hmmm; I was thinking more of a military force," Rich responded.

"Then you would be correct, Mr. Robilliard. Al Quds is a special force of Iran's Revolutionary Guard, sort of like a special force of a Special Forces unit. It's an elite group, and these people are far from stupid. They were formed during the Iran-Iraq War as an intelligence gathering agency. That was during the eighties, almost four decades ago."

"Oh yeah, Dr. B. Didn't President Bush try to tell Congress that al Quds was arming the Iraqis so they could kill our soldiers?"

"Bingo! You got it. You have to realize though, after no weapons of mass destruction were found in Iraq, Bush lost a lot of credibility. Congress and the Senate didn't want to hear anything about 'intelligence' stating anything."

"Yeah, it's always been a war of the egos going on in Washington. I don't think it was supposed to be like that, but maybe it always has been."

"It always has been to an extent, Rich; but not to the extent it is today. The Age of Narcissism has set in. Anyway, al Quds may have the best hacking capabilities in the world, even better than China."

Iran's acquisition of Iraq and Syria, though it wasn't called an "acquisition," allowed al Quds access to military and communication systems designed by U.S. engineers. Something was going on.

"They did find weapons of mass destruction, Dr. B.

"Saddam Hussein was a walkin' talkin' WMD," Rich continued. "He gassed his own people, killed five thousand. He took his gun out and shot parliamentarians in the head; his forces threw dissenters off the tops of buildings and stuffed people into plastic grinders. And oh yeah, excuse me, I almost forgot. There are the two million he killed during that there Iran-Iraq War you mentioned. More killed than all the wars of the eighties put together."

"Nerve agents. He gassed the Kurds with nerve agents. It was the largest chemical weapons attack in world history."

"Exactly. That's what I'm sayin' Dr. B. Hussein *was* a WMD. He also tried to assasinate a U.S. President, George Bush's daddy. Remember that? You'd think nobody remembered. Plus, Israel's Mossad said Hussein moved all his WMD to Lebanon before we ever went into Iraq."

Dan Brunson was at Plant Vogtle for the grand opening of the new reactor. Federal budget cuts and so many federal employees dead from the flu made it necessary for college professors and private specialists to "help out." The government was running out of money.

Suddenly it was back to the John Kennedy days of "Ask not what your country can do for you; ask what you can do for your country." It had worked; and here he was, doing for his country as a volunteer.

The additional nuclear reactor would make the Waynesboro plant the largest provider of electricity in the national grid network. The coolant loss, if there was one, was especially troublesome. After meeting with the control room technical staff and checking alarm sequencing, everything seemed to check out. It made no sense. Maybe Rich had been mistaken, but that would be a first, he figured.

"LOCAs?" Dan asked.

"No LOCAs, Dr. B," Rich replied.

The plant manager had already checked the log for *Loss-of-Coolant Accidents*. Loss of coolant at this plant could cause a really bad day the engineer reckoned. Waynesboro was a small town, but still…

"How much has the coolant temperature risen?" Dan knew there would have to be an increase if there was less coolant.

"That's another puzzle. There hasn't been a temperature increase. That's why the alarms aren't sequencing."

Dan scratched the side of his balding head, noting a small lump that hadn't been there earlier and then remembered the mosquito. He needed to get repellant.

The Plant Vogtle ceremony was a natural choice for him. He was born and raised in Waynesboro and still had family in the area. It hadn't changed much over the years, the blacks still congregating on Saturday night downtown, their pretty ladies always decked out in colorful dresses and ready to go.

Coming to the plant this morning, the moist air smelled of pesticide like it always had in Waynesboro, though they used DDT when he was a kid. DDT smelled much stronger, but childhood memories were stirred nonetheless. Cotton fields were blooming in large fields, left and right, beautifully colored wildflowers along the side of the road. He didn't remember ever seeing so much cotton in bloom, and never in January.

Waynesboro had been a choice location for the Plant Vogtle Nuclear facility. The area was rural with less than 6,000 people within ten miles of the plant, a population that could be easily and quickly evacuated and plenty of water.

Though multiple layers of safety were now incorporated into nuclear plant construction, Vogtle was in a league of its own with all the latest and greatest technology in the industry. Additionally, each generator had a self-contained coolant pool located above that could be operated manually and would not be affected by computer glitches. The cost had been enormous, more than twelve times the original estimate, due to improved safety and environmental regulations. Though accidents were rare, anything was possible with nuclear fission.

"How's Suki?" the woman in the white tunic asked. She held the handrail as the luxury yacht shifted in the rough seas.

The Japanese man was startled as the small but plump woman exited her bedroom. She had been deathly ill an hour earlier. He wondered what his friend saw in this woman. She was a busy-body, always snooping.

"She's not good; but she's better than she was, at least I hope. She's lying down now, trying to get a little sleep. I'm going to tell the captain to submerge and try to avoid this storm. I will see you later."

Slowly and quietly the man entered the yacht's master suite; and as he suspected, his drunken wife was hugging the toilet and didn't hear him enter. As she wretched into the open container, her husband of twelve years approached quietly, out of sight, out of mind. He was sick of this woman.

With the next body spasm, the loving husband held her from behind, the chloroform handkerchief firmly over her mouth as she ingested the remaining waste she had shared earlier with the toilet. Within twenty seconds, the woman with the soft pale skin and jet black hair, a dedicated but *mouthy* wife of twelve years, lay helplessly by the commode on her back. Any autopsy would prove "death by emesis ingestion."

Cautiously the new widower left his suite and nearly ran into the other two associates from Tokyo. They looked pale but better than the last time he saw them.

"Feeling better?" he asked.

"There's a storm," one of the men said, trying to hold down what little, if any, remained in his stomach.

"Yes, we are preparing to dive."

He hoped the two men didn't die on him. They were Japanese Navy men, retired; and they knew all one needed to know about submarines. Their primary mission would be a dive operation.

Exiting the carpeted lounge and onto the yacht's pilot deck, he stopped and took a deep breath. The sky was several shades darker than just a few minutes before and winds were incredible.

"How's the missus?" the captain asked, not as jovial as usual, maybe worried.

"She's fine I guess, finally sleeping like a dog. I hope she will be okay," and the man put on a grim face. "Let's dive, mate."

Two minutes later the hatches were secure and the luxury sub entered the depths of the Atlantic Ocean. They would descend to 200 feet and head back toward Hilton Head, except for the one stop, the one the captain didn't know about. The ship could travel submerged for thirty hours, and the hurricane would be long gone by then.

The captain didn't stare but kept a wary eye on the Japanese man; he had a bad feeling. Any man who would refer to his ailing wife as a dog could not be a good thing. *Sleeping like a dog?* The insult rubbed the Australian the wrong way.

The water two hundred feet below the surface was as calm and quiet as a library; but well above the sea surface, Hurricane

Abby continued to churn toward Category 5, Jacksonville now in her crosshairs.

Chapter Twelve

Jeff's small plane landed at Ken Jones Airport in Port Antonio, now just a two-hour drive to Kingston, Jamaica's often violent capital. The flight from Mobay had been bumpy but otherwise uneventful. The Ken Jones runway was less than 3,500 feet long, so the landing was breathtaking, even to Jeff.

Exiting the small twin-engine Beechcraft, Jeff was glad to see Wild Willy waiting, a black SUV, maybe a Grand Cherokee, idling in one of the ten parking spaces by the fence lined with lavender and white bougainvillea.

Wild Willy loved Jeeps; but then he loved anything drivable or flyable, especially old World War II aircraft. He had his own personal B-29 Stratofortress, reconditioned and garaged in Warner Robins just south of Macon, along with one of the few remaining B-36 Peacemakers, a "J" model he would always clarify.

"Hey, Will. Thanks for meeting me on such short notice."

They shook hands and hugged.

"Still drinking that pink wine?"

"Where are the women?" Will quipped, "and yes, white zin is the only drink for real men. I'm ready for one now!"

"Some things never change, Wild Willy."

"Where are we gonna meet Rosalie?" Will asked. He had not met the cleaning woman and was skeptical of anyone, and anything, he didn't know. It was his nature.

"We're to meet at a small café just to the west of Kingston, *Jammin' Joe's* at Spanish Town. Rosalie's going to call once she can determine the best time to meet. Apparently Melissa is being heavily guarded by a native voodoo group or something. Rosalie's hard to understand. They think Melissa's a goddess, and Rosalie's taking a big chance with her own life by even telling me about Melissa. Let's go check in."

Will drove the Grand Cherokee to Geejam Beach Resort where reservations were confirmed. Driving into the resort, Jeff was admittedly impressed.

"Wow, nice place."

"It should be," Will replied. "And it only costs you six-fifty a day. You said to get a nice place."

Will slapped Jeff on the back and guffawed like he always did. Wild Willy didn't laugh, he vibrated; and he could never finish a joke without breaking out in laughter.

The Jamaican porters showed the two men to their suite, tiled floors, private balcony off both bedrooms with views of the magnificent Caribbean Sea. A single cat lounged at the entryway, not a care in the world.

"That cat needs a diet," Will quipped.

"Yeah, de cat be faht, mon. He be eatin' all de time. He keep de mice away."

Checked in, bags unpacked, Will strolled out to the spacious tiled balcony off the second bedroom; and the king-sized bed was unexpected for a "second" bedroom. He took in the view and walked to the master suite.

"Nice room," Will commented, taking in the suite's amenities, large screen TV and iPad station. Jeff's balcony was large with a small spa, and streaming steam lifted upward. The Jamaican sky was a beautiful blue, as always. The phone rang.

The early afternoon air was stifling among the cotton fields and wide openness of the South Carolina terrain. The Sun seemed angry and scorched the skin of uncovered arms and bald scalps.

Buddy checked out the biplane; and the enhanced spreader would soon be filled to capacity, ready for spraying. Buddy briefly suffered a spontaneous bout of uneasiness, but there seemed nothing to be uneasy about. Just a feeling, he knew; a fleeting thought, like a ghost he once saw at his grandmother's home.

He wanted to complete the spraying today so he could watch the Super Bowl tomorrow without interruption. The Atlanta Falcons were playing, his favorite football team. Farmer Kinsella shouted from the front porch with the huge, white *Gone With the Wind* columns.

"Want me to bring you a glass of sweet tea?"

"Yeah, thanks," Buddy shouted back. "No lemon please."

The old farmer pulled up his blue twill overalls and reentered the home. Buddy took note of his unsteady gait. He worried about the old man and wondered if the farmer's children would take over the ranch when he died. Probably not, he knew. They were always busy it seemed. Three minutes later, maybe less, the farmer returned with the largest glass of tea Buddy had ever seen.

"Hey Sanchez, would you like me to getcha some tea?"

"No. No sir, Mr. Jack. Gracias."

Sanchez continued his day, carrying the scratched leather saddle to the horse barn; and the farmer made his way slowly up the front steps and into the house.

Buddy thought the pesticide seemed a little more syrupy than normal, especially as hot as it was; and he would ask Sanchez about it as soon as he returned from the barn. Possibly the Guatemalan native had delivered the wrong solution, though that was doubtful. Sanchez was thorough, almost obsessively meticulous. Everything always had to be *just right* for the worker, but Buddy considered that to be a positive thing.

Sanchez was dependable, always eager to please. He made a special effort to help on the ranch, going beyond the call of duty; and he never missed Catholic Mass. Buddy wished the newly-arrived crew were like Sanchez, but he knew that wasn't likely.

"Got any work, amigo?" Sanchez asked that day in the parking lot at the Target store in Anderson.

"Didn't I see you during Christmas, up there?" Buddy asked, answering the question with a question and pointing to the Target store entry.

"Si, amigo. I work with Salvation Army during Christmas, a bell ringer." His grin was contagious.

"I remember. I spoke with you during the holidays, stuffed a few bucks in your kettle."

"Si, gracias señor. I no remember."

"You said your son wanted to be a Boy Scout but was only six, I think?"

"Si, si. Yes, he still waiting. He seven now. Then he want to be Marine!"

Buddy hired Sanchez that day, and he had turned out to be a hard and honest worker. He'd never met Sanchez's young son, but he said the boy loved the Boy Scouts. Two years later, he seemed like family.

After a brief nap, his dream interrupted, the farmer left his bedroom, walked slowly down the oak-floored hallway and toward the kitchen to see what the noise was. The oak floor creaked with each step, but the farmer's hearing wasn't what it used to be. He thought he was being quiet and was sure he heard something fall.

The old man missed his wife terribly, but the Super Bowl would take his mind off it for at least a couple of hours. Memories of her should have faded at least a little by now he thought; but they hadn't, and he fought back tears.

Like Buddy, the old man was a Falcons fan and looked forward to the football ass-kickin' that was sure to happen the next day. The Falcons would pour it on and finally win one, at least he hoped so. Entering the kitchen through the swinging door, he was startled to see Sanchez by the pantry.

"What are you doing in here?" the old farmer asked out of curiosity, not anger.

"I came to introduce you to your maker," Sanchez said.

With that, Sanchez covered the old man's mouth with a rag full of ether and held him until he stopped squirming.

Sanchez had severed many throats during this jihad but learned quickly that ether or chloroform worked just as well and wasn't as messy. Dead *is* dead after all.

He was surprised at his feelings of remorse, but he had grown fond of the farmer. Thinking the old man was surely dead and on his journey to hell and his deceased wife, he flushed the rag down the toilet and left the farmer lying on the bathroom floor, face down.

Sanchez liked his Latino name; and for the most part, he liked the Mexicans. They were honorable people, even the drug lords if you didn't cross them. They could be a wrathful bunch if you did. Sanchez was in the United States legally, born twenty-nine years earlier to a pregnant, illegal immigrant, a beneficiary of generous U.S. law. In and out of trouble since age six, Sanchez was sentenced to jail for the first time at fifteen for stabbing the school bully.

"You're gonna get yourself in a heap of trouble son if you aren't careful."

Sanchez remembered the lenient Arizona judge's words well and considered the prospect of being a judge someday. He liked the dark outfit, dark like his mood. What he didn't know is that the school bully had beaten the you-know-what out of the judge's own nephew once, knocking out the kid's two front teeth. For two years the nephew sang "All I want for Christmas is my two front teeth, my two front teeth," over and over again and had nearly driven the family crazy.

A year later, given time off for good behavior, Sanchez began a new journey into the world of gun running. That career came to an abrupt end in southern Arizona, caught by one of Arizona's most notorious sheriffs. He was sentenced as a youthful offender once again and spent three years in the Arizona State Penitentiary. It was this prison stay that introduced Sanchez to Muhammad.

With no religion in his life as a kid, Sanchez dabbled in witchcraft, voodoo and a little Satanism. He even read a little of the Bible once but didn't like all the "rules." Plus, Jesus wasn't mean enough.

Another early release later, again for good behavior, Sanchez applied for a passport; and because of his youth, his felonious record had been wiped clean.

The night of the killings was new for Sanchez, and he worked alone. He entered Golden Age Retirement home through a back entry that was secured, but it wasn't secured enough. The retirement home sat on ten acres and was gated. Without card access or activation by the front desk, no one could enter the property, at least by the driveway. Sanchez found the black, wrought iron fence surrounding the property easily negotiable and was over in a flash.

Golden Age Retirement, just outside Tucson, was an appropriate name, he thought. It was upscale with upscale old ladies and old men, lots of upscale gold and jewelry and diamonds; and cash.

The night was clear but windy, and gusts hid the sound of his entry through the kitchen, at least until he stepped on the cat's tail. The scream could not be hidden by the wind, and one of the two nighttime front desk employees came running.

Sanchez had no choice, though he didn't mean to kill the man. He really hadn't hit him that hard, but the fall killed him as his head hit the stainless trash can, his first murder.

Chapter Thirteen

"I am *soooo* excited!" Jami beamed.

Jenni and Jami had always been obedient twins, at least most of the time, *good* kids. This however was a most-of-the-time moment, because there was no way they would miss the Super Bowl. Their dad was in Jamaica, and they were still bummed that he didn't take them along. Surely he wouldn't expect them to pass up such an opportunity as the Super Bowl.

"Me too," Audry screamed.

Audry, the youngest Ross and very precocious, was growing up fast for a pre-teen. Audry had been adopted by the Ross family after her parents were killed in a drive-by shooting. Melissa read the tragic story in the *Atlanta Constitution*, made some calls to important friends and the adoption happened quickly. Audry had no known blood relatives.

"We have to go get Mr. Hutz," she added.

The statement was redundant. Audry had made it repeatedly during the early afternoon. Game time was 4:00, earlier than normal; and she couldn't wait to attend her first pro-football game.

Audry always was a little *odd*, odd in a good way. She seemed to understand things in a naïve sort of way. She heard Jeff and Melissa discussing her upbringing, what her biological parents might've been like, what her family life had been like… were there any genetic abnormalities? She understood their concerns and knew she would want to know too. When she met

Mr. Hutz and suddenly started understanding and speaking Hebrew, she began to wonder about genetic abnormalities herself.

"I love the Falcon's quarterback," Jenni piped in.

"Yeah you do. You love those tight little pants he wears, that's what you love!" Jami laughed.

"I like his buns! What can I say? I'm normal. Don't you?"

Jenni couldn't deny the statement; and ever since she met the Falcons quarterback at a Cancer Society fund-raiser in the Gwinnett Arena two months earlier, he had occupied her thoughts, which she kept mostly to herself. She had occupied his thoughts too, only she didn't know it.

"I guess. You've been obsessing over him since you met him," Jami whined. "I know these things, because I'm the oldest twin." And she was, by a minute and a half. She was also a little jealous, or a little something. She couldn't quite figure it out.

The sleek Lincoln limousine activated the alarm, and Jami hit the automatic gate-opener with her iPhone app. The driver pulled to the circular, patterned-concrete drive and stopped in front of the house, by the fountain.

The girls, bubbly and talkative, climbed into the back of the black, sixteen-foot-long stretch limo as the chauffeur, height impaired and with a shiny shaved head, held the back door open for the group. He was dressed in a tux and was kind of cute, at least Jami thought so, sort of like a penguin.

In a few minutes they were off to the Super Bowl with only one stop along the way, the Ritz-Carlton in Buckhead. The TV stations always put Hutz up at the Ritz when he appeared for interviews in Atlanta, which was a-ok with him.

"I haven't been this excited in, like forever," Audry said, but a slight case of the worry-wrinkles appeared on her forehead. She felt nauseated. *Dear Jesus, please don't let me puke!* she said silently, a prayer she kept to herself; and the nausea that came out of nowhere, disappeared. *Thank you*, she thought and knew that her thoughts would get to God at the speed of light or faster.

The short chauffeur aimed the limousine southward and merged the behemoth smoothly onto the interstate. A white Mercedes passed on the left, a Falcons flag streaming from both sides of the convertible. Four young men, twenty-somethings it appeared and bare-chested, held up their bottled water in a toast to the limo as they passed. The chauffeur was pretty sure that those bottles weren't filled with water.

"I think that guy's sitting on a pillow," Jami mouthed to Jenni and nodded toward the driver. "Or else he took a growth hormone!"

They snickered, and Audry wondered what they were talking about. They were always talking about *boys*. Yuck.

"Why don't you ask him," Jenni mouthed back, covering her mouth with her hand, hoping the driver wouldn't hear her giggling.

"Are you sitting on a pill,,,?" Audry shouted to the chauffeur before Jami could put her hand over her mouth to stop the question in midair.

"Pardon me, young lady," the chauffeur said through the interior speaker system, looking in the rearview mirror, a broad grin stretching across his face.

"Nothing; nothing," Jami answered. "Kids will be kids," and she gave Audry one of those 'don't embarrass me' looks.

"No problem, ma'am. If you need a pillow, you can use the one I'm sitting on," he offered, and all three girls cracked up.

Vinny pulled into the parking lot. He'd been to The Depot before; but something looked different, he wasn't sure what. He parked in the front where there were plenty of available spaces. He liked the restaurant, the train tracks to the rear and the sounds of the train going by. Plus, the food was great. *I almost got lucky*, he remembered with a smile; but he hadn't given in, praise Allah. The young hooker had been tempting though.

He walked through the heavy, oak doors at the front of the restaurant and the dark-planked floor rocked as a train passed closely behind The Depot and the whistle blew. Vinny loved it. He spotted the large man sitting in a booth, well away from the few other patrons. He walked over and sat down.

"It's a great day in Dalton, do you think?"

Vinny waited for a response.

"Not particularly," came the correct answer; and the men shook hands and shared a fist-bump, procedure. The two men looked anything but Muslim. They just looked like good ol' boys.

Vinny looked the man in the eyes, skeptical of all things, as usual. It paid to be paranoid.

"Is your wife ready for the barbeque?" Vinny asked the Bosnian. "Do we have plenty of chicken?"

Vinny wasn't sure about the middle-aged looking Bosnian or any other Euro-Russian Muslims for that matter. They didn't seem as dedicated and devoted to Allah as Arabs and Persians. The man was white-skinned, scruffy beard and wore a green John Deere cap. His T-shirt was pressed neatly and had a message on the front:

It's America! Love it or Get the Hell Out!

Vinny waited for the man's answer.

"God willin' and the Sun don't rise," the Euro-jihadist said matter-of-factly, just like he was Alabama born and *bred.* That's how he had been described by Bubba, before he got locked up. "He's great, Aboud; you'll like him. He looks like he's Alabama born and bred."

Vinny missed Bubba, who nearly always called him by his birth name. He thought about the Alabama born *bread* and what it might taste like and decided he would have to try it the next time he passed through the state. The Bosnian continued, interrupting Vinny's thoughts of bread. He was hungry, and his stomach reminded him with a grumble.

"The wings are in place, my friend. Original. The chickens are in the coop and ready for the pickin'." He smiled and winked at Vinny.

Vinny glanced around the small, dark restaurant; but as usual, Dalton was asleep and the place was nearly empty. It was after all, past six.

This was Vinny's third visit to the restaurant in two years. Once the carpet capital of the world, the Georgia town had suffered a near-total economic collapse like Europe, and that made Vinny happy. *Pickin'*? Had the Bosnian really said *pickin'*?

He was impressed with the large soldier, at least so far. He spoke good American. Vinny made note of the lone man in the corner booth by the large tropical fish tank. He had seen the man here a year ago; they had a couple of drinks together. The man had laughed when Vinny ordered white zinfandel.

"Men don't drink pink wine my friend, at least not in the mountains of Georgia. Not if he wants to live, that is." The man had laughed again and slapped Vinny on the back. Vinny glanced away as the man looked toward their booth.

"The wings need to be served at the same time. Not *exactly* the same time, but within an hour. Listen carefully, because we don't want it to get too hot."

Vinny's boss, at least he was the boss before getting arrested by the feds, had been Bubba Haskins. Bubba had been one of the largest minority contractors in the Bible-Belt and was loved by everyone. That's why there had been such an uproar when Bubba was arrested for conspiring to blow up the Buford Dam with one of his tourist subs.

Bubba was active in his Baptist church, and his wife Jill was an icon in Atlanta's Jewish community, always helping at food banks and anything to do with helpless or abused children. His close friends, church members and associates knew for sure there was a mistake of some kind.

The man in the corner booth smiled at Vinny, and Vinny acknowledged the man with a nod.

"The first picnic is Easter Sunday," Vinny continued. He hated to even mention the pagan holiday but knew Allah the Merciful would forgive him his duty. He wondered how many Christians knew Easter was named after Ishtar, the goddess of fertility. Probably none.

"You know what to do. The Christians who never go to church always go on Easter Sunday, so all churches will be packed."

"We're ready. Don't be concerned. We have more than five thousand ready, and they all love Kentucky Fried."

"Yes, Kentucky Fried Chicken and seventy-two virgins; that's what they like, my friend," Vinny whispered and winked. The two men laughed.

"Chicken for the pickin' makes for finger lickin'."

The Bosnian laughed at his poem.

Vinny liked the code. It had been Bubba's idea to base it around the fried chicken chain; because everyone loved the "finger lickin' good" chicken, especially Bubba. Wings were soldiers, thighs were weapons, original recipe meant the plan was ready to go, crispy meant a change of plans and so on.

"Bubba and I go back a long way," the Bosnian said. "I used to be one of his air conditioning salesmen. I got him the CDC account, which is how you got your microbes. I also got him the Atlanta airport account. That's where you disbursed the microbes. Trust me, Vinny. Bubba and I had no secrets; and we're going to get him out, soon. There is no security we can't hack into."

The lone waitress, a little thin but not too, compared to previous waitresses Vinny had seen at the restaurant, stood at the showcase full of desserts. She saw the men whispering and didn't want to interrupt; but the coffee cups were empty.

She was so bored with her job, as well as her hometown. She really wanted to go to the police academy and be a detective, but she was *overweight,* at least in her mind. People told her she was skinny, but she always felt overweight. Surely this new diet would work, and she made her way over toward the booth of the whispering men. Just two more hours and she would be off, but not for the night. Then she would go to her other part-time job at Veterinary Clinic just outside town.

"The grenade launchers are for the nurseries, you got that?" Vinny asked. "Do you have a problem with that?"

"Not really," replied the Bosnian. "Little kiddies grow up to be U.S. soldiers. The more we kill now, the less we have to kill when the Big War starts."

"*This* is the year, my friend," and Vinny liked the European's thinking. "This is the year that the West will fall.

When all the women start seeing their children slaughtered, they will demand that the U.S. abandon Israel and withdraw all troops from Muslim lands."

The Bosnian was quiet and thought about Vinny's comments. It seemed to most that the U.S. had already abandoned Israel. They had cut off almost all the foreign aid to the Zionists and had forbidden them from attacking Iran's nuclear facilities. Now Iran had several nukes, maybe more.

World intelligence agencies were well aware that Iran now had nukes and the launching systems to send them anywhere in the world; but the Bosnian knew the West would do nothing. They were weak. They were also sick, millions now dead because of the man sitting with him. Those air conditioning systems that Vinny serviced that day in Atlanta led to world plague, just like the Quran foretold. He was blessed to be a part.

The Twelfth Imam would soon be among them, and they would rule the world, Insha'Allah. The waitress approached the table with coffee pot in hand. The two men waved her off. She dropped the check on the table and said, "I hope everything was good."

"Good? It was finger lickin' good, baby," and the charismatic Bosnian thought he might pat her on the butt. "Just like the chicken." He laughed and contained himself.

The two men walked to the register, paid the bill and exited the restaurant, leaving the skinny waitress a $ 5.00 tip. As the two men were pulling out of The Depot parking lot, the young waitress who wanted to be a detective walked into the kitchen and grabbed the phone out of her knapsack that was hanging on the stainless steel wall hook. She memory-dialed the number, and a lady answered.

"Good morning. May I help you?"

"Mr. Ed Poe?"

"Can I tell him who's calling?" the receptionist asked. "He's in a meeting."

"Yes, tell him it's his niece."

The waitress waited for only a few seconds before her uncle picked up the phone. She found it hard to believe that her Uncle Ed worked with Army Intel when just two years earlier he was homeless and living on the streets of Atlanta. Maybe there was hope for her.

"Hey Uncle Ed. I hate to bother you but think I may have just heard something important."

"Okay, what is it? And you're never a bother, honey."

"I heard a report on FOX News a couple of days ago about the Buford Dam terrorist attack. They mentioned that after the explosion, investigators found a new sleeping bag about two miles from the dam. Along with the sleeping bag there were three empty boxes of Kentucky Fried Chicken."

"Okay," her uncle said. "What about it?"

"You mentioned to Dad last week that there was some 'chatter' of some kind just before the explosion and also the tunnel bombings in New York City, something about finger licking good."

"Yes, that's correct; but keep that under your belt. You weren't supposed to hear that. What about it?"

"Well, this may be nothing; but I just served a couple of guys, and they kept whispering. It was the strangest thing, because only a couple of people are in the whole darn restaurant."

"And?" Uncle Ed asked.

"They kept saying finger lickin' good and laughing."

"Well, honey, that's not a totally unusual thing to say. We think that's why they may have used it for a code of some kind. It was smart on their part to use something so simple."

"Uncle Ed, do you know how good I am at lip reading?"

"Not really. I'm kind of in a hurry, so you need to get to the point. Don't mean to be rude, but we're very busy working on this exact case."

"I learned to read lips, because I wanted to know what people were saying about me, if they were making fun of my weight. I know that's weird since I'm skinny; anyway, I watched the men talking and laughing. I try not to be nosy since it's not my bus…"

"You need to get on with it, honey." Uncle Ed interrupted again.

"They said grenade launcher twice and nuclear explosion at least once. And they kept talking about Kentucky Fried Chicken and some guy named Bubba."

"Bubba? You said Bubba?"

"Yes."

"I'll be there. Don't go anywhere, Janie."

"Are you in Dalton?"

"Atlanta. It won't take long to get there, about an hour. I should be there by 9:00 at the latest." Ed sounded excited and worried at the same time she thought.

"I have to go to my other job. Can you come by the veterinarian clinic? Do you know where it is?"

"On my way." The line went dead.

CHAPTER FOURTEEN

"The second angel sounded his trumpet, and something like a huge mountain, all ablaze, was thrown into the sea. A third of the sea turned into blood, a third of the living creatures in the sea died, and a third of the ships were destroyed."

Revelation 8: 8-9

After flushing the etherized rag, Sanchez didn't notice that the rag had not flushed at all, but instead had clogged the toilet's drain. He also didn't know that you had to jiggle the handle or the toilet would run forever, it was a 1950's model.

Sanchez exited the historic farmhouse through the back door, hidden from the landing strip out front. America's version of football was a stupid sport he thought, not nearly as interesting as soccer; but this would be the mother of all Super Bowls.

While in Pakistan for jihad training, Sanchez hadn't been awarded the name he so cherished, Abdullah. Jamal was so-so but Abdullah would have been much cooler. Maybe after a few kills they would let him be Abdullah.

He circled around to the barn, out of sight of Buddy the pilot-mechanic. Believing that Jamal was really Sanchez from Guatemala, Buddy had instructed him well; and the farmhand assassin was a quick-study if there ever was one. He had now flown the plane solo at least a dozen times, conducting simulated, low-altitude application scenarios.

"That guy's a darn genius, I tell ya," Buddy had told the farmer after the first training flight. "Plus he speaks some other language besides Spanish. It sounded like Asian or something."

The toilet in the hallway bath began to overflow.

"As long as he's not talkin' jihad or somethin' crazy, we'll be alright, Buddy. Stop your worryin'."

It hadn't been Arabic he didn't think, though Buddy wouldn't know Arabic if it hit him smack in the face. He knew that for sure. It was just… Sanchez seemed secretive about it. And he never mentioned his wife.

"Sanchez," Buddy shouted as he saw him entering the gray, weathered barn in the distance. One of the barn doors was askew, another project to solve. "Can you come give me a hand?"

Buddy had waited patiently for the farmer to come assist; but the old man wasn't as reliable as he had once been, when Momma Boss was still alive. He seemed to nap a lot more, but that was okay. Let him sleep.

"Alright, boss, I'm coming." Sanchez-Jamal walked at a brisk pace, knowing that the Latinos were always eager to please the slave masters.

"This chemical seems a little syrupy," Buddy explained as he donned his gas mask to start filling the spreader. "Grab your mask," but after a glance over his shoulder, Buddy realized the request was unnecessary. Sanchez already had his mask and gloves on.

Sanchez-Jamal was now an accomplished flyer, and Buddy loved the interest he expressed in flying the biplane during the past six months. He had been on several training flights, and Sanchez was now qualified to be the *official* spreader and spreading, the man could do. He excelled at low level and night spraying, both extremely dangerous. That's why night spreaders got paid so much. Only Sanchez wasn't in it for the money, he was in it for the *cause*.

Sanchez opened the container of the syrupy pesticide, and it wasn't the kind normally used on the boll weevil. He guessed it could be. It would certainly kill most any pest. Mustard gas and sarin mixture was an unpleasant way to die, but the agony would be brief.

"Hey man! What you doin'?"

In a swift motion, Sanchez-Jamal yanked the gas mask off Buddy and splashed a couple of drops of the fluid in his eyes. Except for the brief screams of agony, those were the last words and almost the last sounds Buddy ever made as the sweet aroma of the unaerated mustard filled his lungs, immediately followed by a three-minute episode of projectile vomiting. Writhing in brief agony, his throat and airway barely open, Buddy looked at Sanchez wide-eyed and finally gurgled. His face gathered in one last spasmodic contortion, and then the look of the dead replaced the smile that had been on his face just five minutes before.

The cool water from the running toilet in the downstairs bathroom crawled slowly along the ceramic tile floor, edging closer to Farmer Kinsella's face and would soon quench his thirst. He would live to see another day.

Three billion miles from planet Earth, the swarm of asteroids swept out of the Kuiper Belt at high speed, victims of an unusual gravitational pull by a rogue and undiscovered planet, a very large object with immense mass. Because of the mass, the gravitational pull was extraordinary.

Similar to the Asteroid Belt between Mars and Jupiter, only much larger and farther away, the Kuiper Belt extended beyond the entire solar system. Within the belt there were millions of asteroids, many larger than 50 miles in diameter. The asteroid that wiped out most life on Earth and killed all the dinosaurs 65 million years earlier was only six miles wide. An asteroid ten times larger could theoretically knock Earth slightly out of orbit.

Rogue planets were unusual, at least so far. Discovered in 2012, they caught most scientists by surprise. They weren't like other planets and roamed through space at high rates of speed, and sometimes not. Sometimes they seemed to poke around, as though waiting for something.

Rogue planets had no sun to orbit and no sibling planets. They were just lone, massive rocky planets zooming through space with no apparent destination or destiny. Most were much larger than Earth and could slam into anything at any moment, and it would be monumental. If the rogue planet now disturbing the Kuiper Belt happened to collide with Earth, there would be no more planet Earth; only another asteroid belt, this one situated between Mars and Venus where Earth had once been.

It was approaching mid-January when the huge swarm of asteroids spun off and headed toward the inner solar system. There were so many, their destinations varied. Some would float through frigid space endlessly, never colliding at all. They would be few, however. Most of this swarm had several planets in its crosshairs.

Since Dark Comet collided with the Moon, debris from the comet and the Moon hit Earth daily. Thankfully most burned in the atmosphere or exploded, but those who lived in a strike zone thought it was Armageddon.

Chad and The Admiral stood in the Goddard Lab examining the latest charts. Except in the rarest instances, the only asteroids that needed to be considered were those that might hit Earth. So far, after billions and billions of research dollars, no life seemed to exist on other planets. They would suffer no "mass extinctions of mankind." The Earth had suffered several, according to geologists, archeologists and geophysicists.

The Hubble Space Telescope was now the only operable space-based telescope. Others had been scheduled to join Hubble, even more sophisticated to see ever deeper into space; but budget cuts had been implemented and observations were curtailed.

Hubble was up to the test though and aimed her technology beyond the Solar System and toward the Kuiper Belt, keeping a close watch. Any aberration caused by previously unknown space objects would activate alarms as soon as detected. Based on new sensor technology, the new telescopes would have already been in alarm state, had they been launched.

The swarm of huge rocks journeyed on, silent like a soft mist crawling along a mountain lake, only faster and not yet detected by anyone except God and his heavenly host. These were the falling mountains and stars that John the Apostle had seen in his visions so long ago at Patmos, and they would cause great havoc on Earth.

Chad picked up the remote and changed one of the large monitors to the *Super Bowl Pregame Show*. The Admiral threw a bag of buttered popcorn in the microwave and hit the popcorn button. Let the game begin.

Sanchez landed the shiny blue and yellow biplane at the private airstrip in Marietta, not far from Dobbins Air Reserve Base.

The airstrip had been secured the night before by fellow jihadists; and the executive who owned the runway and hangars was now deceased, the victim of food poisoning from a spaghetti dinner the previous evening. The man's cook, relatively new to the scene, had served the dinner wearing a short black and white maid's outfit, just like her *boss* demanded. The arrogant and pompous man never had a clue that the salt shaker wasn't really filled with salt.

"Jamal," the young, athletic man with the blue tank-top shouted as Jamal taxied the plane to the makeshift terminal and climbed down the rollup stairs.

"Don't e*ver* mention my name," Jamal said sternly; and the young jihadist cowered at Jamal's sudden anger. "The name is Sanchez, capiche? Where's the banner?"

With less than two hours until game time, Sanchez was getting anxious. Across the field, two accomplices rode an all-terrain vehicle out of the small brick terminal, a large trailer in tow. The banner with 7-foot letters advertising *Free Beer tonight at Jamaica Joe's* was the only cargo.

The banner was neatly laid out and attached to a cable that was then attached to a wire stretched between two telephone-like poles.

"Where's the grapnel hook?" Sanchez asked.

After what seemed like hours of preparation, the plane with grapnel hook was ready to fly. Fifteen minutes later the biplane accelerated down the runway and lifted into the air. The roar of the super-tuned engine was exhilarating, and the fellow jihadists felt a little envy that their job was almost complete.

The plane circled around, swooped in low and decelerated. Like a Navy pilot landing on an aircraft carrier, the plane's grapnel hook made contact with the cable; but instead of landing on a carrier deck Jamal hit the throttle, and the 1001-horsepower engine powered the aircraft upward in a steep climb, keeping the banner from shredding on the runway below.

"I like the plane," one of the three warriors said as the plane circled back toward the executive estate. "She's a beauty. What's he coming back for?"

"Probably wants us to check out the banner, make sure it's not tangled."

The men knew the banner shouldn't get tangled though. They had attached the two tiny parachutes to the end of the banner and the bottom was weighted, so there should be no problem.

As the plane began its descent toward the airstrip, the three men didn't notice the cook who killed the airport owner in her not-so-modest maid's outfit. If they had, they would have probably thought the young lady looked odd in the short dress and the gas mask. She closed the door and windows and taped them so no air could seep in. She opened the door to the basement where she would wait thirty minutes before leaving and walked down the steps.

The men standing to the side of the narrow, asphalt airstrip had no idea what was happening, that they were part of a dry run. Sanchez leveled the plane at fifty feet and aimed the flying machine at the three jihadists below. *They aren't true Muslims*, he justified to himself. *They are Sunnis*.

The men gave Jamal a thumbs-up, excited about the flyover; and Jamal hit the spreader-release button. A mist flowed abundantly like fog from the spreader attached to the bottom wing. The heated liquid turned to gas and poured from beneath the plane.

Before the three men went into a convulsive state, they noticed a sweet smell, sort of mustardy. Then it was over. Jamal didn't smile as the men twitched and vomited in agony, but he knew the men wouldn't suffer long, Insha'Allah. Saddam Hussein, now in the land of seventy-two virgins had gassed his own people in Iraq with mustard gas; but seeing it in action was unnerving.

Sanchez-Jamal considered the jihadists to be sacrificial to the cause. They were, after all, American converts. He would rendezvous with the lovely maid later in Dalton, at least that was the plan. They would have dinner and celebrate at The Depot where they planned to meet Vinny the following day, assuming he made it.

Flying the biplane slowly toward the new Atlanta open-air stadium, the banner extended to the rear. Jamal kept the plane as low to the ground as possible without creating suspicion. Low speed had to be maintained, or the banner would be ripped to shreds.

The stretch limo came to a halt as did the other seven lanes heading southward into Atlanta. Traffic on I-85 was always tentative with traffic accidents more normal than abnormal.

"We're not going to make the kickoff," Jami whined. The traffic was at a dead stop. "Turn on WSB and find out what's up with the traffic." The chauffeur did as requested and the surround-sound system in the large Lincoln did the news justice with enough baritone to make Morgan Freeman envious.

"... and has been taken to Grady Hospital. The young man lost his balance in the upper level of the new stadium and fell forty feet to his death, dragging two people who tried to save him, along. No word on their conditions as rescue vehicles make their way toward the stadium. The fatal accident on 85 South has not helped. The SUV that collided with the concrete barrier by the innermost lane knocked large chunks of concrete into the northbound lanes. Now I-85 has been shut down at the stadium exit; both directions."

"Great. That's just great," Jenni complained, knowing the kickoff might not be the only thing they missed. At this rate they would miss the whole game.

"The Atlanta Police Department is using unmanned drones to patrol the skies around the stadium. The APD told Channel 2 that the drones were not armed. Security is unprecedented though 'there have been no threats' according to Homeland Security."

"It's a gift," Chuck mumbled quietly. "God is giving us a gift."

"What do you mean?" Audry asked.

"I'm sorry, Audry." The twins listened intently. "I don't mean to worry anyone; but I just had a vision, and it's not good. We need to get off this highway *now,* and get far away from the stadium."

Chuck played with his fingers nervously, sweat from his forehead now staining his new madras shirt. He turned to look out the back window, but the tinted glass masked most activity. *What am I looking for? Be calm Chuck, be calm.*

"No! We need to get to the game!" Jenni said, obsessing about her new quarterback friend; and she opened the limo door. "I'll walk; it's only about half a mile."

"No Jenni, come back," Audry cried. "Mr. Hutz is always right." But she was gone, weaving her way through the stalled traffic, horns blowing and irate Super Bowl fans shouting profanities.

Jami exited the stalled limousine next, chasing after Jenni. The traffic didn't move. Above them, the din of the patrolling drones could be heard as they circled the stadium and surrounding areas, on the lookout for anything unusual. The drones were the latest entry from Lockheed and could actually spot concealed weapons.

"Jenni!" Jami shouted, chasing her twin; and surprisingly Jenni stopped, her dark hair now blowing in the sudden breeze. Windy conditions had become the norm. Jami fell to the pavement as she dodged a motorcycle winding through the web of cars, trucks and RVs in the congested mass of vehicles; and Jenni ran back to her aid.

"Jenni, we must get back to the car. Chuck never seems to be wrong about these visions he has. He's been on television for Pete's sake!"

"You sound like Daddy, for Pete's sake!"

Disappointed but also level headed, the twins ran back to the limousine. Audry was frantic with worry, and Chuck was sweating profusely. The news interrupted the pregame show.

CHAPTER FIFTEEN

Sanchez-Jamal flew the shiny crop duster with prodigious skill, low over I-285, the sixteen-lane interstate that circled the perimeter of the city once known as the "Jewel of the South" until the floods had destroyed much of the western half of Atlanta.

The blue and yellow biplane stayed as low as possible, but not low enough to raise concern, the banner extending two hundred feet to the rear. Jamal wished the engine wasn't so loud, and rewrapped the Red Baron bandana around his neck.

Soon he would be in Dalton for the night, a night of mystery and intrigue with the olive skinned beauty who would be waiting patiently at the hotel, watching everything unfold on the news, Insha'Allah. He refocused on his first goal; gas the infidels and escape before anyone knew what happened.

The shiny crop duster with the Jamaica Joe's banner passed low over the Church of the Apostles at Paces Ferry Road and I-75 and would soon begin an ascent toward the new stadium. The wind had picked up, a kink in the otherwise flawless plans. He would have to gain altitude before he could dive.

"Hey, look at that pretty airplane, Momma."

The small girl with the floppy blond curls and Mickey Mouse ears pointed skyward; and the mother looked up just as the blue and yellow plane flew overhead, the droning engine louder than other banner planes she had seen in the past.

"Where's Jamaica Joe's?" the young girl's father asked.

He hadn't heard of the place and had lived in Atlanta his entire life, but free beer was free beer and always had a nice sound to it. He would Google it.

The plane began its slow climb, and Jamal rocked the wings in a "friendly" salute to the backed up traffic on the highways below. Football fans now mingled around outside their cars, and several gave him a thumbs up. He waved and smiled. He liked being a celebrity.

Jamal's devious mind began to wonder how many people would actually be in the stadium. No problem; he would spray the stadium first and then the stalled traffic. That could be even better. Allah was on his side, no doubt about it.

The plane continued toward the stadium just as any other banner plane would do, and Jamal wished he was spraying an infectious disease instead of mustard gas. He would kill a few thousand; Vinny and his brother had killed millions. It was a sin to be envious, but he was. He would pray about it.

He began to circle the stadium, and the jubilant crowds below were dazzled by the sound and beauty of the vintage biplane. The crowds waved, and Jamal waved back and smiled.

With traffic at a complete stop, the limousine was going nowhere; so Chuck insisted they abandon the car and run for it.

"We have to get away from here," Chuck explained again, demanded; but the limo driver wasn't about to abandon his ninety-thousand dollar limousine. Under protest from all but Audry, Chuck once again insisted and opened the rear door.

"Come on, follow me."

Audry followed, as did the twins, though reluctantly. Chuck quickly wormed through the stalled traffic, guiding the girls toward the MARTA train that would take them back north to Dunwoody and safety, leaving the cute-but-short chauffeur behind to guard the Lincoln limousine.

The timing was perfect, almost too perfect; and Chuck knew it was a God thing as the MARTA train pulled into the station just as the entourage arrived.

"What's wrong, Chuck?" the twins asked. "Where are we going? What are we running from?"

"I don't know for sure, just far away from here. Hurry!"

They entered the train, and the sleek vessel moved northward, leaving the traffic nightmare below as they crossed over the interstate.

"Where's Jamaica Joe's?" Jenni asked, pointing out the window at the plane carrying the advertising banner.

Maybe there was still hope, Jenni thought. Possibly the Falcons players would visit the hangout after the game. The train continued northward toward Perimeter Mall, and the plane began to circle the stadium. Kickoff would be in five minutes. Jami and Jenni pulled out their new iPads and had the signal in no time. They would *not* miss the kickoff!

Jamal looked down as he approached the stadium at a slow airspeed, hoping the drones would determine the plane was an authorized advertiser. He would not make a dry run this time, like he did at the airfield in Marietta. A couple of circles around the stadium was all it would take. When he saw the players line up for kickoff, he would dive; and it would be their last kickoff, God willing.

"We have a phantom, sir."

The air-traffic controlman at Dobbins Air Base didn't see the biplane as a threat as the plane, now in the sights of the two patrolling drones, slowly circled the stadium, rocking the wings in salute to the thrill of the crowd below, advertising free beer to one and all after the game.

"Is that plane authorized?" the control center supervisor asked, concerned but calm.

"Not sure, sir. Checking."

Jamal spotted one of the drones in the distance as the teams lined up across the grass-green field below, the Falcons on the receiving end. Most of the crowd, dressed in Falcon-red or Green Bay yellow and green, were oblivious to the coming terror in the sky above. The skimpily clad cheerleaders undulated on the sidelines, and the crowd cheered as the new Falcon receiver caught the football and began his runback.

The drone approached, and Jamal made his move.

Chapter Sixteen

"Be always on the watch, and pray that you may be able to escape all that is about to happen, and that you may be able to stand before the Son of Man."

Luke 21:36

"Abe, what's up? Another hot day in beautiful downtown Duluth."

Abe the Bartender was a favorite of the crowd, even though he was no longer a bartender but manager instead. To most, he would always be Abe the Bartender, and that was fine with the affable Jewish man. He was easy.

The large crowd was unexpected at *The Divide Disco & Café* on the Towne Green; but apparently the word had gotten out. Today, instead of twenty flatscreens spewing the national and international news, for the first time in *The Divide's* history, most TVs were tuned to the Super Bowl instead of international news. It was another hot day in January, and the restaurant's air conditioners were running full-force. Condensate dripped from two of the ceiling vents as humidity increased each time the door opened, and that was often.

"Well hello, Miss Judi!" Abe beamed and was glad to see Judi Ellis, they had become somewhat of an "item." At least he thought they were. She seemed a little distant lately though.

"Is that plane on fire, Abe?" she asked incredulously, pointing to the screen over Abe's shoulder.

Abe wasn't paying attention to the pregame. He was filling in the head bartender's spot for Scott Johnson. Scott was in Haiti with his new missionary honey trying to help tsunami survivors still living on the shores. Abe was surprised at Scott's sudden interest in the missionary thing; but Kara was gorgeous and men were weak. He turned and looked up, focusing on the large flatscreen suspended above the bar.

"Damn! Is it on fire?" He repeated Judi's question, almost. Couldn't be. The crowd took notice and the din became nearly silent.

"Sure looks like it. Earlier it was flying with a banner advertising free beer or something at Jamaica Joe's. Where in the heck is Jamaica Joe's?"

"Never heard of it, Judi," Abe answered, still watching the blue and yellow plane begin a slow dive toward the crowds below.

The gasps of the gathering pregame crowd began to fill the restaurant. Everyone seemed to think the plane was on fire and crashing into the stadium. The planes speed began to increase as the banner was released by Jamal. The white smoke coming from beneath the lower wing of the crop duster increased.

"Allahu Akbar," he shouted, though no one could hear him except Allah. The dark-haired girl in Marietta was far from his mind as the plane approached the waving and jubilant crowd below. The wind calmed briefly.

"Dropped the banner, Sir. The biplane just dropped its banner! She's diving."

This time the Dobbins air-traffic controller *was* concerned, watching the image of the blue and yellow plane suddenly dive toward Atlanta's new open-air stadium and the Super Bowl crowd of sixty thousand below. *What if that's not smoke?* The thought was brief and alarming, but the controlman made no comment. Jamal approached the stadium from the north.

"Wow! Look at the plane," the bearded man yelled, pointing upward. The small stream of smoke spewing from the one-of-a-kind crop duster was almost white but with a greenish tint. It surely had to be part of the pregame show, except… it wasn't pregame anymore.

Hardly anyone heard the bearded man's cry above the din of the screaming football fans, nor did they look skyward. All attention was now on the Falcon receiver's extraordinary runback as he crossed the Green Bay forty yard line with only one Packer now in pursuit. He would score a touchdown before the first play of the Super Bowl.

Jamal approached the stadium and slowed the plane as much as he could without stalling. Dropping his poisonous load at high speed would only dissipate the cloud of terror. A hundred yards from the stadium, Jamal hit the release button; and the payload began a slow but deadly exit beneath the lower wing, no longer just a spew.

"I think that plane's on fire!" someone screamed as the plane came ever closer. "Look at the smoke!"

Still, the crowd watched in mesmerization as the receiver crossed the twenty yard line, dodging the lone defensive Packer's lunge, now on their feet and cheering.

The plane made its pass low over the stadium. The runback would have been the longest in Atlanta Falcon history had it not been for the mustard gas.

As the receiver ran toward the goal and pointed skyward in thanks to the Almighty, the first mist of the sweet-smelling gas entered the front of his football helmet. The receiver breathed deeply, the goal line just a second ahead; and he pondered the sweet smell, not of making the goal but of the suddenly sticky air. He fell immediately to the ground, six yards shy of the goal line; and his body spasmed uncontrollably as he ripped the helmet off and clutched at his throat, trying for just a single breath of fresh air; only there was no fresh air at the stadium at the moment.

Twenty miles to the north, two F-35 Strike Fighters left the runway at Dobbins. The afterburners propelled the planes quickly toward Mach 1. They would intercept the plane in less than a minute.

"Daddy! Daddy!" the little girl screamed.

The kitchen's glassware suddenly broke, and the patio door blew inward as the two jets broke the sound barrier overhead.

"I'm coming, honey!" the father running frantically, wondering what in the world was going on.

He caught just a silver glimpse in the sky; and the jets were gone, but the sonic boom nearly knocked the man to the ground. He was a Lockheed engineer and knew the planes were too low to be breaking the sound barrier, at least by regulation, especially over residential areas. Something was up.

Jamal finished the first and only pass and turned the shiny crop duster southward over I-75 flying low above the stalled traffic. He released another smokescreen of his deadly load of toxic gas.

He smiled at the havoc wreaked below. This would be a great day for Allah. Sixty thousand in the stadium and now all this traffic. He would drop the remaining gas and fly westward at high speed, under the radar. Just past the drop site he would ascend to twenty-five hundred feet, put the plane on automatic pilot and bail out. The dark-haired girl would pick him up in an all-terrain vehicle, which would later be abandoned for the stolen Ford Focus; and they should be in Dalton by dark.

"Oh...My...God..." Judi exclaimed, watching the tragedy unfold before her eyes on the flatscreen above the bar.

She pulled her blond hair back and slid the ponytail through the hole in the back of the Falcons cap. *Hadn't Samarra said she was going to the game? Or was it Audry and the twins?* Her heart raced. No one screamed in *The Divide*, but nearly all were wide-eyed and had their mouths covered.

The crowd in the news helicopter's cameras writhed in a dance of oxygen deprivation on the stadium's grounds, both inside and out. The cameraman continued to film in disbelief.

"Musta been nerve gas or somethin'," one *Divide* patron muttered. "Lousy freakin' A-Rabs."

The opinionated man with the red-checkered shirt slammed his massive fist against the bar, grabbed his cowboy hat and left. He needed to get home to the wife. Something wasn't kosher, that was a fact. The beefy man walked out the front doors of *The Divide* that day, and it would be the last day on this planet for the Vietnam vet.

"Uh oh! Here comes the Air Force," someone in the restaurant shouted, and the helicopter's cameras focused on the rapidly approaching F-35s. The crowd in the restaurant broke out into simultaneous applause.

The beefy man crossed the Duluth Towne Green, entered the parking lot by Chocolate Perks and crawled up into his new pickup truck. He crossed the railroad tracks and turned left on Buford Highway, heading home to Suwanee just a few miles away. The world was ending, he knew that for sure; had been for a while. He and the wife had discussed it often, and what they might do about it. Fact was, there was nothing they could do about it. It was in God's hands, but he and his wife had discussed that too. He felt under the seat, and the handgun was right where it was supposed to be.

While the news-junkie crowd at *The Divide* watched the disaster unfold on multiple big screens, a murder suicide was in this beefy man's plans.

"Missile's been fired!" Judi said, and it was followed by another.

The first missile slammed into the blue and yellow biplane, the multiple metal pieces still shiny; and Jamal began another journey, this one to seventh heaven and seventy-two lovely virgins. He never knew what hit him as the million-dollar biplane was blown out of the sky and onto the traffic below. He would soon find that the virgins were virgins because they weren't so lovely after all, and there was no seventh heaven.

The TV cameras focused on the destroyed plane and the fog still pouring from beneath the bottom wing, and then on the writhing people in the traffic below.

Much of the stadium crowd, realizing the plane was not part of the program, rushed toward the exits, collapsing in desperation to the concrete floor below.

"Several spectators were seen jumping over the railing of the top decks, trying to escape the foggy mist," the news continued. *"The football players below never had a chance as the fog dropped rapidly onto the open field."*

The camera panned away from the writhing and vomiting crowd, by orders of the news production management team, and now focused on the aftermath of the plane crash along I-75 South by Grady Memorial Hospital.

The wind picked up slightly; and the poisonous fog blew to the north, but not before some of the cloud was sucked into the outdoor air vents at Grady Hospital and any other building where the air conditioning might be running.

"Ohhhh, say can you see… by the dawn's early…"

Judi stood up on the other side of *The Divide's* circular bar and began to sing the National Anthem, her hand placed firmly over her heart and a tear dropped down her right cheek. The rest of the crowd stood and joined in, many weeping openly. There would be a high death toll from today's events.

CHAPTER SEVENTEEN

Abe glanced up as the French persimmon doors at the front of the restaurant opened, and the late afternoon glare of the Sun made him squint in order to get a better focus. Everyone else in the crowded disco-restaurant was glued to the flatscreens and the latest devastating news in Atlanta. No one saw the man except Abe.

The stranger stood in the entry, silhouetted by the flaming sunlight, and was not discernible. Suddenly the shadowy silhouette turned a one-eighty and walked toward the Towne Green. The doors shut behind him. A chill ran over Abe like he hadn't felt in a long time, maybe ever. The doors opened again, but this time it was Sheryl Lasseter. She walked up to the crowded bar, and everyone made room. Abe placed a chardonnay on the bar as she sat down, leaned over and kissed her on the cheek.

"How's The Admiral?" Abe asked.

"He's fine, I guess; I hope. He's up at Goddard. He and Chad are scoping out something, not sure what. Nothing from Goddard and JPL has been good lately."

Her brow wrinkled. Judi stopped on her way out to say hello to Sheryl and goodbye to Abe the cute bartender.

"Well, Miss Glummy Poo soon-to-be Mrs. Admiral!"

Abe smiled at her, glancing over her shoulder at one of the other TVs, the carnage still unfolding. Atlanta's airport was now closed.

Sheryl was a good catch for The Admiral, not just because of her political clout but because she was a good woman with a big heart. Plus, she loved animals; and Abe knew from his life's experiences, if you love dogs you gotta be a good person.

"Who wouldn't be? Glum, I mean. Abe, what's going on in the world? Since you believe in God, do you think God has anything to do with all these terrible tragedies?"

"... still waiting to find out what kind of chemical the plane sprayed. Some doctors who escaped Grady said the sweet-garlicky smell means it may have been mustard gas, used as a weapon as far back as... World War I, I think?"

"Of course he does. Oh, by the way; when you came in did you happen to see a man, I think it was a man, walking around that seemed maybe a little 'strange'?"

"...deaths into the thousands; women, children, pets. It's awful."

The news faded to yet another scene of horror, ambulances and rescue vehicles prohibited from entering the now restricted zone because of the imminent danger from the lingering gas.

The interior lights dimmed, just slightly; only the lights weren't programmed to dim for another hour. A couple of the flatscreens pixilated but recovered. He would check the timing system later.

"Hmmm... No one but the man dressed in black with the black hat; oh, and a sign-board draped over his shoulders."

Sheryl's look went from casual to concerned, and she stood and walked back over to the front doors. The man was standing by the fountain, looking around at the few people strolling around the Green. The day was nice, very warm; but people were scared. A few of the strollers wore surgical face masks, purchased at the local drug store, as though that would save them from wandering viruses.

The news was interrupted with yet another news alert, and *The Divide's* crowd waited to learn what was happening now that could be more important than what would become known as the *Super Bowl 9/11*. Condi Zimmerman appeared on the screen, and her stress was plain to see.

"In other bad news of the day, a nuclear power plant in the Augusta, Georgia area has apparently suffered a failure of some kind. We have a nuclear expert on the line. Dr. Brunson, what can you tell us?"

"Thanks Condi, and I wish I could say it was nice talking with you again. There has been an attempted breach in security at the nuclear plant in Waynesboro, just east of Augusta. Some of the intel folk think it may have been another attempt to hack into the networks at the plant. It's been tried before."

This was not the news the crowd anticipated, and most wondered why the *real* news was interrupted. The din became a low mumble.

"Reports claim that the core's coolant system began a 'slow drain' possibly two days ago; and emergency measures to import additional coolant were stymied because the manual valves were welded shut and the automatically controlled valve operation system has apparently been 'hacked,' according to an anonymous source. Not sure what that's about, and we are awaiting further news.

"Waynesboro and surrounding areas are being evacuated; and the plant's reactors are shutting down exactly as designed, according to the plant's PR department."

Dr. Brunson pondered the PR department's statement. He knew those guys would say anything, more often fiction than truth. The valves had been welded shut, but he was sure the culprit wasn't a welding rod; too much light, too much noise and too much smoke. It was probably as simple as the empty tube of Liquid Nail he found in the bathroom trash that he turned over to plant security.

"I guess the concern is, will we have a meltdown, a China Syndrome if you will?" Condi continued, sipping her bottled water.

"No, no... nothing like that will or could happen, even in the worst of conditions," the doctor replied, *"and besides that, the Waynesboro facilities are the most advanced in the world. The plant has multiple backup systems. Everyone will be safe and sound, we're just taking precautions."*

Dan didn't mention the other nuclear plants in the United States that had been breached within the last twenty-four hours; or the breached plants in Europe. These older plants didn't have the technical safeguards now implemented at the nation's most advanced power generator in Waynesboro, the Birddog Capital of the World. Obvious terrorism, he knew.

Abe paid no attention to the news, and his stare followed Sheryl to the front entrance and then down the steps to the Towne Green. He hurriedly served the waiting patrons; and the drinking seemed heavier than normal, even for Super Bowl Sunday.

Standing on the last step, Sheryl swatted a mosquito and stared at the man. She thought he kind of resembled Abraham Lincoln, except for the hat. The hat was more Wyatt Earpish.

The man with the sign-board turned to face her as a loud peal of thunder came from somewhere faraway, and the front of the sign was clear: *THE END IS NEAR*

She had seen plenty of these signs in her life, but lately they were commonplace. Something was different about this man though, or maybe it was his glowing sign. Her body tingled but not a good tingle, and she made her way down the final step and toward the man.

The Abraham Lincoln-looking man turned, showing Sheryl and the sparse crowd with donned face masks the back part of his sign, hanging down to his backside. The message was chilling, not just because of the message itself but because the message glowed like blue neon lights on a Saturday night in Las Vegas.

Are you ready for the Day of God's Wrath?

The man looked back briefly, and Sheryl was sure he was crying. He threw her a kiss, which was unnerving; but the tears pouring from the stranger's eyes were plain to see.

"Sheryl!"

Sheryl turned toward the shout and saw Abe standing on the front steps.

"Is anything wrong?" he yelled, concern spreading over his face. He ran toward her.

"No, I'm fine. It's just the man's sign."

"What man?" Abe asked, and thought Sheryl seemed a little confused. Maybe she was on pain meds or something; she hadn't touched her wine.

"The strange man you mentioned, *that* man," and she turned to point.

No man. The man in black and his large sign had simply disappeared.

"Where did he go?"

She was in awe at how quickly the man and sign could make it 50 yards from the fountain to the nearest parking lot and out of sight. It wasn't possible in the three seconds or so she was turned toward Abe. *Very strange,* she thought, but the whole world seemed strange.

"What did the sign say?" Abe asked. They turned and strolled back toward the restaurant.

"It said 'the end is near' and 'get ready for God' or something like that." She was light-headed and momentarily felt faint but continued.

"The writing glowed; the letters glowed like blue neon against a black sky. And you know what, Abe? I think I've seen that man at *The Divide* before, at least once. Where did he go? Very strange. He was there, and then he wasn't. I'm gettin' too old for this stuff, Abe."

Sheryl mused and massaged the back of her neck as they walked up the steps toward the ever-gathering crowd. Everyone knew where to come to hear the latest news. She retook her seat at the bar, her chardonnay still untouched; and the news continued on and on and on. She was weary.

Contemplating the irony of her situation, it was a little comical. She had waited many years to meet a man like The Admiral; and now that it happened, the whole world was going berserk. *I think the world really is ending*, and the fleeting thought flashed through her mind.

Abe's thoughts remained with the stranger in black; and he recalled another visitor to the club, also dressed in black. He had visited a couple of times actually, and his exits had been remarkable, like the man with the sign. He simply vanished. The lights dimmed further, and three more TVs went blank.

"... Bowl in Atlanta has been taken off the air; and reports are flooding in via Twitter that a small advertising plane caught fire or exploded and has crashed into the new Falcon's stadium. Reporters were on the way to the site but have been stopped by the Atlanta Police Department and the National Guard.

"As we now know, the plane didn't catch fire until it was shot down by a fighter jet from Dobbins and did not, I repeat Did Not crash into the new stadium. The smoke from the small biplane, we are now told, may have been mustard gas. The estimated tolls speculated so far: 'more than ten thousand dead or injured.' I'm Amber Michelle with the Apocalypse News Channel.

"In other news, Charleston, South Carolina has suffered another small earthqua..."

Sheryl sipped her chardonnay, but her mood had become dismal. Her light headedness persisted. She reached in her larger-than-life, black leather purse and searched for her ringing phone. She found it before the last ring that would send the caller to voicemail. It was The Admiral, and her mood changed for the better.

"Hey!"

"Hey Babe. Just landed at Briscoe Field. Where are you?"

"Watching the news at *The Divide.* It's been a big news day. I'm so glad you're back."

"What news? I've been on a private plane for three hours. Who's winning the Super Bowl?"

CHAPTER EIGHTEEN

"There will be signs in the sun, moon and stars. On the earth, nations will be in anguish and perplexity at the roaring and tossing of the sea."

Luke 21:25

Admiral Justin Philip McLemore was known as "The Admiral" to most people, including his close friends. He never married anyone other than the U.S. Navy but had fallen hard for Sheryl. It hadn't been love at first sight, but there had been something right from the beginning. Maybe those pheromones he read about. Mature, bright and intelligent, he never knew women like Sheryl existed and found himself severely smitten. The scenery was pretty good too.

The Super Bowl tragedy the day before had killed an estimated twenty-five thousand and counting, now the nation's deadliest terrorist attack. *Seems like that record is being broken on a regular basis*, he thought silently. However, the other news about the nuclear plant hackings was also quite worrisome. He was glad to be back *home* and gently squeezed her hand.

"The same thing's going on in Europe, according to the White House. It has to be terrorism, but the President refused to call it such in the press conference. He won't even call the Super Bowl attack terrorism; says it's a 'domestic' issue. It can't be a coincidence that nuclear power plants all over the world are having simultaneous problems."

Sheryl paused and wiped her forehead. She ran her fingers through her long red hair, damp from the humidity. She would get a haircut this week.

"It's hot in here, let's go outside."

"It's hotter outside," The Admiral said as he stood and slid Sheryl's chair from the table. She perspired profusely, and he worried about her health. He told Abe they would be back and to keep the tab open.

Sheryl's position as Public Affairs Liaison to the President had been long and stressful, especially the Spanish Flu outbreak; and the stress was becoming more apparent each day.

They walked down the steps hand-in-hand, toward the fountain. Two kids in red bathing suits ran through the water, giggling as though nothing was wrong; and in their young world, there probably was nothing wrong.

The Towne Green's newly-installed weather station displayed 87 degrees and 76% humidity in large blue figures, another record temperature for January. At least there was a good breeze. It seemed there was always a breeze these days. He leaned over and kissed her.

"Well thank you, Mr. Admiral Sir. What was *that* for?"

"It was an 'I love you bunches kiss'."

"Well alrighty then. Can we do it again?" And they did.

A sudden gust blew the pizza sign down in front of Steverinos, and the smell of fine Italian food wafted across the Towne Green. Two kittens frolicked in the Children's Park on the left, the two kids in the red bathing suits now playing on the swings. A lone man, heavy and wearing sunglasses sat on a bench adjacent to the Children's Park and read the newspaper, at least it appeared so.

"Chadbo said the winds are picking up all over the world. Last week he said the high-altitude winds were almost black, the darkest he's ever seen," The Admiral continued. "Said the high-altitude winds were diving farther south than normal and were probably driving all the hailstorms we've been having. He also said that's why Hurricane Abby made the U-turn toward Florida."

They sat on one of the benches under the large white-oak tree by the Living Honorarium Memorial. Most of the other large oaks that once surrounded City Hall had died from heat and drought. The conversation was silent for the moment, and Sheryl wondered what it must be like to actually be able to see the wind.

"Philip," Sheryl asked, "what's going on in the world?"

"I don't know, Sheryl." He paused in thought.

"Remember how things were just before the comet hit the Moon?" Sheryl asked.

"Whaddaya mean there, Miss Duluth?" The Admiral winked and squeezed her hand, speaking in his best John Wayne voice. "Ya look great; did I tell ya that?"

Sheryl ignored the compliment at first and then said, "Thanks, John;" and the worry-wrinkles appeared again on her forehead as she continued.

"I mean everyone seemed so passive and peaceful. Most of the terrorist attacks stopped, even the Muslims seemed to get along with each other. There were a few gangs roaming, but not many. The whole world seemed to come together, but now… Now the world is falling apart like never before."

The mood was melancholy. Thunder rumbled in the distance, but the sky remained azure blue. The Moon journeyed slowly across the daytime sky, now hovering over City Hall. The Moon's rings were clearly visible, even in the afternoon sunlight.

"So what other mischief did you and Chad discover? Anymore asteroids headed our way?"

"As a matter of fact, that's likely."

"What do you mean?"

The Admiral looked deep into Sheryl's sea-blue eyes. He really didn't want to tell her what they had discovered, but she was conditioned to receive bad news. Working directly for the President was often a world of bad news and cover-ups. Thunder rang out again, this time closer.

"Something massive has forced a large swarm of asteroids out of the Kuiper Belt. It's actually a large cloud of debris."

"Kuiper Belt?" Sheryl asked. "Isn't that where the Dark Comet came from?"

"No, they think that was from the Oort Cloud. Of course the Oort Cloud is only a theory, but indications are that it exists and holds the remnants of many asteroids and comets. It's much more distant than Kuiper."

Sheryl was thankful for the breeze, no matter what the wind might portend. At least it made it seem cooler.

"Oh yeah, I remember. Chuck Hutz mentioned the Oort Cloud during one of his trances."

"The scientists at Jet Propulsion Labs and Goddard think the asteroid cloud was pulled out of the Kuiper Belt by an undiscovered rogue planet, possibly as large as Jupiter. The gravitational pull, if this is what truly happened, pulled the cloud inward toward the inner solar system."

"And a 'rogue' planet is?"

"Rogue planets were only discovered a couple of years ago, but we're learning more every day," The Admiral explained. "They're also called 'nomads' because they wander around with no home star."

"You mean they don't orbit a star? They just float around in space?"

"That's correct. We've only detected a few, but they've been theorized for years. There could be billions. Anyway, this is Chadbo's guess… a rogue planet, probably well beyond Neptune and maybe seven times bigger than Jupiter…"

"Wow! That's big!" Sheryl interrupted.

"Yep, it is. The planet could have pushed or pulled this large cloud of asteroids and small comets toward the inner solar system.

"That would be us?" Sheryl asked.

"Possibly. We *are* sure that most of these objects will fly harmlessly through space and never hit anything. Many of the asteroids will never make it by Jupiter. Jupiter's gravity is so strong, anything semi-close will be sucked in as they pass."

"Where's the 'however'?"

"However," he continued, "there is a high probability that Mars and Earth will get some hits."

"Lovely."

"That's not all. When the Dark Comet hit the Moon, most of the debris field from the collision began to orbit the Moon and formed the rings. We were hoping that all the debris would remain in lunar orbit, but that didn't happen. We know some debris took out the space station, and it was most likely debris from the collision."

"I know all that already."

"Yes, I know you do; but you don't know this. At least one large boulder has come out of lunar orbit and will pass very near Earth, if it doesn't actually hit."

"Where will it hit if it does hit? Any idea?" Her worry-wrinkles grew horizontally on her forehead, becoming deeper.

"Southern Hemisphere, possibly Antarctica. That's where the probability lies."

"So," Sheryl asked, "we have a moon rock that's an NEO now headed toward Earth that may obliterate Antarctica; we have a large cloud of asteroids or comets headed toward the Sun that may hit us; we have meteor showers now being forecast on *The Weather Channel*; the world is on the verge of war; HIV, Ebola, Spanish Flu and smallpox have killed millions in the past three years; crime has skyrocketed; so what's to worry about?" They didn't laugh.

"What happens if this rogue planet heads toward Earth? I mean, is there any way to know this early? The Bible talked about *signs in the sky*; and that would certainly be one, a new planet bigger than Jupiter."

"So is a pink moon with rings," The Admiral said looking up into the sky.

"Philip, didn't the Bible say something about the Moon turning red in the last days?"

"Yes, it did. That was just one of the many signs to come. No one really knew how this could possibly happen, so the prophecy was ignored. Who would've ever figured that a comet crashing into the Moon would begin to turn the Moon red?"

Another clap of thunder to the east but no hail, thankfully.

Chapter Nineteen

Carrying Samarra's small and limp body through the rear entrance of her expansive home, Vinny hoped he hadn't hit her too hard during the brief struggle. He didn't want her dead, at least not yet. He had plans and laid her gently on the couch, her purse still draped around her left shoulder; and a small trickle of bright red escaped her now swollen lip.

Samarra let out a soft moan as he laid her on the leather couch, but her semi-consciousness was a delusion. She moaned again and whined softly.

"Please don't take me in there, please don't take me in that room," she slurred softly and pointed down the hall to the left of the extravagant entertainment center. Samarra remembered that the cleaning lady would be there any moment and worried.

The woman's incoherent, Vinny thought. He visually searched the large living room but didn't have a clue what room the woman was talking about. Where was she pointing? He would definitely take her to the dreaded room if he only knew where it was.

Vinny gently slapped Samarra's face, hoping to wake her from her semi-consciousness. She was laying on her carry-purse, and the small Derringer dug into her side. She didn't respond to the slap, other than another moan.

"Please don't take me in that room," she whimpered and again pointed down the dark hallway that lead to the first floor master suite.

"Don't die on me you infidel whore," Vinny hissed. "I want to know where your son is; you know, the son with the missing finger. I should have cut his pretty little red head off then, but it's never too late. The pudding is in the proof." Vinnie laughed.

As she recalled *that* day, Samarra's act of being out-of-it was in dire straits. Her blood began to boil, and she only hoped this madman couldn't hear it bubbling in her heart.

She would always be haunted by that scene, a missing nanny and a Valentine's candy box on the kitchen counter with Thomas' ring finger inside with ring still on; and the note. That's how all this started. She had to keep her cool or young Thomas would be without a finger, without a mother and a father in prison for lewd sex acts with young boys. She silently thanked God that Thomas was with his grandmother in Israel.

"Where's the boy!" Vinny hissed again, this time louder.

Vinny spotted the granite-topped bar across the room and the Baccarat crystal pitcher filled with water. *Good taste* he said to no one and admired the abundant glassware lining the dark mahogany bar. A bottle of Duckhorn merlot sat at the end, and Vinny was sure he had seen the name before but couldn't recall.

He grabbed the pitcher. A splash or two of cold water and the now-not-so-lovely woman would be wide-awake. As he journeyed back toward the couch, he glanced down the hallway and noticed a closed door at the far end. *Maybe that's it* he thought, and he detoured down the hall to find the room the woman feared.

Out of sight, Samarra slowly secured her carry-purse. Unlike other purses, her Hermes Matte Crocodile purse was designed with a concealed holster. In the holster was her *Bond Ranger II* Derringer, a gift from Jeff. She could hear the madman making his way down the hall, and she rapidly regained her faculties.

Reaching inside the expensive designer purse, she felt the holstered firearm, heavy for such a small gun, just over a pound of lethality. She quietly cocked the .45 Derringer while still in the purse, withdrew it and waited. Loaded with two rounds, the gun was deadly and *very* loud. She probably wouldn't have to use it if the well-tanned man opened the right door.

Jeff always worried about Samarra's safety with all the kooks threatening to kill her after the Spanish Flu was loosed on the nation and other parts of the world. The threat of beheading her young son had stirred Samarra to steal the virus from the Centers for Disease Control, and fortunately young Thomas only lost a finger. In addition to the Derringer Jeff gave her, when he was away from home overnight he would let Samarra keep his Great Dane at her home; and the large dog was no longer a puppy.

The strange noises going on in the other room had not escaped the Dane's attention, and his ears perked as he heard someone with an unusual gait and smell walking toward his room.

Samarra waited as patiently as possible, and her heart pounded. This could be the day her life ended, she was sure of that. Why was she being targeted again? She had given them what they wanted, and now millions were dead or in the process.

Vinny secured the small, Egyptian stiletto in his right hand and slowly turned the doorknob on the large, heavy oak door with his left. Cautiously he pushed the door open. There was no sound, and Vinny began to think it might be the next room instead.

Great Danes are not barkers like smaller dogs, don't need to be; and the large gray dog silently stirred as the knob turned, waiting for the stranger to open the door. He slowly rose as the door crept open. With one of the keenest senses of smell of all breeds, the Great Dane smelled evil; and the hair on the back of his neck and spine stood up. The dog made no sound but salivated heavily, now in protection mode.

Vinny tightened the grip on his 4-inch stiletto and flung the door open. The large dog leaped as Vinny swung the knife and caught the Dane's right ear. Harley didn't cry out but let out a growl like nothing Vinny had ever heard. He tried to pull the door shut but couldn't secure it.

Vinny tore up the hallway fast as he could toward the living room, and he never realized until then how truly fast his short legs could propel him. He had a tremendous fear of dogs, and this one looked vaguely familiar. He would take care of the lady later.

Bounding past Samarra, no longer laying on the couch, he glimpsed the silver gun in her hand just before the gun exploded in a loud boom that sounded like a cannon.

The Great Dane, now out of the bedroom that he thought was his own, galloped like a small horse down the hallway. Vinny wished he could deal with the gun rather than the large dog, but the choice was not his.

The first slug missed as Vinny opened the door to the front yard; but the second made contact, ripping through his right buttocks, a glancing but painful encounter. He did not slow much, but his run became more of a fast limp; and he tried to shut the heavy front door behind him, heading for the black Mercedes and hoping the key was still in the ignition.

Vinny made it to the car, slammed the door behind him as he limp-crawled in to the plush leather seat and blood streamed down his leg onto the floor. No key. *Great* he thought and looked left as he saw the Great Dane galloping in a full sprint toward the car. Then he spotted the round START button and pushed. The key fob was on the center console, and the Mercedes started instantly.

CHAPTER TWENTY

"For he spoke and stirred up a tempest that lifted high the waves."

Psalm 107:25

"F*olks, I know it's only January, but Hurricane Abigail is a Category 5 storm with sustained winds of 178 miles per hour, one of the strongest in history. The barometric pressure is now 870 millibars and falling rapidly, the lowest ever recorded. Wind gusts are topping 210 miles per hour, and the Outer Banks of North Carolina are virtually underwater with the unprecedented sea surge."*

Jeff watched the satellite weather channel in his airy Jamaican villa, noting the sudden increase in the hurricane's forward speed, now heading south but still well east of Charleston. He was restless, anxious and confused and paid little attention to the weather report. His mind was elsewhere.

"The forward motion of Abby is now nine miles per hour as she is pushed southward by an unusual jet stream. The storm is still well out to sea but now heading south-southwest. Abby is relatively compact, and the eye is perfectly symmetrical. Though Georgia..."

"What's up?" Wild Willy asked as he entered the living room with coffee in hand.

"Just watching this hurricane. Georgia has hurricane storm warnings up along the coast, all the way in to Macon."

"Thought that thing was headed toward Bermuda." Will searched for creamer.

"That was yesterday; now it's made a U-turn. I don't think I heard the wind speeds right, because they sounded awfully high."

Jeff channel surfed in a search for FOX News but stopped briefly when he saw Chuck Hutz on a religious channel.

"Hal Lindsey," Will said walking back into the room, stirring his almost white coffee.

"Who?"

"Hal Lindsey, that's who Chuck is talking to. Ol' Chuck's been talking a lot more about end-of-the- world stuff lately. I see his smiling face all over Israeli TV, talking about Ezekiel, Jeremiah, Isaiah and Jesus. Hal Lindsey's an expert on all those Bible predictions."

"Prophecies," Jeff added.

"Yeah, that's right. Do you know anything about… you don't know anything about prophecies. You don't believe the Bible. Must've lost my head."

Will took a sip, but the coffee was already too cold. Jeff surfed more and found FOX News.

"...blew the plane out of the sky. Thousands are believed dead as well as most of the players."

"What the hell?" Will took a gulp from the hibiscus decorated coffee cup, burning the back of his throat. "Is that the Super Bowl?"

Jeff and Will breathed in silence as they continued to watch, taking in the scenes displayed on the screen.

"CDC is saying the crop duster may have carried mustard gas or possibly another chemical weapon mixture of some kind.

Rich, do you have anything on that?" Condi asked. *"Let's go to Rich Badey in Atlanta. Rich, can you hear me?"*

Rich Badey, the award-winning journalist, had covered disasters all over the world. Jeff had seen the correspondent many times and thought he looked worried, which couldn't be a good thing.

"I hear you Condi. I was heading for the stadium, but the police and National Guard have set up a perimeter several miles around the area of attack."

The cameraman panned the traffic and then focused on the mist that was suddenly headed their way.

"Before the crop duster was blown out of the sky, we're not sure if it was one of the F-18s or possibly an armed drone, it appears the cargo was mustard gas or possibly a mixture of mustard gas and a nerve agent. Mustard gas has a garlicky-sweet smell, kind of like mustard; and that was the gas Saddam Hussein used on the Kurds in Iraq when he gassed and killed five thousand of them. Mustard gas is a blistering agent and causes burns to the skin and inside the lungs when inhaled, but a lot of reports have indicated that many people were 'twitching and falling' as they tried to escape the area. That's why there are some who say a nerve agent was involved.

"The plane made one pass over the stadium and then flew down I-75 south, dumping the rest on the stalled traffic below."

Rich paused and began coughing and wheezing as the winds pushed the gas outward; and then he collapsed. The camera continued to roll automatically as the cameraman also fell to the ground, twitching uncontrollably, out of sight of the camera.

"Rich? Are you there? Did we lose him?" The news faded and went to commercial.

Jeff reached for his phone and began texting Jenni, Jami and Audry. *They better not have gone to that game* was the only thing on his mind. He had given them orders to stay away. Will turned to CNN which had satellite images of the stadium, and bodies were everywhere. The scene was total death and destruction.

With no response from the kids, Jeff phoned Samarra who answered on the third ring.

Vinny headed north on I-75 toward Chattanooga, hoping to make it to Dalton before he bled to death. He had to get rid of the Mercedes and would at first chance. The car was too obvious. The Sun was setting, and he exited the interstate near Cartersville. He would use secondary roads.

Seventeen miles later, Vinny's head spinning as his blood pressure continued to drop, he spotted a mosque. *Really? A mosque in the north Georgia foothills?*

There were no cars in the parking lot, so he continued northward, hoping he wouldn't pass out. Then he spotted the emergency veterinarian clinic he had seen during a past journey to Dalton. Only two cars were at the clinic as twilight evolved into darkness. The Moon wasn't quite full, but the pink rings were beautiful. Hadn't the Christians mentioned something about signs in the sky? This one was beautiful.

He pulled the black, V-12 behemoth behind the building and took a hit of speed, his last. Like a rush of adrenalin, the height-impaired Vinny felt a renewal of strength and opened the car door.

"Dr. Chafin?" the young veterinarian attendant asked. "Since we aren't busy, can I run home a minute? I forgot my laptop."

Janie Marsh wasn't related to the veterinarian, but she loved the elderly man like her own grandfather. He had been a friend of her family for years. It had been a hard time for the elderly man since his son had been killed a year or so before in a biking accident, somewhere in Europe. His body was never found.

"Sure Janie, but be careful. Don't let the boogeyman get you." He winked.

She laughed at the comment. He always told her that, but there weren't many boogeymen in this area of Georgia.

"I won't be gone long. I'm taking a Bible course on-line and have three lessons to finish."

"Oh really? Which books are you studying?"

"*Revelation* and *Daniel*," she stated.

"Good for you, Janie. Most Christians avoid *Revelation* like the plague. It's *tooo scaaarry*. That's what they say alright."

"Maybe that's because it talks about the coming plagues and the end of the world," the young girl said with a smile.

Vivacious Jane, as her friends called her, grabbed her pink, patent-leather purse and exited the front door of the faux stucco-sided building. Walking to her new Honda, also pink, she thought she heard a door slam, maybe a car door and glanced around the parking lot, seeing nada. She started the engine and turned right on Dalton Highway.

Vinny had secured the stiletto before exiting the black Mercedes when he noticed a shiny object on the floor, highlighted by the interior LED lighting system, a loose bullet in front of the passenger seat. He picked the bullet up and felt the Glock under the seat.

Praise Allah, he thought as he pocketed the black polymer-framed pistol, closed the car door and nearly fell down. He was weak, but the speed was doing what speed does.

Vinny was a lucky man, except for the shot in the ass he received an hour or so earlier, he thought. The back door was unlocked.

Glancing through the window, he saw a man with white hair, maybe six feet tall, sitting at a gray metal desk. It looked like the old man was reading. Vinny pulled the gun though it was not his intent to use it; too noisy. The old man turned as Vinny came in the back door, but he did not look startled. Vinny staggered and fell but regained his composure and pointed the Glock at the doctor.

"Antibiotics and pain medication," Vinny stated matter-of-factly. Blood continued down his leg and onto the gray, linoleum floor.

"What happened?" the old man asked and came to Vinny's aid. Vinny waved the doctor away with the Glock.

"I have a bullet in my ass, hurts like hell. I need you to remove it and sew me up."

The old man walked calmly to the stainless-steel medicine cabinet and removed a small container of oxycodone. He handed two of the pills and a glass of water to the wounded man and told him to put the gun away.

"How'd you get shot, young man?"

"Doesn't matter. I won't hurt you, but you must help." Vinny paused and breathed deeply. "Why are you reading the *Quran*? Are you Muslim?"

Sweat began to make tiny pathways down Vinny's back, each droplet slowly creeping toward his wounded behind.

"I've read it several times, young man. No, I'm a Christian."

"Stop calling me 'young man.' So why are you reading it?"

Vinny held the gun but stopped pointing it at the veterinarian.

"Curiosity, mostly," the veterinarian quipped. "Islam is said to be one of the world's great religions. Since you guys kill so many of us, I wanted to find out why. That's all. Get on the gurney, and I'll take a look."

Vinny did as the doc instructed. The doctor began his exam, and Vinny winced in pain. The veterinarian filled a small syringe with lidocaine; and Vinny watched closely, wondering how the doctor knew he was a Muslim.

"No shot," Vinny demanded. "Just sew me up, and I'll leave."

Outside, the wind began to howl, and thunder sounded in the distance. The lights flickered, as Vinny and the doc both hoped another hailstorm wasn't imminent. Recent hailstorms were car destroyers, along with barns and livestock. He would take the doctor's car that was in the garage.

Samarra answered on the third ring and was glad it was Jeff.

"Samarra, what's going on? Are you okay?"

Samarra was anything but okay. The police had left, except for two Atlanta police officers who would remain out front for the night, just in case. Whoever the monster was, she doubted he would be back *this* night. She had tried to kill the short, little man but guessed she must have shot him in the rear. He had screamed something about shot in the ass, and that brought a smile to her face.

"Hey Jeffrey, no I'm fine. Don't panic, the girls are at your house; and I'm headed there in an hour or so. I have to clean up the mess."

"What mess?"

Darn, she thought; she hadn't wanted to tell him about the strange man with the sore butt. He had too much on his mind, and the Jamaica trip would solve a lot of it. But then, how could she keep it from him?

"Jeffrey, the girls are safe and sound. They picked up Mr. Hutz this afternoon. They were going to the game but traffic was stopped on the interstates. Chuck or Audry, not quite sure who, had a feeling or a vision of something terrible happening; so the group went back home. I still don't have the details of what happened at the game."

"I told them not to go to the game."

"Jeff, did you really think they would miss the Super Bowl? They're young. I know you would've done the same."

"What's the mess you have to clean up?" Jeff asked again.

"Just a little accident by the front door."

"Harley peed on your floor? He never does that." Jeff was surprised and knew something odd must have happened.

"Oh, it wasn't Harley." She changed the subject. "How are things in Jamaica? Have you seen Melissa?"

"What scared him? He doesn't frighten easy."

"Jeff, I had a break-in today. I'm fine; don't worry. I am not hurt."

"I'm coming home."

"You can't come home, Jeff! You have to take care of Jamaica matters first. There is a reason for all this. I'm fine. Just a petty thief. Don't worry, Harley scared the… well, he scared the pee out of him. See, I said it wasn't Harley. Stay where you are, and just keep me posted."

An hour later, Jeff stood on the balcony of the master suite, the fresh Jamaican air not quite as fresh as last time, and waited patiently for Rosalie's call. The sky was dark except for the pinpoint lights of faraway stars and planets, and things that bump into the earth at night. The Moon was a vivid pink now and seemed to get pinker by the month. *Who would've ever thought the Moon would be pink and have rings.* They were beautiful though, but dangerous.

He stared at Earth's moon, and beads of moisture swelled on his forehead. Then he remembered what his mom had once told him, and the words flowed through his mind at the speed of light.

"Jeffrey my sonny-boy," she said, "when the end-times starts approachin,'… I know you think that's a joke… you mark my words. You'll see some strange things in the sky at night, maybe the daytime too. You watch the Moon. When it turns red, you'll know the time is near, just a breath away. Says so right in the Bible, 'course you wouldn't know that. I pray for you Jeffrey, I really do."

The phone rang.

Chapter Twenty-One

The morning was beautiful as most Jamaican mornings are, but the climate was far from Jeff's mind. It would be a busy day, the day he would find out if Rosalie was right about Melissa. Maybe it wasn't Melissa at all. Things had gotten complicated and confused. The TV now monitored the weather twenty-four seven.

"Hurricane Abigail has grown into a massive event almost overnight. The hurricane-force wind field now extends one hundred miles from the large but well-formed eye, and tropical force winds extend all the way to the north Georgia mountains and into eastern Tennessee. Let's go to the National Hurricane Center. Dr. Whited? Are you there?"

Day two in Jamaica should be more productive, Jeff thought; at least he hoped. Rosalie had called the evening before, just after he spoke with Samarra. She would have contact information this morning.

Wild Willy and Jeff watched the weather with renewed interest. The storm was growing rapidly, and its predicted movement would take it along the Atlantic coast of Georgia and Florida and then toward Cuba, at least according to the models. The high winds aloft in the upper atmosphere were abnormal, not just the wind speed but the southerly thrust of the jet stream so early in the year.

"Wow! Who *is* that lady?" Will asked as the TV screen faded to the National Hurricane Center and *that lady* appeared front and center on the screen. "She's gorgeous!"

"Will, you think they're all gorgeous, my friend."

Dr. Jenni Whited *was* gorgeous and was used to flattery and compliments. She was from *upper stock,* and her family was none too happy when she decided to move from Monaco to the United States and major in meteorology. Her parents had different plans. Now here she was, working with the Hurricane Center; and she couldn't be happier.

Behind her was the mother of all arrays of flatscreen monitors, each tuned to specific charts, graphs and live video of the huge storm, as well as two in the Pacific that appeared almost out of nowhere.

"Yes, I'm here watching closely. The last twelve hours have been monumental. Abby is breaking all the records in the history books, though records do only go back about a hundred and fifty years. If she continues to drop in pressure and maintain direction, it could be a rough few days for the Southern Atlantic Coast. The storm has moved more westward; so the states of South Carolina, Georgia and Florida are in for a rough time.

"Some evacuations are..."

"How do the weather channels get these gorgeous babes?" Will interrupted.

"Don't get excited, Wild Willy; whoaaaa boy," Jeff said with a laugh. "You haven't seen her before? She's on a lot with all the windstorm news. We've been having a lot in case you haven't noticed."

The weather girl was the perfect picture of fashion. Dressed in an ebony dress to match her ebony hair, she was new to the Hurricane Center. Her popularity among weather-interested viewers had grown quickly, and she had become a regular player in the world of meteorology. She seemed to be everywhere there was severe weather.

"Nope, I haven't," Will replied. "I would remember her, believe me. We'd probably be married by now!"

"Pardon the interruption, Jenni; but are evacuations being planned? We haven't heard much."

"Yes, that's correct," Jenni explained. *"Evacuations are beginning along the Atlantic Seaboard from South Carolina to Key West, as her forward motion has increased from seven knots to ten."*

"Will, stop drooling. She's way too young for you; and besides that, she's a princess from Monaco. She's the daughter of the Royal Family."

"My goodness, she just takes my breath away," Will sighed and looked up to the ceiling, his hands folded as if in prayer. "You really did good with this one, Lord. Is she married?"

Wild Willy was worldly in the sense that he had traveled the world, seen many cultures and was well aware of Monaco. He was also aware of the dire financial straits in France and the rest of Europe, barely staying alive. The West was broke.

"Did you know that Monaco is the smallest country in the world? And the most densely populated?" Will asked.

"Second smallest," Jeff answered. "You are correct about the population though. Monaco's bordered by France on three sides, and the Mediterranean on the fourth. Ever been to Monte Carlo?"

"Of course; several times. It's a great resort town, and the beaches are magnifique," Will answered in his best French accent. "And the ladies are also magnifique."

Will watched the screen closely as Princess Jenni began her report, her French accent adding to Wild Willy's intrigue. Jeff and Will had been friends for years, and Jeff knew how intrigued Wild Willy would always get over the unattainable.

"You're exactly right," the Princess continued. "The South Carolina and Georgia interstates have been converted to one-way for evacuation to the west; but Florida interstates for the most part are north and south, with the exception of I-10.

"This hurricane is now the strongest on record for the Atlantic, and the wind field is wide. The situation has quickly become critical. South Florida, already suffering from the destruction caused by the Cayman Tsunami, is in a... how do you say in America... heck of a mess? For those who don't heed the warnings, there is really no escape. Because of the collapsing time frame, some are taking fishing boats and charter boats out to sea; but this too is very dangero..."

The in-suite phone rang, and Jeff picked it up on the first. His heart pounded. Will continued to watch the princess.

"This is Jeff." It was Rosalie.

"Mistuh Jeffy, I have 'ranged fo Miss Melissa to meet wit you, but it is veddy dangeous. Can you meet at J- Joe's Café at 2:00? It is not fah fum you."

"J- Joe's? Jeff repeated.

"Yes suh. Jamaica Joe's. We call it J-Joes."

"No problem. Can you give me directions?"

Jeff took directions and thought the place sounded familiar but couldn't place it.

"Why is it dangerous?" he asked.

"Cause, Mistuh Jeffy. De witch doctuh is potective of de lady. Ya know we have lot of voodoo in Jamaica, Mistuh Jeffy. Miss Melissa, she be talkin' to de witch doctuh 'bout Chistianity. She be witnissin'. De witch doctuh, he be thinkin' she be de angel fum God."

Witch doctor? Jeff knew voodoo was rampant in Jamaica, at least in the north and throughout the mountains. He also knew that voodoo mythology had a strong effect on its adherents. This could be a problem.

"Okay, Rosalie, we will be there at 2:00."

"We? Mistuh Jeffy, you got to come alone," Rosalie said. "You *must* come alone."

"Okay, Rosalie, I'll be alone." The phone went silent, and Jeff hung up.

"I think I'm in love with this woman," Will said as Jeff reentered the room.

"Yeah, right; you love them all Wild Willy. I'm meeting Rosalie and Melissa at 2:00. Rosalie insisted I come alone."

"Why?" Will demanded.

"Don't know. That's just what she said."

"I don't think that's a good idea, Jeff. Some of these Jamaican haunts can be pretty dangerous."

"Dangeous,"Jeff said with a smile. "That's what Rosy says. It's dangeous. I love dangeous."

"Me too, let's go!" Will piped in; and if anyone in this world loved danger it was Wild Willy, Jeff knew.

"I'll go alone, Will. She was insistent. It'll be alright."

Will left the room but returned in a few seconds with a small hard-case pouch.

"Take these with you," and he handed Jeff the case.

"What is it?" Jeff asked, opening the case to find what looked like three small bugs of some sort. One looked like a small dragonfly.

"It's the latest and greatest from our good friends in Israel. Each bug is a micro-robot. They look so real they are almost undetectable. The Israelis have been developing these spybots for years; and they're now in use to track jihadist groups in Greater Iran and Pakistan."

"Is this what you used to track Sheryl down when she was kidnapped?" Jeff asked.

"Yep. Freaked her out when that bug came flying in, but the video told me exactly where she was."

"You're a real hero," Jeff complimented.

"Yeah, so what's new?" Will asked. They laughed. Will had an uneasy feeling.

"So what do you think I should do with the spybots?" Jeff asked.

"They're activated and just waiting. If Rosalie won't tell you where they're keeping Melissa, and she won't; the spybots can follow her. See the small keyboard? Just hit that little green icon and they're good to go. These babies are Google-map ready with Jamaica's terrain programmed in. I have your cell phone linked, so just take a picture of Rosalie's car, license plate would be good; and the data will automatically be input to the three bugs. They will follow her and send back real-time data."

"How fast can they fly?" Jeff asked.

"Classified; I'd have to kill ya." Will slapped Jeff on the shoulder and guffawed as he usually did at his own jokes.

At 1:00 Jeff started Will's rental SUV to let the AC cool the Grand Cherokee down. Five minutes later he pulled onto Kingston Highway and drove east toward Jamaica Joe's.

Then he remembered why the name was familiar; the news report from the Super Bowl. The crop duster was carrying a banner about free drinks at Jamaica Joe's, and he reasoned that there might be a connection of some kind. He remembered a man named Jamal, a Jamaican who spoke perfect French. *Had that been a dream?*

The trip would take about twenty minutes if the directions were correct. The afternoon sun bore down, but the breezes from the sea were refreshingly cool. It seemed like a nice day at the beach, other than the intermittent odor of dead fish. He couldn't recall ever smelling dead fish anywhere in Jamaica.

An hour later, Rosalie and Melissa walked in the small café. Sitting in the round booth at the rear as instructed, Jeff's heart fluttered briefly; and he felt his face flush. *Why do I feel so uncomfortable?*

Melissa, dressed in a coral sundress and sandals, was just as stunning as the last time he saw her; but that wasn't totally true he knew. The last time he saw Melissa was more than two years earlier when she washed over the roof of the four-story Cayman Grand Hotel. She didn't look stunning that day, just terrified; and he shut the memories down. He had gotten good at that.

From the instant Jeff saw her until she walked the thirty feet to his booth, it seemed an eternity as his memories, *their memories,* were restored from the depths of somewhere in his mind. They could not be restrained and no memory abatement control could douse this fire.

There was no doubt this was Melissa; and in a twinkling of an eye, Jeff recalled all the reasons he had loved her so much. It wasn't just the beauty or the smell of her skin, or the lust, but the kindness and lovingness in her eyes. Why had he never realized that?

Rosalie and Melissa moved closer, in slow motion it seemed and passed the three palm trees in the center of the empty dance floor by the pool table. Christmas lights hung down from the ceiling, looping in long arches from place to place. Jeff was amazed at all the things he remembered about their life together in such a brief period of time.

"Jeffrey, if you ever drown, and you better not, they say your whole life passes before you," his mom used to say, so maybe this was the same.

Then they were there.

Chapter Twenty-Two

The introduction was uneasy. Jeff gave Rosalie a hug but did not attempt the same with Melissa as they shook hands. Melissa smiled.

They sat down at the small round table, ordered glasses of water and an appetizer, then sat in silence, each waiting for the other to start the conversation.

"Do you remember me?" Jeff asked, looking into Melissa's eyes, trying to analyze what was going on inside her head. The pause was brief but didn't seem so. Time seemed to be crawling, almost like in a dream state.

Melissa looked at Rosalie, nodded her head and Rosalie excused herself and moved to the Tiki bar where her brother was bartender. There was only two other patrons in the small café.

"Mr. Ross," Melissa started.

"Please don't call me Mr. Ross. I was your husband for twenty-five years, Melissa. For Pete's sake! Would you mind calling me Jeffrey? That's what you used to call me."

Jeff had to get control of his out-of-control feelings. Melissa's hands were folded on the table, fingers intertwined; and Jeff started to reach over to hold them but then decided better. It was reflex he guessed.

"No, Jeffrey, I don't. I'm so sorry. I know this is difficult for you, more so than me. I just don't remember about the life before the wave."

"Do you remember the girls?" he asked, dreading the answer. "The twins and Audry?"

"No, Jeffrey. Rosalie showed me, gave me a photo of you. I thought you were so handsome, but I had no memories." She paused. "Will you refresh my memories?"

She reached over and touched his hand, placing hers on top of his.

"Can I ask you some questions?" he asked.

"Of course," and she smiled as she looked into his eyes, searching for … something.

Do you remember Robert?" he probed.

"No. Who is he?"

"Hmmm… this is going to be tougher than I thought. You and I were married, then we were divorced, then you married Robert, a missionary…."

They talked for two hours as Jeff tried to explain Melissa back into his world. He was surprised she remembered what the rapture of the church was, she remembered God and the scriptures; but she had no memories of him or the children. She didn't even remember Wild Willy, and no one seemed to forget him.

"I want to ask you something Melissa. It's personal, but I know you've thought about it."

"Sure Jeffrey, ask me anything."

Jeff paused as a crack of thunder echoed in the background, and rain began to fall along the perimeter of the mostly open café.

"Do you ever wonder if you will be raptured? I ask because so many people seem to think it has already happened, or maybe is in the process. I don't know. There's a lot of talk going around."

"Don't you believe in the rapture, Jeffrey?" Melissa asked.

Jeff guessed Melissa didn't remember he didn't believe in God and the stories, why would she? Before he could answer though, she continued; and he let out a silent sigh of relief.

"I have heard the talk that the rapture has started or has happened. Who really knows how this will happen? I just know that if it has, I'm still here."

"It's not just you, Melissa. There are people all over the world wondering why they are still here. It's all over TV. Most believe it hasn't started, but Chuck the Hutz says it has."

"Who?" she asked.

"Never mind; a story for another time."

"I don't watch TV, Jeffrey. I have thought about why I would not have been raptured if it has started. I know there is a reason, if it's true. I've had some memories I can't explain."

She paused a few seconds, trying to absorb the conversation and the thoughts in her head.

"Maybe it's an ongoing process," he piped in.

"Maybe. That would be different than I have learned though. I do have a theory though, in case it has started, or happened."

"What theory?" Jeff asked.

"I don't remember my life, Jeffrey. You say I was a great person, a wonderful mom, in Church helping others all the time. I don't remember any of that, and really, any of my past. Maybe there were sins I didn't know about?'

"What sins?" he asked. "You didn't do sins! You were as pure as snow. I'm the sinner, if there is such a thing as sin."

"What? You don't believe in sin either? Oh Jeffrey, I need to help you." She squeezed his hands, more friendly-gesture than any kind of attraction.

"I don't know, Jeffrey. I know God has a plan. I do remember the prophecies and the predictions that all came true. They prove that God is reality, Jeffrey, at least for anyone who wants to open his mind and recognize it.

"I have been living under the care of a group of people here, the people who rescued me from the sea."

"So I heard. They call you the Lady of the Sea. The voodoo people."

"Yes, the voodoo people. They are so confused, but they too are loving people, at least most. I have helped them so much the last years, not sure how long it's been. The witch doctor himself is beginning to come around. I am helping these people hear the truth about the God of Abraham and his Son. Until I showed up, they killed missionaries with their spells or zombie powder."

"Zombie powder?" Jeff asked with a look of amusement. His eyes explored every inch of Melissa's face.

"Zombie powder," she repeated. "It's a powder that, should one inhale it, makes them appear dead. The victim's pulse and breathing can't be detected. They blow this in their enemy's face. Twenty-four hours later, the person is buried, only to wake up a few hours later."

"I guess there's not much chance you'll fly back to Atlanta with me." Jeff said, dejectedly.

"No, Jeffrey, not this time. I can't. God pulled me from the sea, and he used the voodoo people to do it. I think it was for a reason. There isn't much time left for the world as we know it, or have known it. That I do know."

Melissa stood as Rosalie walked back to the booth with the round table. She turned to Jeff, wrapped her arms around him and squeezed. Her smell, the memories, almost knocked him off his feet.

"Let's meet again, maybe in a few months. God will lead me I am sure. If he has a plan for us in the future, it will happen. I am safe right now. They think I'm supernatural or something. Rosalie knows how to get in touch with you.

"Jeffrey, I don't know the future. Please get on with your life. Marry Samarra if you feel it's right. I'm sorry I don't remember her, but she must have been a good friend. She sounds like she's been through hell and back."

They walked together out to the parking lot, and Jeff opened the car door.

"Thanks, Melissa. Thanks for meeting me." He leaned down to hug her once again and then turned to leave. He did not look back.

Rosalie started the small car and turned west on Kingston Highway. She had a million questions and could not hold back.

"Oh Miss Melissa, mistuh Jeffy so handsome. He veddy nice man. What you think?"

Melissa thought about the meeting. Her heart ached for Jeffrey and knew his difficulty was worse than hers.

"I don't know, Rosalie. Let me close my eyes and think a few minutes."

"You think, Miss Melissa; I drive, zoom zoom. You no worry."

The small car sped down the highway, as a meteor flashed through the darkening sky high above.

The Lady of the Sea laid her head back on the small headrest and closed her eyes. Soon she was in the land of dreams, but the dreams were different. Dreams of another place and another time, children playing, the smell of a man's skin she once knew and a saying she had heard so many times at some point in her life.

For Pete's sake.

Chapter Twenty-Three

"Now let's go to Dalton, Georgia. A local veterinarian, Dr. Ralph Chafin, was accosted last night at his clinic by a man who had been shot in the... I can't say that!" The young man glared at the programmer, then laughed. *"Let me rephrase.*

Taci had no interest in Dalton news as the north Florida sky became darker and darker. Her VW Beetle churned along with no weather worries; but hers grew, as did the traffic.

"The doctor was accosted by a man who had been shot in the gluteus-maximus. This matches a report out of Atlanta claiming that Samarra Russell shot an intruder in the... gluteus maximus. You remember Samarra Russell. She was the CDC doctor who stole the Spanish Flu virus after terrorists threatened to cut her little boy's head off. Millions have died as a result, and she continues to live in luxury. Go figure."

Taci changed the station back to the weather. Concerned, she thought these were the darkest clouds she had ever seen. A strong gust hit her VW like a ton of bricks as she traveled north toward the Alligator Alley exit three miles ahead. Maybe she would take the AA Highway and head west to safer ground.

"... the South Georgia Coast. Tropical storm gusts, if you can believe this, reach all the way to Texas. If you are in Florida, evacuate now. Do not take I-95 North. Take I-10 West toward Alabama. This storm is just below the strength of what meteorologists are calling a hyper-cane.

"Hurricane Abigail's forward speed has slowed with her eye aimed directly down the eastern Florida Coast. Folks, this thing's going to hit the coast like a buzz saw; and with wind gusts of two-hundred, two-fifty miles per hour, nothing much is expected to remain standing, even some high rises. Storm surges will be unprecedented. Wilmington, North Carolina had a twenty foot storm surge with seven hundred thirty drownings reported so far. Now listen to this story."

Taci took the Alligator Alley exit toward the Gulf Coast. There she could ride out the storm in Naples or if possible, continue north toward Atlanta. The small car was blown from lane to lane, and she was thankful no one was headed east. Still, it had not started to rain. Traffic was manageable; but had she seen the blue Miata a few cars back get blown into the Everglades, she would have surely been frightened.

The luxury submarine could no longer feel the super-hurricane above as the ship settled near the sea floor, somewhere between Bermuda and Charleston. The good captain should have followed the orders of his Japanese clients, but he didn't and was now dead and buried at sea. Though the submarine-yacht had no torpedo tubes, there was a pressurized discharge system. The captain had been discharged.

The two-man submersible on the lower deck was prepped and ready. The water-proof compartment was pressurized to a slightly greater depth than they actually were, and the submersible chamber slowly opened beneath. The greater pressure worked like a charm, keeping the sea from rushing in.

The two Japanese pilots guided the submersible with ease. The dark blue, bubble-like craft moved slowly beneath the submarine, nearly invisible; and the surrounding glass dome was completely see-through. This craft wasn't built for speed, it was built to take high pressure and could go three times deeper than the submarine a few feet above.

The Seattle 1000 submarine was a beauty; but at the depths they were going today, she would fold up like an empty beer can at a Saturday night fraternity party. They were only thirty feet above the sea floor, but that didn't really matter. At two-hundred fifty feet down, everything was deep blue along the Bermuda Rise. They explored and listened. Finally, a *ping*.

The GPS low-frequency detector had the signal locked-in and secured. Fifteen minutes later the submersible hovered over one of the many ledges along the line of ancient, undersea volcanos. The two small, sand-camouflaged boxes were six-hundred twelve feet below.

They began a slow descent. The water was coal-black outside the Plexiglas hybrid enclosure. Occasionally the darkness of the surrounding sea would be interrupted with pinpoints of light, like distant stars in the night sky. Tiny bioluminescent organisms floated easily in the depths, some blinking on and off like a beacon, a sex attractant.

Another twenty minutes passed before the GPS locator signaled they were above the *package*, now highlighted by the sub's powerful LED searchlights. This had been too easy, the men thought but didn't discuss.

The small submersible's robot arm had the ability of lifting up to one thousand pounds. However, the submersible could not surface with that much payload. It was limited to about three-hundred pounds plus crew of two, and additional weight meant a slower ascent back to the sub.

The mechanical arm scooped up the two small containers with ease and placed them in the storage compartment. Each was the size of a child's shoebox but weighed in at a whopping one hundred twenty pounds. The submersible began its slow ascent and was back to the sub in twenty-five minutes. Safely and secretly stored aboard the luxury submarine, the crew high-fived and began their underwater journey southeastward toward Hilton Head.

The two lead-lined containers confined most of the radiation emitted from the three-inch perfectly round plutonium ball and the two smaller cores. Any portable radiation detector would have to be within three feet to detect a potential leak, and that wouldn't happen at the resort island.

The *Select* members cheered their great success with a champagne toast. The submarine, beautiful but slow would be at Hilton Head Island in less than three days. They would pull into harbor, followed by curiosity-seekers, as always; and the small crew would wave to the crowds enthusiastically as reggae music blared from the sound system, just a group of friends trying out their new submarine.

"Looks like Vinny will have his bombs."

Oh my God.. oh my God.. oh my God!" Taci cried out and covered her mouth. She fainted and collapsed, the carpet cushioning her fall.

The man with the dark hair, the one she had noticed and thought quite attractive, quickly slid behind her and slowed her fall. He had seen the same thing and felt light-headed too, but he maintained his composure. Two others brought cool-compresses. It had started with a simple weather report, the kind one sees every time there's a hurricane.

It was late afternoon when Taci made reservations as she crossed south Florida on Alligator Alley. The Marriott in Naples only had one room left, and she took it.

Immediately after checking in, she returned to the lobby to pick up a newspaper. The skies were darkening, but then it *was* late afternoon; so she didn't know if it was the storm or the approaching night. The winds gusted, and the Marriott's flag stood horizontal in the strong wind from the north. The large glass windows in the TV lounge seemed to bow in and out with each heavy gust.

Taci entered the carpeted lounge, pink sandals slapping the bottom of her feet; and the men talking outside the conference room stopped to watch. Even after a day of driving, she was something else. She was also surprised by the crowded hotel; it seemed no one was evacuating. The traffic on the streets of Naples was like any other day. No one seemed worried.

The soft cushion beneath her feet felt good after all the time in the cramped VW. She tried not to stare at the tall slender man with the dark hair, blue golf shirt, no wedding band and Victoria's Secret shopping bag in his hand. She hardly noticed.

Taci searched for a newspaper but found none. That's when the TV meteorologist went to the hurricane-hunter, *live* in Jacksonville, Florida. The picture became *live* alright; wind, rain, hail and continuous flashes of lightning in the background. The rain and golf ball sized hail blew almost parallel with the ground.

The young hurricane-hunter-turned-weather man reported from outside, his rain parka nearly blowing off, his hair pointing southward in a wedge and large palm fronds flying down the oceanfront street behind him. He held firmly onto a metal pole in front of the *Tiki Tiki Lounge* where a hurricane party was going strong. The ocean in the background was a world of white, foamy froth; and sand rapidly infiltrated the inland streets, alleyways and any nook-and-cranny the gritty particles could hide. Water lapped at the reporter's feet.

A few minutes earlier, the weatherman had been interviewing partiers inside, most saying the same.

"Why should we evacuate, dude? We evacuated the last two hurricanes; and they didn't even hit, man. We gonna drink tequila and party-hardy, right?"

The twenty-something man held his shot glass up, and the crowd roared. The latest hip-hop/reggae blend blared from the Bose sound system, life was grand. Evacuation fatigue had set in among the population.

But *that was then, and this was now*, the reporter thought, frightened for the first time in his brief stint as a weatherman; and the sounds of the wind were deafening. Sand blasted the No Parking sign, now barely standing; and the letters were nearly sanded away.

The large section of sheet metal came out of nowhere, flying horizontal to the street about four feet above the pavement, making a *whipping* sound. All edges were sharp, and the ocean frothed in the background as the reporter wrapped both arms around the No Parking sign, trying to maintain for television. The ratings would be great.

"Folks, I'm going in," the reporter finally yelled into the wind-filtered microphone, his all-weather parka in shreds. "I've been in hurricanes before, but nothing like…"

The pause got Taci's attention, and she looked up at the flatscreen. In the blink of an eye, the sheet metal slammed into the reporter about waist-high; but it happened so fast, Taci wasn't really sure she saw what she thought she saw. Then she was sure, as she screamed and started yelling, "Oh my God," and fainted.

Taci's handsome rescuer-to-be had known it was just a matter of time before tragedy struck. He was an avid weather fan and often mused at the idiocy of weather reporters standing in hundred-plus mile per hour winds. Anything to get ratings he guessed; but the inevitable was bound to happen, and it had. Darrell swooped down and caught the young lady just before she hit the floor, protecting her head-with-sun-visor in the crook of his arm.

The sheet metal went through the weatherman like a hot knife going through soft butter. It was so fast, the weatherman kept yelling into the microphone for a second, until he knew something was gravely wrong. Before his knees could collapse to the pavement, the top half of his body flew down the street, gone in an instant in the 140 mile per hour gust. The club full of kids followed.

Chapter Twenty-Four

Mother's Day
<u>A Day of Tribulation</u>

"Certainly is a lovely mawnin', Miss Elma."

The pastor's handkerchief was soaked, and the Kansas humidity was high as an elephant's eye. He wished for a breeze and said a silent prayer.

"Yessiree, Pastor John, it tis, it tis."

"I see you have the granchillin' wid ya."

The Sunday morning air was still and stifling, even for Mountainview; and not a breeze stirred. Except for the bright yellow daffodils in the surrounding fields, most of the church's landscape was dirt-brown from drought and heat.

Elma turned and smiled at her eight grandchildren frolicking on the church lawn like young puppies on a spring day. The three boys were dressed in their navy blue shorts, white shirt and tie; and the girls in yellow, white and light blue dresses. There were no shirttails tucked in properly now, when only a few moments earlier the boys had been dressed perfectly; and their shoes were no longer shiny. The young girls were immaculate, as always.

"I sure do Pastor John. They always come visit on Mother's Day, yes they do."

Rural was rural; and at 68 years old, Elma reckoned rural Kansas wasn't much different from rural Georgia or rural Wyoming. People were good, honest and churchgoing.

The church service would be crowded she reckoned, the gravel parking lot was already full. One small red station wagon had even parked in the circular driveway at the entrance by the No Parking sign. Lordy mercy, it was gonna be a hot one.

Ten minutes later everyone was seated in the white-oak pews with Bible and songbook holder, about three hundred and fifteen or so, at least by Pastor John's estimate, standing room only in the small white church.

Looking out one of the open windows, Elma thought the fields looked like they were flowing with butter and was mesmerized by God's beauty.

Daffodils bloomed freely in the large fields behind the church, ignoring the season and drought. The white-wood siding of Mountainview Church of the Nazarene glowed in the yellow reflection of the surrounding jonquils, at least that's what her mother had called daffodils.

The church choir began to sing the first stanza of *Fairest Lord Jesus*. New mothers with their infant children sat in the front two rows with their husbands.

All the mothers in Mountainview had husbands, except Miss Johnson whose husband was killed last year by a hit-and-run driver in a white Chevrolet, maybe an Impala; they never did find the car. Mountainview was just that kind of place, God's Country.

A blue Dodge van, radio blaring with the latest rap, passed by the front of the church as the choir began the second stanza.

Fair are the meadows, fairer still the woodlands,
robed in the blooming garb of spring:
Jesus is fairer, Jesus is purer
who makes the woeful heart to sing.

The bearded man riding shotgun in the van entered a number in his new cell phone, recently purchased at the convenience mart. The choir sang exuberantly as they started the third stanza.

Fair is the sunshine, fairer still the moonlight,
and all the twinkling starry host:
Jesus shines brighter, Jesus shines purer
than all the angels heaven can boast.

With the phone number entered, the bearded man waited until the van was a quarter-mile away from the yellowish-white church and then keyed the green arrow.

As the choir began the last stanza, a cell phone in the red station wagon by the No Parking sign at the church's front entrance rang once.

Elma had noticed the red car earlier but didn't pay much attention. People were always parking by the No Parking sign. She had noted the darker-than-normal tinted windows, but nothing else indicated the station wagon was equipped, not with just a Bose twelve-speaker sound system but also, a 250 pound diesel-fertilizer bomb.

This was the last car that Elma would ever recognize as the station wagon exploded in what she would've thought was Hell had she not been deceased from blast and shrapnel injuries. The yellow-white church was no more, and the wooden siding was now strewn across what had been just a minute earlier, pristine fields of yellow flowers, the prettiest flowers Elma had ever seen.

The church steeple, though not large, had been stately; but now it was suspended in an oak tree at the side of the property, burning violently. The tree fire spread to the next tree and soon Mountainview, population 2,000, was ablaze.

In the distance the blue van disappeared over the horizon. They had another mission to complete, the day was young. The bearded man felt no remorse about the women and children. To him a Christian woman was just a terrorist propagating machine; and the children would grow up to hate Islam. They were being programmed. Islam would soon rule America. Islam would soon rule the world. *Allahu Akbar*.

A small chain hung from beneath the van, and occasional sparks could be seen by a lone farmer in a field of yellow daffodils as the van crested the hill.

New Orleans

Sally Greenfield slapped at another mosquito and held her daughter's hand firmly as she filled her minivan with gas. She kept a close watch on her five-year old because of all the gang activity. Stores were closed down, and the homeless were everywhere. Her eyes searched the surroundings, on the lookout for anything odd. At $9.00 a gallon, it would cost the single mother about a hundred fifty bucks, more than she could afford.

"These *New Ahleans* mosquitos sure are big this year, Mimi."

"Sure are, sweetie. Did you spray?"

The Louisiana mosquitos were known to be big, but this year it seemed that the small ones were the biters. Dengue fever was now common place, and the young mother of one massaged her aching elbow as the minivan drank and drank from the Citgo-Valero pump.

"I always spray, Mimi. You told me to, so I always do what you say."

Mimi knew that wasn't true; but all-in-all, her little blue-eyed and blond-haired daughter was almost perfect! Apparently she was also modeling material. Sally planned to pursue that course since being contacted by some modeling agencies. She had no idea when she posted the YouTube video of her daughter playing Chopsticks on the keyboard and singing to Kermit the Frog that it would've ever gone viral; but it had.

She topped off the tank and would meet the agency to sign the contract at 2:00. She couldn't wait. Soon her old minivan would go the way of the Dodo bird; and she would buy an SUV, something safer. It was going to be a great Mother's Day. Spring was in the air.

Six hundred feet away, the small-statured man was virtually invisible as he lay prone in a vacant field of weedy dandelions and wild daisies.

The sniper rifle was equipped with a silencer, thanks to Vinny. Today would be a day of havoc. The Bosnian man wasn't keen on killing people for his beloved religion; but what must be done, must be done. It was for God. He braced and took aim at the back of the faded-blue minivan.

The Bosnian would lots rather be killing Jews instead of common folk. Vinny was the boss though, and the slogan was *Create Havoc and Fear*. That worked for him. Maybe he would escape, maybe not. He would gladly give his life for Allah. His finger closed on the trigger. Would he kill the woman and the kid with a single shot, or would he blow up the van and let them burn to death?

Sally secured the nozzle to the red cradle on the Citgo pump and screwed the silver gas cap on. She moved to the front of the minivan and secured her daughter in the front seat, closed the door and walked around the front and to the driver's side door.

A black Lexus pulled up on the other side of the pump, and three young boys, maybe late teens, climbed out. *This is getting better* the sniper thought. He decided on an explosion. He loved explosions.

The man gently squeezed the trigger, and the sound-suppression system hid the sound of the rifle relatively well, considering the caliber. The bullet traveled toward the target, the minivan gas tank, at 2,500 feet per second. In less than half a second the Bosnian fired the second round at the pavement beneath the minivan. The second round ignited the now leaking gas tank, and the blast wave swept over the sniper's head.

Sally and her model-worthy young daughter never knew what hit them and didn't even have time to disengage the seat belts. The young boys standing at the rear of the Lexus thought they heard a car backfire; but before they could look toward the field of weeds, all three were running through the parking lot, on fire.

I didn't want to be cremated was Sally Greenfield's last thought.

<u>Atlanta</u>

Jacob Peyton, an honors grad student at Georgia Tech finished his term paper. Proofing the paper one last time, he decided it was as good as it gets. Organic chemistry just wasn't that interesting to many, but he loved it. His new theory about increasing explosive yield in chemical reactions was leading edge.

The paper, *More Bang for the Buck* would be published in the next edition of *Military Technology* magazine. The newly discovered reaction, caused by a simple chemical catalyst, made the explosive strength of C4, ammonium nitrate and other high explosives significantly greater. An ounce of C4 could be transformed in a matter of seconds into the equivalent of ten pounds, enough to blow up a building if small charges were placed near support structures. An ounce of explosives to drop a five-story building to the ground in an instant, and the average drone could carry well over an ounce. This would revolutionize war.

However, Jacob wasn't in it for the fame and fortune. He was a strong Christian man, especially to be so young and brilliant; and his duty was to God, not recognition.

Jacob grabbed his backpack and secured it tightly. The thirty-pound backpack, adorned with the Georgia Tech Yellow Jacket logo would be heavy after a while. Jacob was tall with floppy-blond hair but of small frame, and his skinniness had always caused problems with the community bullies. They would get theirs, he knew that for a fact.

The grad student made sure his pistol was loaded with one in the chamber. It had gotten to be a jungle out there, and street crime was rampant. With the ongoing budget cuts, Atlanta just didn't have the money to provide police patrols like they once did.

Walking to the MARTA train station, the Sunday weather was cloudy with an annoying, umbrella-proof drizzle. The day was cool for a change; and the Mother's Day celebrants crowded on the train, destined for the celebration at Centennial

Park. Jacob removed his backpack and grabbed a seat at the rear of the train module. He slid the backpack under the blue vinyl seat in front of him, unfolded the day's newspaper and pretended to read. He didn't feel like talking with anyone but nodded at the MARTA policeman walking down the center aisle, through the rear door and into the next module.

Two stops later the sleek, silver MARTA train slowed as it entered MARTA's busiest station, Five Points. MARTA was the nation's eighth largest rapid-transit system, and Five Points was where the East-West trains met with the North-South trains. The station was packed with Sunday revelers; and tropical colored dresses adorned the little girls, most clinging to Mom's hand, overwhelmed by the hustle-bustle and the noise.

Jacob got up as the train slowed and made his way to the door. The smelly man sitting next to him had snored through three stops but awoke as the train slowed. The pneumatic module doors opened with a whoosh, and Jacob started to exit.

"Hey man, you left your backpack." It wasn't a shout, but the smelly man did his part to help.

Jacob didn't hear smelly-man's half-hearted shout and moved into the large crowd. He headed toward the three story escalator and glanced back at the train. The train would remain in the station, because of the holiday, a full five minutes to accommodate the rush.

Exiting the top of the escalator, the young graduate student walked out to Peachtree Street, turned right and caught the first cab.

"Hartsfield-Jackson please," he said to the taxi driver.

"Hey man, you could take the MARTA train you know. You would get there faster," the cabby replied.

"Too many people, my man; too many people. Every stop would be ten minutes. Let's go."

Smelly-man started to reach for the backpack but was interrupted when a fat guy in beige corduroy shorts, at least three hundred and fifty pounds, sat down in the seat that Jacob had just relinquished. He would have to explore the goodies in the backpack later. The fat man's butt slowly oozed into Smelly-man's seat.

"Hey jerkhead, your ass is in my seat."

The fat man in cordurory shorts turned to the left and stared at the odorous, loud-mouthed passenger with the scruffy beard.

"Tough stuff, Mr. Smellgood. It is what it is."

Jacob Peyton, graduate student and scholar, took the phone from his blue jean's pocket and punched in the 10-digit phone number, waiting for the ring. The taxi made good time as it merged onto I-75 South. They would be at Hartsfield in fifteen-twenty minutes and should have no trouble catching his flight to Belize. No ring. Jacob tried again.

"What the hell's wrong with you, Jacob?"

Student Peyton remembered the words from his mother and his father. They thought his Christian beliefs were a little extremist, and maybe they were. His parents were well educated, college professors and atheists. They were beside themselves when their son told them he had joined a *Christian group.*

The Army of the Christian Soldier though was probably different than Jacob's parents' expectations. They weren't a turn-the-other-cheek type of organization and were well armed. The group spoke the truth, and the truth was never politically correct. The truth to Jacob was this: God does not like queers.

The Westborough Church had tried to tell people that for years, but they were ridiculed by the libs. Atlanta's gay and transgender populations had grown tremendously since recent court rulings and were definitely out of the closet; and from the number, Jason guessed the closet must have been really big.

The ruling last week lowered the age of consent for pedophilia from sixteen to twelve, and Jacob wished death to all the perverts. It would come soon.

The phone at the other end rang three times, and Jacob waited.

"Is that your phone ringing?" Fat-man asked Smelly-man and tried to lean over to pull the backpack from under the seat; but he was too fat to bend over far enough. The phone rang a second time.

"Yeah man, it's mine. Don't worry 'bout it. They'll call back." The train doors whooshed again, this time to close; and the train started to move slowly southward toward the airport. The phone rang a third time.

Jacob listened intently as the third ring transited the wireless network. At first he wasn't sure of the practicality of the relationship that had formed between The Army of the Christian Soldier and the Muslim extremist group, Jihad's Warriors. However, their goals were similar. Kill the perverts, overthrow the United States government and wait for Jesus' return in glory. The Muslim group thought Jesus' return would herald the return of Muhammad, who would show Jesus how to pray. Now that was funny.

"The enemy of my enemy is my friend."

Jacob had only met the man once… was his name Vinny? Yeah. Vinny appeared to be the top dog in the jihadist group, and this was one of his sayings.

"Suppose you have two enemies, but one you especially hate. It turns out that your other enemy also hates the enemy that you especially hate," Vinny had explained in the brief meeting. "Form a kinship with the lesser enemy, because in reality he is your friend. He will help you kill your bigger enemy.

"Muslims and Christians have a common enemy, Satan and the Jew. Satan is the West, the United States and Europe. For the good of the cause, remember this Arab saying."

The fat man used his foot to lure the backpack from beneath the MARTA train seat as the phone rang for the third time. His tennis shoe nudged the backpack, and then his foot disappeared.

Jacob's explosive concoction had now been lab tested in a *real* environment and worked like a charm. The twelve pounds of modified C4 exploded on the fourth ring, and the Five Points MARTA station was pretty much destroyed in a flash, at least the common areas. All trains in the station at the time were destroyed and now burned, black smoke pouring onto the streets above.

The heat wave melted much of the MARTA train module; and the blast created a shock wave that burst up the escalators. A cloud of debris, dust and fire blasted out the multiple entrances and into the middle of Peachtree Street, Forsyth Street and Alabama. The streets were crowded with Mother's Day partiers, or at least they had been. Many now lay in the street, some screaming, some dead.

The Catholic priest and two nuns were exiting onto Peachtree when the blast paid a visit. The three, along with several others, were lifted off their feet, thrown across the six-lane street and embedded into the large glass windows that had a few minutes encased *The Sportslife Rock Café*. The priest was decapitated in the explosion; and while his body seemed intact from the street angle, the old priest's head and upper torso were nowhere to be found.

"Be bold," Vinny had told the Christian group. "This war isn't for the weak. Killing the women and children will bring America to her knees, and the same thing will be happening in Paris, London and Rome. Think about it," he continued. "How much more can the West spend? They're out of money.

"The women, they are only whores of Satan. They produce babies; the babies become teenagers; the teenagers become Crusaders who kill Muslims. Why do you think Allah told the Israelites to kill all the Canaanites? I will answer. Because the Canaanite children would grow up to kill the Israelites, and the women would just have more children. It's simple."

"When will America and the West fall?" Jacob asked Vinny in their one and only meeting.

Jacob in no way hated Jews. Quite the opposite. Maybe Vinny didn't know that Jesus was a Jew. *The enemy of my enemy is my friend*, and the anything-goes U.S. government was definitely God's enemy.

"Soon, my friend, soon. The world will get an ultimatum to either convert to Islam or die, Insha'Allah. The Christians and Jews are People of the Book. Their lives will be spared, and they will be free to worship in the New World."

"How many jihadists are here?" Jacob asked, then thought he probably shouldn't have. He was surprised that Vinny answered.

"Thirty, maybe thirty-five thousand. Many hold vital positions in the U.S. infrastructure, power generation, water purification, food distribution and the government itself. If the people in Washington and Warner Robins knew who they discussed plans with every day, they would have a duck."

"Cow."

"Pardon?" Vinny asked.

"Cow. They would have a cow, not a duck." Jacob explained and winked at Vinny. Vinny thought he might like Jacob, except he would probably have to kill him when all was done and said.

"Wonder what the heck happened back there?" the taxi driver asked, staring hard in the rearview mirror.

Dark, nearly black smoke was pouring from the MARTA station he had just left a few minutes before, though he didn't know that. To him it was just another big fire in downtown Atlanta. News helicopters were seen rushing to the scene.

Cushing, Oklahoma

"Ready, amigos?" Dejan asked.

"Ready!"

The six men answered in unison, but none were *amigos*. They were all from Mecca, the *city of seven hills* in the middle of the Saudi Arabian Desert, except for Dejan, who was from Bosnia. They did speak perfect Spanish. Though dressed as construction workers, the men were destruction workers instead.

"You know the plan. Just after sunset you open the can."

"Insha'Allah," again in unison, a whisper.

The waitress brought more coffee to the table. She was fluent in Spanish and wondered what kind of *can* the men were talking about when she was sure she heard something… something about Allah. She'd heard it before.

Nellie was young, maybe nineteen with bright red pigtails and a face full of freckles. This was her second week on the job. She liked waitressing, because she had great ears. She would hear some of the most interesting gossip in the small rural restaurant. She could even hear people whisper. By the time she was five, her parents had figured out that she could hear the wind blowing from far away, long before the wind would reach them. It was eerie.

Nellie carried the coffee pot to the kitchen after filling the only other customer's cup and walked into the manager's office. Her friend Gina manned the front door in case anyone showed up, but restaurants in the dying economy were a dying industry. They only *wished* a paying customer would come in.

The men continued in whispers as they totaled the checks. The failure of the Easter plot to materialize had been disappointing to the warriors, but today's campaign had been orchestrated well in advance of the narcissistic Mother's Day, another pagan holiday celebrated in the Land of the Infidel. The snipers were eager, and they were good. Very good.

"I think the seven guys at the front might be up to no good," Nellie told the manager. "Every time I hear 'Allah' now, I get really nervous. They said it. Also, they were talking in Spanish before that."

Nellie's manager, a distinguished-looking woman with wire-rimmed glasses, was young herself at only thirty-two. She listened intently. She knew of Nellie's trauma when the plane had crashed in East Point last year. No one may have ever known what happened had the investigators not found the little girl's camera. She filmed the whole thing, two small bright lights far beneath the plane that were racing her way as she filmed.

"Look at the Roman candles, Mama." That's what was on the recording. It was a sad memory. The little girl had only been eight.

The plane never made it to the Hartsfield-Jackson runway that night in Atlanta, and Nellie's parents and brother were killed in the crash.

"Let's go check it out. Want me to call 911?"

"Nah, it's probably nothing. You know how paranoid I am."

"I know how right you are about a lot of things, Nellie. That's why I'm calling Charlie at the sheriff's office."

With the call finished and Charlie on his way, the two women noticed that the men were totaling their checks to leave.

"You go out the back, Nell. I'll take care of their checks, see if I can detect anything odd." She laughed. "Isn't this fun? I always wanted to be Matlock. Make sure you get the license numbers, but stay out of sight." She couldn't wait to get home and tell her hubby *this* story.

The time was six-thirty, and the sun was gaining speed toward the hot pink western horizon of Cushing, a small town of less than ten thousand, just a hundred miles south of the Oklahoma-Kansas border.

"Did you men enjoy your meals?"

The bespectacled manager remained cool and calm as Nellie made her way to the persimmon tree at the edge of the parking area, hardly what one would call a parking *lot*.

"Si. Esta delicioso."

The smaller man, stocky with a pock-marked face said he loved the food, only they didn't have food, they had coffee.

"Well thank you kind sir. You boys from around here?"

The silence was deafening as the men, maybe migrant workers, maybe not, looked at the friendly lady, not really knowing what to say. Most cashiers took the money and avoided talking to "furiners," at least from what Dejan had experienced.

Dejan was the leader of the small group, a Muslim-jihadist from the Bosnia-Serbia area in Eastern Europe. Ever since

American president Bill Clinton bombed his small village back in the nineties, Dejan had vowed revenge. The sight of his parents and two sisters, only parts of their bodies remaining contiguous, still haunted his young mind. He had only been six at the time, and the smart-bombs ended life as he then knew it.

"I guess not. Alrighty then." The manager restrained herself, though she had questions.

She gave the men change. In the process, she squeezed one of the coins hard and gave it to the short guy; she just had a feeling. It wasn't really a coin; it just looked like one. It was one of Nellie's numerous tracking devices that her Uncle Will insisted she keep with her at all times. The manager developed a nervous twitch over her left eye, and the spasm didn't go unnoticed by Dejan. He glanced at the lone customer sitting in the booth and wondered where the waitress was.

"Where's the waitress?" Dejan said in perfect English.

The manager was caught off-guard and remained speechless for a few seconds. The pause also didn't go unnoticed by Dejan or the other men. Something was up.

"She got sick; went home."

The manager spoke in staccato-English, short sentences, a sign of anxiety. Just a moment before, she was Miss Talkative. Her eyebrow twitched three times as the manager faked a smile. That's when she found out the short, stocky man wasn't really overweight at all and wondered why in the world these heavily armed men would be in Cushing.

Cushing, Oklahoma was a small, quaint town and had been founded in 1891 by a man named "Billy Rae" Little. The oil boom began in 1912, and before long Cushing was an oil refining center.

Once the Keystone Pipeline had been completed, Cushing became one of the few rural areas in the United States to have a boom instead of economic bust. The pipeline shipped five-hundred thousand gallons of potential fuel each day and had helped make the country more energy independent.

The oil from Canada, as many Americans suspected, turned out to be a great asset. More jobs and cheaper oil, only the gas wasn't cheaper. It had only gone up, though around Cushing gas was less than most places. The Cushing Tank Farm had become the world's largest oil storage facility.

Nellie waited at the edge of the parking lot, well-concealed, for something to happen; but the men hadn't come out. *What's taking them so long?*

She walked cautiously across the gravel lot to get a better view of the entrance. She used her cell phone to photograph the license plates of the seven pickup trucks and the single car parked in the lot. Employees parked in the back. She recalled a conversation with her uncle.

"Nellie, remember this if you're ever tracking someone."

Uncle Will was advising her, like he always did; and he would load her up with paranoid cautions, at least that's what she called them.

"Be careful on gravel. You think it's quiet, but the sound of gravel-contact travels farther than you would think."

Nellie looked down at the ground, placing her feet carefully around the small rocks. She thought she heard something at the rear of the restaurant and looked, but there was nothing.

Inside the group of seven men picked up their change, but they continued to stare at the cashier-manager. One of the seven walked calmly over to the lone customer reading the paper, an older gentleman with a Keystone Pipeline uniform.

"How you doing, man?"

The Keystone employee glanced up from the *Cushing Gazette*. That's when the one-of-seven slammed the dagger into the old man's throat, a perfect and instantaneous kill. The manager couldn't believe what she just saw, and the twitch went into hypermode across her lower forehead.

The short, stocky man opened his jacket, and the manager realized the stockiness was really the work of the two compact automatic weapons secreted beneath the light-weight coat. Her mouth dropped open, her eyes wide in fear. The patron slumped over the table and only made a few gurgling sounds. Nellie remained outside, oblivious to the goings-on inside.

"And remember this, Nellie," her uncle instructed, "when you're tracking somebody, every shiny surface is a mirror. The paint job on a shiny car is a mirror, a car's side-view mirror is a mirror for your use, a store's plate glass windows. Almost every surface can be a mirror. Keep an eye out for reflections, they're everywhere. It'll save your life."

She paid attention to Uncle Will's advice, *Wild Willy* to his friends; and she guessed he was pretty wild at times, at least from some of the stories she had heard over the years. He spent a lot of time in Israel, and she often wondered why. She didn't think it likely that she would ever be "tracking someone," but here she was tracking seven.

Nellie saw a reflection, a single man coming out the front door. It wasn't the old guy who had been reading the paper; and she began to worry, even more than she was already worried.

"Don't be afraid, my dear," Dejan spoke calmly to the manager. "You are safe."

"What do you want?" The manager began to cry. "Please don't kill me. I have a husband and a baby; please, please."

She begged.

"I'm not going to kill you, *ma'am*. Just do what I say, and I won't hurt you, I promise."

The men ushered Gina the receptionist and the manager into the kitchen. Dejan hadn't paid much attention to the manager until then, but he thought she looked pretty *fine*. They would rape her and the young receptionist, all of them. He smiled in anticipation. They had done it before.

Outside the front entrance Nellie waited, hidden behind the worn, gray dumpster privacy fence. She monitored the reflection of the man, *was that a gun?* Her heartbeat suddenly raced. *What was taking them so long?*

In the distance she was sure she heard a siren, maybe Charlie; but the sound faded in and out with the wind. Inside the small restaurant, five of the men did have their way with the two women while two kept guard at the front and back entrances. The women pleaded and cried, but they had no choice but comply. Then it was over.

"Throw them in the freezer." Dejan said.

Dejan lived up to his Serbian namesake *to take action*, and he always did. He never hesitated.

The two women continued to cry and plead; but Dejan only thought about the sex. It hadn't been that great, too rushed. He didn't care, the women were whores; and he felt a small twinge of guilt. He knew that Allah had spoken against whores, and he would probably suffer the consequences of his actions sometime down the road. He would worry about it then.

"Kill them," Dejan commanded.

"No, no… please." The manager pleaded for her life. "You said you wouldn't kill me.

"I'm not," Dejan said in a near whisper. "He is."

Less than thirty seconds later, the men climbed into their seven made-in-the-USA pickups. The sniper rifles, scopes and wind-speed indicators were all securely stored in a hidden compartment between the exhaust pipes on the bottom of the trucks. The rear windows had Oklahoma University decals and a couple of redneck humor stickers, one showing a little boy wearing a Chevy shirt and peeing on a Ford. All seven had *Support your Local Police* decals on the back bumper.

Nellie waited until the men left, then ran into the restaurant. No one was there except the Gazette-reading man. He was slumped over the table, lying in a large pool of blood. He was silent, but the patter of the blood hitting the floor was deafening. The sound of the siren grew closer but suddenly stopped. She didn't know why.

Mother's Day had been a hot one in North Carolina, and Rabbi Akiva Rosen left his home in one of Raleigh's numerous gated communities about 6:00. Dusk was approaching; and the rabbi glanced up at the pink moon as he walked to his brand new Chevy Volt III, the newest Chevrolet hybrid. He still found himself in awe of the *sign in the sky*, a dark pink moon with rings like Saturn. He was well aware of the term.

At just twenty-six, Akiva was one of the younger rabbis in the Research Triangle area of North Carolina; and he loved the attention the community showered on his wife and their three-year-old triplets. *Three girls in one swoop, game over.* That's what he would tell his friends.

It was hard to believe he got to North Carolina the way he did, and he thought about that often. Who would've ever figured a barbeque pork sandwich would entice a young Jewish rabbi-to-be to come back to the state for a visit? But that's the way it was.

Kepley's Barbeque in High Point was as good as barbeque pork could get. He was only six at the time, but his parents stopped at Kepley's shortly after they became Reform Jews. That opened a whole new world of dietary law-breaking-with-no-consequences and twenty years later, here he was.

Grandpa Akiva would not be impressed, as the young rabbi was named after Akiva ben Joseph, a first century founder of Rabbinic Judaism. Akiva ben Joseph would've certainly turned down the pork sandwich.

"Bye, Aki!" He turned around, swatted another mosquito and waved to his wife standing with the three girls on the front stoop. He loved her greatly and thanked God every day for bringing her into his life. He waved again, swatted another bug and thought maybe mosquitos were becoming immune to the insecticide sprays the cities and counties were using.

Somewhere in the distance he heard thunder, but that had become normal in today's odd world. Thunder without lightning, giant pieces of hail dropping out of a clear sky and the shopping center last week in Dallas that disappeared in less than five minutes. Sinkhole.

Rabbi Aki opened the Volt's door, the three girls giggling up a storm. That was normal too, and a smile overcame his face. They would be joining him at tonight's Mother's Day service. Ahhh, life was grand.

Aki's wife thought the same of Aki. He was her very best friend and a wonderful father. He graduated from rabbinical school with honors and went on to study early first-century Christianity, when only Jews were Christians. He volunteered his time every second Saturday to visit the federal penitentiary in Butner where he taught Bible History 101. The prisoners loved him too. Plus, that olive skin, jet-black hair and those lips… She felt she was a lucky woman. She turned and headed the girls back inside the house.

That's when it happened.

Dejan waited; and the siren crept closer, changing in pitch according to Doppler's effect. He had instructed the other six to go to the targeted oil storage fields and get situated. He would take care of the cop. He didn't plan on letting the police make it to the scene of the crime, and he sneered the way evil people do.

Manipulating the scene, Dejan knew that the cop wouldn't stop for roadside assistance; because he had more important things to do. Opening his hood wouldn't work, so Dejan's plan evolved. He would do something desperate.

The siren, louder by the second, approached the curve where Dejan parked the made-in-America truck at an angle, as though he had run off the road. He grabbed six packets of large size fast-food ketchup, spread the ketchup on his face and on his bare arms, opened the truck door and lay on the pavement just in front of the truck as though he had been ejected. He looked like the victim of a terrible accident, he was sure. With his left hand contorted under his stomach, the pistol was tightly secured in his hand. The siren screamed in the not-so-distant approach.

Charlie drove his patrol car proudly and assertively, but also safely. The brand new, charcoal gray Dodge Charger was his pride and joy, so he didn't do anything foolish, nothing that would put a scratch or door-ding on the beauty. Rounding the curve at 50 miles per hour was easily doable, unless someone was lying in the road.

Charlie tried to slow the patrol car as best he could in the short time before he would hit the truck, and he did; but not slow enough. Dejan the Terrorist, with fake blood all over his face, now had real blood frothing from his mouth. He didn't have time to scream Allahu'Akbar before the car slammed into his truck with him between the two. He was now dead and would stop twitching as soon as his brain figured it out, muscle-laden neurons firing and misfiring.

Charlie pulled the man from beneath his patrol car and noticed the revolver still tucked in the killer's hand, though Charlie didn't know the man was a killer at the time. A business card from the restaurant a mile away lay beside him.

An hour later, Charlie and Nellie had discovered the bodies; and Charlie mused about the sniper rifle and accessories he found stashed in the secret compartment below the dead man's truck. It was now dark, except for the constant showers of microscopic meteors lighting up the sky.

The six other men didn't know of their leader's sudden demise. They all had a different location targeted, and the large oil storage tanks dotted the landscape.

The plan was simple and would be carried out all over Europe and the United States. The sniper men would fire a single high-powered round into the targeted storage tanks, about twelve to fifteen feet above the ground and wait exactly five minutes until 9:05 Central Mountain Time. It was doubtful that any workers would hear the distant shots, because each sniper rifle was silencer equipped.

After glancing at the sky, multiple meteors streaming horizontally high above, the men from Mecca took aim and prepared to fire. The shots were well aimed and penetrated the double-hulled fuel containers with no problem. A stream of flammable liquid poured from each penetration and splattered on the gravel-covered ground below, pooling around each storage tank.

Five minutes later the marksmen fired a specialized phosphor-round at the base of the previously punctured storage tanks, igniting large fires before the workers knew what was happening. As the industrial workers scrambled for the fire equipment, the six warriors packed their gear and escaped into the darkness. Each would gladly be a martyr for their cause but would rather not.

Rabbi Aki pushed the start button, but the Chevy Volt didn't start. That was odd. It always started, it was electric. He pressed the button again.

The explosion was loud, but Aki never heard it. The bomb had been secured beneath the Volt in the dead of night and was really too large for the small car. The gated community had been easy to beat, and Latif's threats to his Muslim brother's had paid off: *Get me the names of every rabbi in your community.*

Rabbi Aki was well aware that each major city in the United States had an Islamic community; and while they were considered moderate, most really weren't moderate as much as they were fearful of not obeying the fanatics. Most Muslims, at least in the West, just wanted to get along. They neither hated Jews nor wanted to destroy Israel. Like every religion, the rabbi knew, they thought they were right; and everyone else was wrong. Just like Jews, Christians and Hindus. He also knew they couldn't *all* be right.

Being a "moderate Muslim" had not been so easy since Osama bin Laden did his evil. With U.S. borders weaker than ever, especially the southern, the jihadists had invaded like a locust plague in Egypt. They sought out the *moderates,* as they were called and threatened them with the death of their children, wives or parents in Pakistan. Their reach was long, violent and permanent. One video of a family member having a hand or arm amputated, sans anesthesia, usually worked.

Upon hearing the large explosion, Rabbi Aki's wife ran out the front door of her home in the not-so-secure gated community but was overcome by the heat. Her house was now in flames, as was the house on the other side of the driveway and the house across the street. The gates of the gated community were blown across Hilandale Lane and were now suspended in the top of a large dogwood tree, guarding a nest of parenting robins.

Chapter Twenty-Five

Three Months Later
Duluth, Georgia

"Here you are my man, a chilled Duckhorn on a really hot, late summer afternoon."

Abe set the glass of merlot on the bar and pondered the weather. He never remembered it being a hundred and twelve degrees at four in the afternoon. He didn't remember it ever being that hot in Duluth, *ever*. Atlanta's streets were melting.

"When's your next trip to Jamaica?"

The Divide Disco & Café was nearly empty, considering Happy Hour was just ten minutes away. Jeff sat alone at the bar, alternating his thoughts from Melissa to Samarra and back to Melissa. What a dilemma this had been. Two couples were being served on the upper level.

Abe the Bartender wiped down the counter and prepared the ice for the afternoon crowd, though the crowds had dwindled. He had been Abe the Manager for a while when Scott took over the head-bartender position; but now that Scott was hot-to-trot for Kara the Haiti missionary, Scott was on extended leave to help distribute light bulbs, shoes, toilet paper and dry food items to the starving masses. Abe remembered Scott's stories about the huge Haitian rats, so bold they were prevalent even during the day. No thanks.

"Next weekend," Jeff replied and ran his index finger around the rim of the wine glass, a habit of late. His mood was upbeat, and he would be glad when Samarra arrived. The wedding was on again, this time for New Year's Eve.

"Labor Day? Taking the kids this time?"

The three girls and Samarra the bride-to-be had all visited at Melissa's request during the Mother's Day weekend three months earlier, a weekend that changed the world, again; seemed to be happening more-and-more.

"Nope. This is my third trip, and she asked me to come by myself. It's just as well. Flying's getting dangerous, three planes shot down over South Asia last week, compliments of some enemy that we give aid to. She's beginning to remember things about our marriage, the kids and especially Audry. We've also spoken on the phone a couple of times. Taking the girls and Samarra last time was therapeutic for all of us, but stressful."

"How's Audry holdin' up?"

Jeff paused, thinking about the way he would, or should, answer Abe's question. He and Abe had become great friends since the Park Place Café bombing three years earlier, and Abe had been a great help in trying to clarify the God-myth. Maybe it wasn't a myth at all, and the thought crossed his mind more often lately. *What if it's not a myth?*

"Audry's an amazing kid. Adopting her was a great gift for Melissa and me, the twins too. She says some of the most amazing things…"

"And she speaks fluent Hebrew, not bad for pre-teen," Abe interrupted.

"Yeah… she does." Jeff's thoughts drifted. "When we were flying back from Montego Bay on Mother's Day after visiting Melissa, Audry got a sudden sadness in her eyes and then began to cry, not a boo-hoo cry, a small cry, kind of a whimper."

"Was she sick?"

"No," Jeff continued. "I asked her what was wrong, and she said…" Jeff's thoughts drifted again.

"And?" Abe asked.

"And she said, 'Mom will be raptured soon. God gave her a mission, and it's almost through.'"

"Wow, that's deep for a little kid."

"Abe, I know we talked about this once; but do you believe the rapture is really gonna happen? Do Messianic Jews believe that Christians are going to instantaneously disappear like they do in those rapture movies?"

"Messianic Jews believe what the very early Christians believed, the ones of the first and early second century. Our views on the rapture and a few other things differ, but not that much. I know that my religion is not perfect, because none is. By the way, not all Christians believe in the rapture."

Abe swatted a fly and told the new waitress to make sure the air blowers over the front entrance were on. He spotted The Admiral, Sheryl and Wild Willy walking across the Towne Green, making their way toward *The Divide* and some cool air. The fountains were going medium-force, and several children ran through the water. Abe was glad the fountains were finally on again. Since the Buford Dam had been blown up, fresh water had been scarce, especially for decorative fountains, and medium-force was better than no-force.

"Here's what I think, but it's just my opinion," Abe continued. "I try not to debate people, because some think they have it all figured out. I do believe the last third of the Bible, and the New Testament plainly states that it will.

"The followers of Jesus at the time of his return, maybe sooner, will join him in heaven with the final army. I know that's hard to believe, but that's what it says. By the way, the term never appears in the Bible."

"What term?" Jeff asked.

"The rapture."

"Really? I've heard it did. But you believe that people will suddenly disappear in a flash."

"Not *people*; followers of Christ. They will disappear, and yes it will be very quick, in a flash, in my opinion I might add."

"In a flash to who? To God? To man? How long is a *flash* to God?"

"Let me finish, before I lose my thoughts," Abe answered.

The Admiral and friends began the trek to the front steps of the disco café, and Abe prepared their lemonades.

"You brought these questions up last time we talked about this, about what is God's time frame compared to our time frame? I've thought about that a lot, good question by the way, and have come to a conclusion, right or wrong."

The group of three opened the French doors and made their way toward Jeff. They were not smiling, and Will dabbed his perspiring forehead with a *45 Main Street* napkin.

"I think the rapture-process," Abe continued, setting the lemonades and one glass of zinfandel on the bar, "may go on throughout the Tribulation, but the disappearances will be rapid, bam… gone in an instant."

"The Tribulation?" Jeff asked.

"According to the ancient prophets, just before the end comes, the last days, there will be a period of unprecedented horror. That period of time is to be seven years. The first three-and-a-half would be really bad, and the last three-and-a-half would be much, much worse."

Jeff listened intently to Abe's explanation.

"So you believe the scripture that says two will be in a field and one will be taken, the *good* one. You think that 'one' will just disappear?" Jeff asked. "Now if I could see *that* I might believe in God."

"This just in from AP News," Condi continued as the TV over the circular bar had yet another News Alert.

Condi was no longer just a news anchor but had her very own news show, *The Condi Zimmerman Hour*. Every cloud has a silver lining she often thought, knowing her sudden rise to stardom wasn't just about looks. All the tragedies and terrorism had made her a star. That aspect was depressing, and she prayed for the victims every day.

"Apparently we now know why an Easter massacre didn't take place in spite of the internet chatter. News sources say that evidence was planted to throw everyone off guard. The Mother's Day Massacre, which killed..."

Jeff continued to rub his finger around the rim of his wine glass, and a small hum could be heard.

"Oh my goodness, have you been reading that Gideons Bible? Jeff, you're my bestest buddy; but everyone wants a 'sign,' been demanding them every generation since Moses walked the deserts of ancient Israel. And yes, I do believe two will be in a field, maybe more; and some will suddenly disappear. It will be mind-blowing for any left in the field, don't ya think?"

Abe smiled, the left corner of his mouth quirked and pointing toward the asteroid belt high above, like it always did.

"Then why haven't *you* disappeared, Abe? You don't drink, you don't go out with wild women, you don't go on dates with men, you talk about religion and help others. I don't understand why you're still here if Chuck Hutz was right about the *rapture has begun* thing. Why is Melissa still here?"

"And why is Chuck still here?" Abe added. "I'm not sure, my friend; but I have my ghosts, we all do, things that only you and God know about. Maybe God has further plans for me. Who knows the mechanism of the rapture? All I know is…"

Abe waved to his friends as they approached the bamboo-finished bar. The Admiral still limped slightly from his encounter with the Pants-on-the-Ground gang awhile back.

"About 150,000 of the Messianic Jews did disappear, in a matter of hours, maybe faster; but not all. It seems that all the MJs who were preaching in Israel disappeared."

"How many Messianic Jews were there in Israel?" Jeff asked.

"Hey guys and gal. It's the Magnificent Three, so what can I get ya? Why so glum?" Abe asked.

Abe knew his question was rhetorical; there were many reasons to be glum. Bombs going off, looting and arson, gang violence, the national forests on fire, meteorites… and those great big hailstones. Now *that* was scary.

"Hi Abe," the three said in unison.

"A cool ice water would be nice," Sheryl piped in and picked up one of the glasses of lemonade. She and The Admiral held hands, but there was no happiness in their eyes like there had been for the last year.

Abe set another Duckhorn in front of Jeff and said, "One hundred forty-four thousand."

"Say what?" Jeff asked.

"One hundred forty-four thousand Messianic Jews lived in Israel, until they disappeared. No one knows where they went."

"But you do," Jeff said.

"I'm not sure."

"You mean you don't think they were raptured?"

"We need to talk," Wild Willy interrupted, talking directly to Jeff with only a glance at Abe.

"Okay, can we talk here; or do we need to get a table?" Jeff asked.

Wild Willy looked around, and *The Divide* was nearly empty. Almost anywhere should be fine, he thought.

"Up there," he said and pointed to the most remote part of the disco-café.

"What are we talking about?" Jeff asked.

"Nothing good," Sheryl stated matter-of-factly as she always did when troubled. It seemed to her that no news had been good for the last few years and was getting especially bad all of a sudden. They walked toward the large, round booth. Multiple mirror balls rotated from the ceiling, disbursing tiny beads of light throughout.

"... seven-teen hundred forty-five dead. And it sadly didn't end there," Condi said and sipped her bottled water.

"No, it didn't," the guest said. *"The Mother's Day Massacre was a day-long event. By the time the day was over, churches, synagogues, shopping malls and rapid transit systems were bombed or shot up, almost any place with a gathering of innocent people."*

"And the fuel storage facilities," Condi added.

"And the fuel storage facilities, yes. Gas prices are through the roof, as though they weren't already. The Cushing Oil Storage Fields, the largest in the world, are no more. Forty-two killed there, mostly workers."

Abe loved the friends he had made over his years of bartending all over the United States, but he especially loved this group. You just learn so much about people when you tend bar. He had faced his share of anti-Semitism in his life, being a Jew from Israel; that's why he went by Abe instead of Abraham, *too much 'splainin' to do*. But never had there been a sign of dislike or distrust from them. They were patriotic and moral, dedicated to their country, God fearing; except for Jeff who thought God was a figment of someone's imagination long ago.

Then he had to face the reality of anti-Semitic Semitism when he decided that Jesus really was the foretold Jewish Savior. His family rejected him, his friends rejected him, there were even fistfights… fighting for God. He figured that's the way it had always been, probably since the very beginning.

Being a Jewish Christian in a world where most rabbis said it was impossible to be a Jew *and* a Christian, even though the rabbis admitted that Jesus was Jewish, was difficult to say the least; and the Jews for Jesus group must have been brave to take their Jesus-message to the Jewish country, at least until they disappeared. He wondered again what happened to them, here one day; gone the next.

Abe thought The Admiral looked typically *stately* as he always did, white hair and dark golf shirt; but Sheryl's face was splotched with small red whelps, probably mosquito bites.

The waitress took their drinks to the booth in the corner overlooking Duluth City Hall. Will looked unusually stressed, and Abe wondered what was going on. Seemed to him like there were a lot of things happening.

"So what's up?" Jeff asked.

Sheryl spoke first after making brief eye contact with the other two.

"We have been given an ultimatum. There appears to be a significant contingency of militant Christians and Islamic radicals that have banded together under the label, 'The enemy of my enemy is my friend', some Arab saying or something.

The contingency is worldwide. Europe has been given the same ultimatum, and…"

"What ultimatum?" Jeff interrupted.

There was a pause; then Will continued.

"Israel got the same ultimatum. It's a 'final warning' to surrender or be destroyed and was issued by an unknown group based somewhere in Asia, maybe Afghanistan or Pakistan."

"Oh bull dooky," Jeff said. "We should've let Israel take care of Iran and Syria long ago. Now Damascus is a hot-bed of al Qaeda, Hizbullah and God only knows how many other nutty groups that want to take over the world."

"*Bull dooky*?" Sheryl inquired.

"There are an estimated thirty thousand Islamists in the United States," Will continued. "Border security is being tightened as we speak, but it's way too late. They're here, blending in, looking American, hanging out at strip joints and Little League games, the friendly neighbor next door. It's been going on since Iran's Islamic Revolution in 1979.

"Mossad believes there are more than a hundred briefcase nukes already in the United States. There is also rumored intelligence that there may be a real bomb here."

"Real bomb?" Jeff asked.

"Real bomb," The Admiral added. "The Russian sub that was hijacked may have dropped a plutonium core somewhere in the waters of Bermuda. If true and it can be successfully picked up somehow, it's destined for the U.S."

The Admiral had been in the Submarine Service and knew the waters were deep off the shores of Bermuda; but with new mini-sub technology, should the rumors be substantiated, would make retrieval pretty simple.

"A large plutonium bomb could destroy most of even the largest metropolitan areas. A one-megaton bomb could flatten a city the size of Atlanta, if they could get it high enough in the air."

"How likely is that?" Jeff asked. "How would they get a two-thousand pound bomb in the air? A hot air balloon can't carry a two-thousand pound payload."

"Maybe they won't put it in the air. They could take it to the top of a building or parking deck and greatly increase the damage," Will said. "Here's the deal and the concern of many in Israel. What if they blow up a small town with a small 2-K briefcase nuke, somewhere in rural America or Europe? Then they issue another ultimatum."

"Okay," Jeff said, listening.

A few people began to drift in to *The Divide*, but none moved up to the second level where they talked privately.

"Obviously we wouldn't surrender," Sheryl said. "We would rant and rave and threaten retaliation; but the facts are, we don't know who to retaliate against."

"So they blow up another town, maybe a little larger, kill five to ten thousand people in an instant and wound God only knows how many," The Admiral contributed. "The terror and the agony of survivors will get tremendous media play. When they start showing people with their skin blown off and their bones white as ash, people will begin to consider surrender. The greatest addiction of all is the addiction to live."

"But of course we won't," Sheryl said. "Then they take their large plutonium bomb and annihilate Chicago, possibly killing a million. That's what they really want to do, kill a million infidels. The outcry to surrender could take over."

"The same with Europe and Asia. What if Paris is flattened, or London? They're already so broke and so populated with

Muslims, surrender will be a no-brainer. Then the world works its way toward the long-predicted One World Government, and it will be Islamic. The moderate Muslims, and there are many, will subjugate to the radicals out of fear."

"Exactly," Will interrupted, "and that's what the Israelis fear. Wouldn't surprise me if they blow the hell out of Damascus. You know the prophecy about Damascus, don't you?"

"Refresh my memory," Jeff laughed and sipped his merlot.

"You laugh, but these prophecies all come true; and this one is specific for Damascus. Think about that. The prediction was made almost three thousand years ago."

"So what was the prediction?" Jeff asked again, rubbing his finger around the rim of his glass.

"Will you stop that please," Sheryl demanded as she grabbed Jeff's hand. "That noise drives me crazy."

"Here's the prediction, ready?"

"Ready," the other three said.

"A prophecy against Damascus: See, Damascus will no longer be a city but will become a heap of ruins," Will quoted from heart.

There was a pause, and Jeff began to applaud.

"Very good Wild Willy. That's it?" Jeff asked. "Did it ever happen?"

"Not yet," Will said. "And that's what I was talking about. Israel may make it happen. Bible predictions always come true."

"So back to the ultimatum," Jeff said. "When do the Feds plan to tell us little-people?"

"Not anytime soon," Sheryl said.

They all knew that Sheryl had the real inside scoop. She had worked directly with the President for several years as Director of Public Relations.

Sheryl didn't particularly like the President and hoped he wouldn't run yet again. Since the 22nd Amendment had been repealed last year, the President could run for another two terms. Sixteen years of *this* President would surely dissolve the Constitution, and she hoped in her heart-of-hearts that he would take the rumored post as President of the United Nations. Then he could rule the world, and that was depressing.

"Is there a time frame on the ultimatum?" Jeff asked.

"Yeah," Sheryl answered. "Twenty-four hours."

Chapter Twenty-Six

Naples, Italy

Mohammed Rehza's mission was complete, at least *this* mission. The meltdown of the French nuclear power plants earlier in the year had caused extensive damage, and radiation wafted in the wind in France's worst nuclear disaster. Power to large parts of western France including vast sections of Paris remained out and had been for months. Gangs now ruled the streets of Paris, and the population struggled to find food and water. Murders were rampant, as was looting; only there wasn't much left to loot.

Twin brother Vinny hadn't been so fortunate in the States. All three nuclear plants that were hacked had new security measures and bypasses that made it impossible to take over. There had been some intermittent power outages and flickering lights, but that was about it.

Plant Vogtle was the United States' newest reactor; and Vinny should've known the redundant safeties would be difficult, at least that was Mohammed's opinion.

The French military did the best they could under the circumstances, and with a near-zero budget; but the large Muslim population thought the latest calamity, like all calamities that happened to anyone non-Muslim, was a sign from Allah. Islamic communities were the only communities around Paris that maintained some semblance of control.

Europe was a disaster, and Mohammed was proud of his work for Allah. No power meant no hospitals, no grocery stores, no water system, no emergency services. The military's backup generators managed to keep military vehicles fueled and ready, but it hadn't been easy.

The Saudi's and other large Middle East oil producers blackmailed the free world with sky-high prices; and as a result, while the rest of the world languished in economic distress, as well as the AIDS, flu and smallpox plagues, the Middle East oil barons raked in the dough. It was Allah who had protected the Islamic nations from the devastating plagues sweeping the world, and gold was their gift. Mohammed also knew that the Jews in Israel had escaped the plagues too, and that was confusing. Maybe it was a Semitic trait, or maybe Allah was just making it interesting as He often did.

Mohammed started his bright red Vespa scooter and headed to Viva's, his favorite Italian coffee shop, overlooking the sea on the foothills of Mount Vesuvius. There he would meet Dmitry, the Chechen arms dealer. Twenty minutes later, he parked the red scooter in the moped section of the small parking lot, entered the café and spotted Dmitry in the back.

"How are you my good friend," Dmitry said as he greeted *The Preacher*.

"I am fine, Dmitry, thanks be to Allah and His blessings," Mohammed answered.

"How do you like being called a preacher?"

"I love it. I always wanted to be a preacher when I grew up," Mohammed lied. The two men laughed and ordered coffee and a cheese bagel.

"Looks like you've been busy," Dmitry continued.

The Bastille Day bombings in London, Copenhagen and Berlin caught security off guard. It was a French holiday, so other European cities had no reason to take special precautions.

"Yes, I have been busy doing God's work."

"Yeah, I noticed. France is beginning to glow in the dark."

They laughed again, before getting down to business.

Jaffa, Israel

Naomi and Aludra's journey had been long and arduous, and dangerous. The Korengal Valley of Death along the Afghanistan-Pakistan border seemed so long ago to Aludra, and she wondered if her brother had survived the nuclear holocaust.

Aludra didn't miss her home or the smell of the Spring poppy plants; but she did miss Muhammed. She and her brother had been so close, at least until she showed him her New Testament, a crime punishable by death along the border.

At first Pakistan and the Arab world blamed Israel and the United States, but Pakistan finally admitted to the three nuclear explosions. One thing for certain, Aludra knew; the Valley of Death had lived up to its name. She was sure Muhammed hadn't survived, and the news had been of thousands of deaths in the Valley.

"We are safe now Aludra," Naomi reassured as she made her bed in their new home in Jaffa. Getting into Israel had been miraculously simple, and Naomi silently thanked the God of Abraham.

"It's beautiful here, Naomi," and Aludra peered over the balcony railing. "The Mediterranean is so blue. I've never been to Israel. Muhammed would *not* be happy," she said nervously.

Aludra could only imagine what her brother would think of her presence in Israel, the land he wanted destroyed, or at least the Jews.

"It is beautiful, and historic."

"Tell me," Aludra asked, and she did feel safe for the first time in years. Her depression was lifted, but she still thought often of the Christian friend she met in Tajikistan. He had given her roses and date nuts, but then an Islamist killed him. He had been the first man she had loved; but the marriage she hoped for came to a sudden end when the AK-47 exploded over the hills that night. One less Christian for her religion to kill.

"Jaffa used to be called Joppa in the ancient days and was a grand port city before becoming a part of Tel Aviv. In the 1400's, Joppa was captured by Egypt. Have you ever heard the story about Jonah, the Prophet?"

"Jonah and the whale?" Aludra asked.

"That's the one, only the Tanach never said it was a whale that swallowed him.

"What is the Tanach, Naomi?"

"The Tanach is the Old Testament. Jonah was instructed by God to go to Nineveh and warn the people to change their decadent ways. Jonah didn't want to follow God's instructions and tried to escape. The Israelis had a habit of killing the prophets; they didn't like their messages. Jonah tried to take a boat from the port of Joppa to Tarshish."

"Tarshish?" Aludra had never heard of the city.

"Some scholars believe that Tarshish was along the Sea of Galilee or in Asia Minor, but no archeological evidence has been found there. Many believe Jonah was trying to escape across the Mediterranean to Tarshish in Spain. That's when the crew of the fishing boat threw him over the side, at Jonah's request if you can believe that. Can you imagine?

"The big fish swallowed him and three days later, spit him out along the shores of Joppa. Then of course, many don't believe the story at all and think it's just mythology. It is hard to believe if you really think about it, a man being swallowed by a fish for three days and living to tell about it. The same thing happened to Jesus."

Aludra was awed at the vast knowledge of the old Jewish woman but had come to expect it since their daring escape from Korengal Valley. She still thanked Allah every day for the miracle of the lone donkey and the meeting of Naomi. It now seemed like a dream.

Aludra began to feel guilt about her Muslim beliefs and her upbringing, mainly because of the doubts she now had about Muhammad the Prophet. She found herself wondering, what did Muhammad prophecy? What predictions had he made that came true? Other than the predictions of beheadings and enslavement of the infidels, who seemed to be anyone who wasn't a Muslim, she could think of none.

"Jesus was swallowed by a whale too?"

"No, that's not what I meant," Naomi patiently explained with a smile. The question tickled her funny bone, but she held back her laughter.

"Jesus was swallowed up by the grave for three days; and then, like Jonah, he miraculously appeared again, alive and healthy. No one could believe their eyes, and that is why so many early followers of Jesus were willing to give their lives. They had seen this miracle, death and then life, with their own eyes. When someone actually *sees* a miracle, it makes quite an impression.

"Aludra, I want to take you on a tour. I haven't been to Israel in many years, but there is so much history here. You will love it."

They had become close friends during the escape, almost like a mother-daughter relationship. Aludra liked it.

"I want to go to the Holocaust Museum, Naomi. Can we do that? My brother never believed in the holocaust, so I want to see for myself."

Aludra prepared for her day and entered the ceramic-tiled shower, an experience she relished thoroughly. She hadn't been able to shower since she visited Paris several years earlier. As the warm water flowed over her soft, olive skin, Aludra's thoughts overwhelmed her as hurt invaded her spirit once again.

Though the relationship had been brief, she was sure she loved Ahmed, the Christian-convert son of the Muslim leader of the small village in Tajikistan. She was sure of it; and then he was killed in an instant, judged to be an infidel by another Muslim, a singular judge, jury and executioner.

That night in the hills of Tajikistan was a night she would always remember, a haunting night. The sky had been cool for a change, the air brisk and the stars shooting across the sky. She would never forget the loud crack as the AK-47 assault rifle shouted across the hills, and the blood had rushed from Ahmed's neck.

Aludra finished her shower, wrapped a soft Egyptian-cotton towel around her head and waited for her hair to dry. She felt reenergized and couldn't wait to get to the Holocaust Museum.

"Ready to go, my dear?" Naomi asked after Aludra finished dressing.

Naomi thought Aludra to be quite beautiful in her new dress, tropically mango with a modestly cut neckline. She glowed with happiness.

"Yes, I'm ready. Naomi, I'm so excited that God brought you into my life. I feel free for the first time ever. I can say what I want, do what I want… it's the way it should be."

Naomi had explained that the red flags indicated a high alert for missiles coming in from the north, an everyday occurrence. At the insistence of the West, Israel refrained from taking action, except for the Iron Dome Defense System. The IDDS had become so effective, missile launches had slowed significantly. The accuracy rate was about 90%.

As soon as the two women exited their apartment building onto Haifa Street the high-pitched, oscillating scream of a defense siren assaulted the surrounding air. Aludra covered her ears, her eyes suddenly wide with fear.

The crowded streets of Jaffa became empty as the well-trained Israelis ran for shelter. Though nine out of ten rockets were destroyed by the anti-missile system, the Israelis knew that just one could be life changing for many.

Across the street, a lone man scanned the skies for incoming missiles about the same time he spotted the two women leaving the apartment building. An elderly gentleman stood outside the *153 Mazarin Bakery* next door, about ten feet away from the women who still covered their ears and cowered in fear.

The man across the street spotted three missiles, small specks of white light clearly visible in the sky, even with the bright morning Sun. He ran toward the women, who were clearly more fearful of the loud siren than the incoming missiles.

The old man with the white hair and baggy, beige Bermuda shorts appeared confused.

Crossing the street at a full trot, the man saw one, then two of the missiles explode in balls of flame well above the city, victims of Iron Dome. The third continued toward the street, and the rescuer-to-be began to think he wouldn't make it.

۞

Dmitry sipped his coffee and waited for the waitress to leave. He was sure he felt the floor vibrate but thought it probably was a compressor vibration of some kind.

"How was your trip to Disneyland?" Mohammed asked.

"It was a success. Space Mountain was closed, but Pluto is alive and well."

Mohammed concealed his happiness at *that* news but was smiling on the inside. This was good. Brother Vinny would have his *big* bombs.

"Did Pluto have any puppies?"

"Yes, my friend. There was Pluto and two small Plutos."

The code probably wasn't necessary, but the Japanese financiers insisted. No one seemed to know of the group, but *Select* provided the money for the hijacked nuclear sub. Though the submarine didn't complete its mission, the Panama Canal remained shut and the large U.S. air base in the Indian Ocean remained closed "until further notice," thanks to the nuclear missiles from the Nerpa-class sub. Radiation levels still remained high.

Pluto and two pups. That was good. Three plutonium cores had been delivered to Vinny's cement plant just north of the U.S.-Mexican border. Space Mountain referred to the delivery system; but Dmitry had warned that getting an ICBM launcher would be next to impossible; and how would they hide it.

Mohammed was confident Vinny would figure it out, and the Japanese Babies of World War II would finally get their revenge for Hiroshima. In return, the jihadists had unlimited funds.

"What about us?" Mohammed asked, and Dmitry handed *The Preacher* a small Bible with coded instructions located in the Book of Psalms.

Dmitry didn't have the ability to feel guilt. He didn't care who blew up who, as long as it wasn't him. He didn't particularly like or dislike Jews, Muslims, Christians, stone worshippers, whatever. This was pure business; but this time there was a twinge of something, if not guilt.

He knew, if things worked according to the jihadist plan, World War III was right around the corner; and that *could* affect him. When these super-bombs went off, Pandora's Box would surely have opened.

"Psalm 23," Dmitry answered.

Chapter Twenty-Seven

Jeff's flight to Montego Bay was uneventful, and he hoped Wild Willy would have the rental car. He was glad Will had decided to join him on such short notice. Just the week before they were discussing the ultimatum that had been sent to the President. The 24-hour deadline had come and gone with no renewed attacks.

The Mother's Day Massacre had rallied the troops, and the American Legion Post in Duluth had come alive with activity, as had American Legion and VFW Posts all over the United States.

Jeff spotted Will, waiting in a Grand Cherokee at the roundabout in front of the baggage area.

"You made it!" Jeff noticed the scrapes on the side of Will's face.

"Always on time my man, always. Wish I could say the same about you."

Will glanced at his Timex and said "Geejam Beach Resort" which activated the GPS system.

"Yeah, we had some bad weather to skirt, according to the pilot. Probably a meteor shower since there were no clouds. Looks like you've been in a cat fight."

Wild Willy's demeanor was unusually happy, just the opposite from a week earlier when they were talking about ultimatums from the jihadists trying to take control of the world.

"How was your week in Israel?"

"Fandamtastic!" Will said after a pause, and a big grin formed across his tanned face. That's when Jeff noticed the bandage on Will's right leg.

"You're pretty smiley to have all these injuries. What happened?"

Turn left in 300 meters said the GPS, and Will activated the left-turn signal. He made no comment as they both watched a couple of meteors flying along the horizon. It had become commonplace, but the majority burned up in the atmosphere.

"I'm in love man, and it's *real* this time!"

They both laughed at the comment, Jeff had heard it many times.

"Looks like she beat the dickens out of ya. You sure can pick 'em Wild Willy. So tell me about Miss Fandamtastic. Is she an Israeli?"

Will contemplated.

"She's a Muslim, but I did meet her in Israel."

"Yeah, right."

"No, really. I met her last week."

"What color's her burqa?"

Will glanced at Jeff and gave him the evil eye.

"I'm just kiddin' Wild Willy. Whoa! You almost hit that cow. They drive on the left here in case you didn't know. Tell me the story; we have another hour.

Turn right on Mandeville Highway at next light, five hundred meters.

"I think it was a God thing, definitely," Will explained in as sincere a voice as Jeff had ever heard from Wild Willy.

"It started with a missile attack. I was in Jaffa to check out some property. I'm thinkin' about buying a condo since I'm in Israel so much."

"A God thing? So you think you were fortunate to come under missile attack? You really *are* wild, Wild Willy."

Please continue one hundred twenty-seven kilometers.

"When do you see Melissa?" Will asked.

"Not until tomorrow afternoon. She's doing some kind of voodoo baptism ceremony tonight. I can't believe I'm even saying that."

And he couldn't, my-o-my how quickly things change. Two years ago she was dead, then she was alive; and now she's baptizing voodoo people.

"I just wanted to get here a day early and wind down. I get keyed up, know what I mean? Stop changing the subject."

The two had been friends since the *last century*, Will liked to say; and they rode in comfortable silence. Will really was pretty wild if you got right down to it… master's degree from Georgia Tech, ex-CIA and now a consultant with Israel's intelligence network. His cover was great, a repo-man of luxury vehicles: yachts, Ferraris and Lear Jets. Will could pretty much fly, float or drive anything on the planet.

"I was standing on the corner of Jaffa Street last Monday morning when the missile warning system went off. It's extremely loud. There weren't many people on the streets because of the Red Flag warning for incoming rockets from the north.

"I looked across the street at these two ladies coming out of an apartment building just as the sirens sounded, and they froze. One of the poor ladies covered her ears and squatted on the ground, about the worst thing you can do in a missile attack. Then, just a few yards away was this old guy with saggy pants looking in the bakery. He seemed oblivious."

"Did the new Iron Dome make the intercept?" Jeff interrupted.

"Got two out of three. Anyway, I ran… I was really scared man, it was gonna be close."

"And you saved them," Jeff interrupted again. "You're the save-a-life King! You're always doing that."

"What can I say man, I'm just in the right place at the right time. So I do a booty-haul across the street, grabbed the old man and the two ladies and shoved them into the apartment building and under the stairwell.

"Next thing you know, there's a huge detonation about a hundred feet from us, just up the street. Blew two people in a car into the next block. They were the only two casualties.

"The front door of the apartment building flew open, windows broke and the marquis collapsed out front."

"Were they injured?"

"Only the old man. He broke his arm when I shoved him inside, but he was thankful nonetheless. One of the women was an old Jewish lady named Naomi, probably eighty, been around some tough blocks, you could tell.

"The lady who covered her ears stood up and held out her hand. She was nervous and scared but clearly happy to be alive. Jeff, she's the prettiest girl that I ever did see, I swear. Dark hair, almond eyes. Now I know that's *shallow*, but I can't help it that she's so beautiful.

"Well, it turns out that she and Naomi share an apartment. I shook her hand since she kept holding it out, but we had chemistry right from the start. I could just tell. I hugged Naomi and told her to stay close to a shelter when the Red Flags are out and said goodbye to Aludra, that was the younger girl's name; but it seemed so strange that this old Jewish woman and the young Muslim girl were such friends, almost like mother and daughter. Really weird."

"So you like her?" Jeff prodded.

"Like her? I love her! We had dinner every single night last week. The last night, we had dinner alone in a quaint little Italian restaurant, and…"

"I hope you didn't order that pink girlie wine you always drink."

"Will you stop interrupting, and it's called zinfandel. The last night we stayed out until almost midnight. Now, let me tell you this: That pink moon with rings is unbelievably romantic. She didn't even know about the comet hitting the Moon."

"Did you kiss her?"

"You just ask way too many questions, Jeff. And no, I didn't. She's Muslim, for Pete's sake!"

"Muslims don't kiss?" Jeff laughed.

"We had a passionate hug."

Will smiled again, and Jeff could tell he was definitely smitten.

"And I'm not smitten. I know what you're thinking."

Fifteen minutes later, Will turned into the luxury resort. Jeff thought it didn't seem quite as luxurious as during the Mother's Day trip; and scattered weeds sprouted in the usually impeccable lawn, a banana tree leaning way over, broken at the top.

"Man, this place is a dump," Will said. "Just kidding, since you're paying. There's hardly anyone here."

"Does look like they need a little landscaping," Jeff agreed.

Jake the Bellman had been there during Jeff's previous visits, and they had become friends quickly. Jeff gave the bellman a fist-bump and a small shopping bag with six watches, one for each of Jake's children, and hoped the kids would like the colorful bands.

The afternoon passed, Will talked about Aludra and talked about Aludra and talked about Aludra more. Never had Jeff seen a more smitten Wild Willy, and Will had always had lots of girlfriends.

Jeff put on his bathing suit. He would go down to the white sandy beach and take a nap. Maybe he could relax a little. Then Will mentioned Bubba Haskins.

"What about Bubba Haskins?"

"You haven't heard? That's hard to believe, news-junkie. Last night he escaped from that new high-security terrorist prison out west. All of them escaped, about seventy people awaiting trial."

"Those guys have been in there two years and still haven't gone to trial? Bubba's a *bad* man. How'd they do it?" Jeff asked.

"Bubba's a bad man, but a guy named Vinny is worse.

"Who?"

"We have a lead on a guy who goes by 'Vinny'. Before the Pakistanis nuked the Korengal Valley, the Israelis sent in dozens of nano-bots."

"The little bugs that spy? Like the dragonflies you used to rescue Sheryl last year?

"Exactly," Will answered.

"This Vinny-guy is really Aboud Rehza, a Saudi. He and Bubba are in charge of North American Operations, including Mexico and Canada for some jihadist group. Aboud's supposedly brilliant, according to recordings; and his twin brother Mohammed is in charge of Euro-Asian operations. Mohammed was responsible for the meltdown of the French and German nuclear plants a few months ago according to Mossad."

"How'd they do it?" Jeff asked again.

"EMP bomb. U.S. Intel doesn't know how they got one, but EMP bombs are easy to construct."

"Really?" Jeff was incredulous. An electromagnetic pulse would disrupt most electronics for miles.

"Yep. Seems they used some method of elevating the EMP generator to about half a mile and set it off. Of course, this isn't a bomb that actually explodes like other bombs; it just generates a constant electromagnetic pulse. Anything with solid-state circuits within range stops operating. That would be cell phones, automobiles, aircraft, you name it.

"With the phones out and security circuits fried, the reports I got indicated a group of men in seven old pickup trucks, trucks that were built prior to solid-state electronics, raided the prison with grenade launchers, assault rifles and mortars. They killed every prison guard except one who faked his death. They also killed three of the imprisoned jihadists that were actually informants for the FBI."

Jeff mulled over the information. Bubba Haskins had been the largest minority contractor in Georgia at one time and seemed like a nice guy. Bubba's wife was good friends with both Melissa and Samarra. Only, Jill was Bubba's ex-wife now; and Bubba wasn't really his name.

"Does anyone know Bubba's real name?"

"Nope, not yet. Now, let me tell you more about Aludra.

Jeff gave Will the *look*, grabbed a towel and headed to the beach. He had heard enough about Will's new flame.

CHAPTER TWENTY-EIGHT

"Listen, I tell you a mystery: We will not all sleep, but we will all be changed- in a flash, in the twinkling of an eye, at the last trumpet. For the trumpet will sound, the dead will be raised imperishable, and we will be changed."

1 Corinthians 15: 51-52

"I don't understand why we ain't been raptured? Ever'body's talkin' 'bout it."

The plump and short choir director cried as she spoke, clearly upset. Her yellow and orange bonnet sat askew on her poufy gray hair, and her bright blue dress blew in the breeze flowing through the open church windows.

"They sho 'nuff are. People been dis'pearin' fo years 'round heah, yes dey have, jus' like dat," the young man, dressed in his Sunday-best said, snapping his fingers. His fingers were long and slender, and Melissa thought he might've been the piano player.

The church television was the largest flatscreen TV she had seen. But then it hit her; how could she have *that* thought since she had no memory. She did have a memory, however; and visions of young women in short dresses, dancing on a grand piano, *somewhere…*

Melissa's memory drifted. It had been for several days as past memories enveloped her mind. *Somewhere with flashing lights, a ball of mirrors hanging from the ceiling and a dance floor... and lots of big screen TVs all tuned to news stations.*

"Didn't you see the interview last night with that Chuck Hutz fella?" The choir director continued to cry, and tears flowed down her face, ruining her Sunday makeup.

"I wuz drivin' my horse an' wagon down de road, jus' last week," the young black man continued, and Melissa thought he spoke more like an old man. He also didn't sound like a Jamaican, maybe Haitian; or *Southern*. Another memory.

"Yessiree Bob," the young man continued, "They wuz three ladies an' a gentle man sittin' by de side a de road, sittin' on de bench waitin' fo de bus. I sneezed and looked up and..."

"Go on boy, go on," cried another member.

"An' de man an' one a de ladies had dis'peared, jus' like dat," and he snapped his fingers again.

Melissa looked around the sanctuary of the small, white church. She surely didn't remember walking in, and no one seemed to notice her. She sat next to a lady with a floral hat and thought the lady smelled a little like the bathroom deodorant spray she used to smell on some of the poor ladies at church when she was a little girl in... it almost came back to her.

"Excuse me, do you know the name of this church?"

Melissa had been to several churches around Kingston, but this one stirred no memories. The woman wearing bathroom deodorizer kept knitting, or crocheting or whatever. She ignored Melissa as though she wasn't there.

This was just too weird. The last thing she remembered was driving from Kingston toward Drapers, the small village where she would meet Jeff. She smiled at the thought, something was there, in her heart. She could feel it.

"Excuse me," she said again, this time louder. No response. Maybe the lady was deaf, she thought.

"There it is; there it is now!"

The choir director screamed; and for a short woman, the scream was penetrating. The whole crowd became silent and took a seat. The church interior glowed in soft yellow, as the fields of daffodils surrounding the small church shared their yellow tint.

"Mr. Hutz, are you telling your fans that the rapture is an ongoing process?"

"Condi, I am only saying what I see in these visions I have. Three years ago I didn't even know what the rapture was. It wasn't mentioned in the Bible, at least by that name; because I have searched thoroughly. Now I know that it was mentioned somewhere in the New Testament that just before the end, the last days, some people will disappear in an instant, a flash if you will. I think it said at the last trumpet.

Chuck paused and sipped his bottled water.

"Plus, I'm losing fans fast with these visions of mine. It is in defiance of commonly accepted beliefs."

The TV lights glistened off Chuck's nearly bald head, and only a trace of his once red hair remained. His trademark seersucker shirt was showing signs of perspiration, and Chuck sweated profusely as he always did. He would go on a diet next week.

"Let me interrupt you, if I may, Condi said and studied her small Samsung Six display after keying in "trumpet."

"What is this 'last trumpet' you mentioned?"

Melissa listened intently to Chuck's vision. The congregation, if that's what it was, stared at the large screen as though hypnotized, maybe even hopeful, hopeful that Chuck was right. Otherwise, why would they all still be here? Why was *she* still here?

"Condi, many have avoided studying the last book of the Bible, for various reasons. It's not the easiest to follow, much less understand. It's also quite frightening. There is a coming time of troubles when the world, not the United States, the 'world' will undergo grave changes. Those who experience these days will be forced into making some difficult choices if they want to continue to live.

"These 'troubles' are described in Revelation as seals, trumpets and bowls. There are seven of each, and..."

"Mr. Hutz, I hate to interrupt you; but we have a commercial break. Before we break, are you saying the rapture will be an instantaneous event or an ongoing event? I know our listeners are eager to hear."

"Condi, there are Christians and Messianic Jews who believe the event known as the rapture will definitely happen. The conflict is 'when does it happen?' Most believe the rapture will occur before these times of Jacob's trouble. That's how it's described in the Bible."

"But what do you think, Chuck? You have these visions, so what do you see?"

"The Bible seems to indicate that it will be in an instant at the 'last trumpet'. God does not make things particularly easy to figure out. There are the pre-tribs who believe the rapture will happen before the bad stuff starts..."

"Yes, I think we all hope for that!" Condi interrupted.

"Exactly," Chuck continued. *"We all hope for that. However, and there always seems to be a 'however,' there are those who believe the rapture will occur right in the middle of this Tribulation. And then there are those who believe it will be at the last trumpet or at the very end of the Tribulation period, which is to last seven years."*

A time of *Jacob's trouble*... Melissa well knew that scripture from the ancient prophet, and Jacob's trouble would not be a pleasant experience. Jeremiah had described it.

"How awful that day will be! No other will be like it.
It will be a time of trouble for Jacob, but he will be saved out of it."

No other would be like it, she was sure. She had prayed many times to be raptured before the times of Tribulation, but maybe God hadn't listened. Or maybe he had, and the answer was "no."

"From my own discernment, I think the rapture happens in a flash, here one second and gone the next, just like it says. But I also think it will occur all through the times of Jacob's trouble. I'm not sure why or what the process will be, but I think some will be left behind just to help save others and to prove they really are worthy."

"'Really are worthy' Mr. Hutz?"

"It's easy to talk the talk, Condi. It's hard to walk the walk."

Thank you, Mr. Hutz. We will pause for three min... wait! We have a news alert. There have been three large earthquakes, two in the United States and one in Europe. The one in Yellowstone was the largest at 6.7 magnitude. There are no reports of casualties. We will be right back."

Melissa had been on her way to meet Jeff, so why had she stopped here? She watched the screen, as mesmerized as everyone else when suddenly, just before the break, Chuck went into one of his trances and started talking in Hebrew. The lights flickered as high winds buffeted the studio.

"What do you think?"

Melissa looked to her left, and a young woman with black hair was sitting next to her. She had the palest skin and wore a white smock.

"Pardon me?" Melissa said. At least this woman wasn't deaf.

From the rear of the church she heard a man shout, something about the missing Messianic Jews.

"What do you think of Mr. Hutz? Do you believe he sees all these things in visions?"

The church floor seemed to shift, but the pendant lamps shaped like crucifixes with Jesus remained steady. She was sure she felt something.

"I don't know. I'm not sure why he would make it up, but this story is different than some of the things I learned… I think. Do you know the name of this church?"

The commercial break ended in less than a minute, and Condi reappeared, a look of stress across her face. Chuck Hutz was nowhere to be seen.

"Breaking news, folks. There has been an eruption of Mt. Vesuvius in Italy. There are casualties reported, and Naples is being evacuated. It doesn't appear to be in time, as a pyroclastic flow of super-heated ash and debris are approaching Naples at more than two hundred miles per hour. Naples is only thirteen miles from the volcano.

"Yellowstone's eruption was magnitude 6.7; and many tourists and animals have been killed, apparently from poisonous hydrogen sulfide and carbon dioxide gases. There is great concern that this sudden activity might be a precursor to a Yellowstone eruption, according to Lynn Tomay, one of the world's leading geologists. Yellowstone is designated as the largest supervolcano in the world and has erupted two…"

"I'm Melissa," Melissa said to the pale-but-stunning woman and stuck her hand out in greeting.

"I know who you are Melissa, and you will have a fine meeting today with Jeffrey. You have done well, but your time here is nearly over. Do not worry about Jeff. He hasn't discovered his role in the coming events, but he has one and will soon figure it out."

"Who in the world *are* you?" Melissa asked.

"My name is Missy T. Tell Jeffrey that Missy and Kipper said hello, and we will see him soon."

Melissa was startled; but before she could answer, Missy disappeared. As she glanced around the small church, others were disappearing, like Chuck had said. It was instantaneous. As the last person in the church disappeared, Melissa remained alone and began to cry. *Did I disappoint you Lord?*

"Lady du Mer?" The gentle rocking took her thoughts from the disappearing church.

"Lady du Mer?" This time it was louder. "Are you alright, deah?"

Melissa rubbed her eyes and tried to focus.

"You have bad dream? You be cryin' in de sleep."

Melissa sat up and asked where she was, then realized she was in her cabin. It had all been a strange dream. Her dreams of late had all seemed so real. Twenty minutes later she drove toward Drapers. It seemed like her second trip of the day.

CHAPTER TWENTY-NINE

"Coffee?"

Jeff stirred, looked around and couldn't believe he spent the night on the beach. *Must've been more tired than I thought.* He stood, stumbled and squinted in the bright morning light. Will walked toward him carrying a small tray with two cups and a silver coffee carafe.

"Man. I can't believe I crashed out here all night. What time is it?"

Will glanced at the Sun, looked at one of the shadows of a nearby palm and said, "It's about 9:16."

"You always were good with that sun-time thing. What time is it really?"

Will glanced at his watch. "9:22. I'm gettin' better."

They sat silently, drinking the Jamaica Blue Mountain blend and watched the tropical birds stir in the flowering bushes. The morning sky was cloudless but with a slight haze, unusual for the Islands.

"What's the itinerary?" Will asked.

"I'm meeting Melissa at noon, probably have lunch and see if any memories might be stirring. You want go with me? It might stir something."

"Nope, I'm gonna hang out at the beach and think about my new girlfriend. You need to be alone anyway."

After breakfast, a shower and shave, Jeff was headed south toward Drapers and the small restaurant overlooking Blue Lake.

It was an okay place, small and quiet with strings of Christmas lights hanging across the ceiling. He drove and thought, contemplating. He wasn't sure what he expected the end result to be and wished he could look Melissa in the eyes and tell her he loved her and God, but she would know.

Why am I so resistant to God he wondered. *Is it a rebellion? Do I have a dark side that just won't let me go there?*

He knew that wasn't true. He wasn't dark and was reading his Gideons Bible for the second time. Recently he had subscribed to an internet newsletter about biblical archeology. Still… The stories were hard to believe; mysterious hands appearing in thin air and writing messages on a wall and people walking on water or feeding five thousand people with a couple of loaves of bread and a fish.

If I could only see a sign... He hadn't even seen the bright blip in the sky for a long time; had it been two years? Maybe it was gone, or imaginary. The bright light wasn't imaginary though, because Abe the Bartender had seen it about the time he had. Gray and Andi saw it when they rescued him the night of the Cayman Tsunami, said the light guided them to where he was floating in the sea.

Two miles outside Drapers, Jeff heard a disturbance and looked to the left. Several men were fighting with knives and a woman lay on the ground. A small child cried over the still body.

Jeff hit the brake and pulled the SUV to a stop on the left side of the road. He opened the door and exited but not before retrieving Will's new Callaway four-iron.

The three Jamaican men watched in amusement, flashing their machetes and knives as the gray-haired Jeff walked calmly across the narrow, two-lane road, carrying a golf club. The child continued to weep and another man bled as he lay in the dirt, stabbed earlier by one of the three.

"You gone t'play a leetle golf, mon?" the taller man asked and laughed; but none were ready for the rapid fluidity of the ex-Navy SEAL's response.

"Yeah, mon; I be gonna tee off on your Rasta head, hero."

With that, Jeff kicked the shorter of the three squarely in the groin; and he knew from the crushing sound the young man wouldn't be making babies for a long time.

He swung the four-iron at the kneecap of the taller man, and he dropped to the dirt in a raging howl. Jeff hit the last man with the back swing and the sound of shattered teeth filled the morning air. Just like that, it was over.

The stabbed man lying in the dirt moaned in thanks as Jeff came over to check his wound. He would live. The woman, however, was already deceased. Jeff picked up the little girl and hugged her close to his body, trying to make her secure. She sobbed uncontrollably.

"Mistuh, mistuh, you gimme de baby."

"Who are you?" he asked.

"She be de baby's granmutter," the stabbed man moaned. "That be her daughter, layin' on de dirt over dere."

Within five minutes a Bluefields Police car pulled to the side of the road, put an orange traffic cone in the street and walked to the gathering crowd. A small, white sedan pulled behind the police car, and Jeff recognized Melissa right away. She walked toward the crowd, but before the policeman began to question, Melissa spoke up.

"Jamal, Jamal."

The policeman turned toward Melissa and a big smile grew across his slender, dark face.

"De Lady uh de Sea!" He beamed, and she gave him a hug. Jeff thought they appeared to be friends, and Jamal looked very familiar.

"Jamal, this is… my friend Jeffrey. We were to meet at JJ's in Drapers. What happened, Jeffrey?"

"Well, I was headed to Jamaica Joe's when I saw these men beating the guy over there," and Jeff pointed to the injured man who was now staggering toward the dead lady. "The lady was on the ground and appeared dead. I stopped to see if there was a misunderstanding."

Jamal looked at the three men. One was holding both knees, clearly shattered and crying like a child. The other two lay on the ground, one moaning and holding his golden-boys and the other trying to find his two front teeth in the sand.

"Dat's what I call de inte'vention, mon. Dat def'nitely be some inte'vention goin' on, I mean."

They finished up what little paperwork was required, and Jeff gave the policeman a Timex watch with a colored band for the little boy sitting in the front seat of the Toyota patrol car. Then he walked over to the grandmother holding the small girl, still sobbing. He reached into his pocket and pulled out his last Timex, this one with a hot pink band and handed it to the little girl. The grandmother smiled as the child stopped crying, and Jeff leaned over and gave her a small kiss on her wet cheek. He walked back toward Melissa and Jamal, still talking at the edge of the road.

"Jamal, you look familiar; ever been to the States?"

"I have been dere, mon. I had de helicopta bidness in New York a while ago. I flew de people 'round de city. Maybe I fly you?"

"Maybe you did, Jamal; maybe you did."

Jamal made the arrests and threw the men in the back of his patrol car. No ambulance for these guys. They said their goodbyes, Jamal gave Melissa another hug and they were on the way to JJs. Jeff was ready after a morning he had not expected.

Jamal *had* flown him on *de helicopta.* Jeff smiled and wished he could talk like that. He had tried, but the Jamaican's just laughed. Hard to talk Jamaican with a Southern accent, he knew.

As Jeff's Mensa-mind searched his internal memory files, he recalled Jamal as a Jamaican with a French accent. That certainly wasn't the case today, and he also remembered a dream he had a few months earlier, a terrible nightmare. When Samarra woke him, he was drenched in sweat. Jamal was in that dream too.

Following Melissa's car into Jamaica Joe's small parking lot, the fine hair on the back of his neck stood at attention. Something was going on.

Chapter Thirty

"Listen, I tell you a mystery: We will not all sleep, but we will all be changed— in a flash, in the twinkling of an eye, at the last trumpet. For the trumpet will sound, the dead will be raised imperishable, and we will be changed."

1 Corinthians 15:51-52

"How was your trip, Jeffrey? I mean except for what just happened?"

They chuckled. Suddenly Jeff was overwhelmed with a warmth of some kind, not severe but noticeable, and internal. He had an acute desire to hold Melissa, hug her, kiss her… he contained himself but confusion set in. She reached across the rose-topped table, putting her hand on his.

"I'm glad you're here, Jeff." She smiled, a smile he so well remembered.

"Really?" He tried not to sound surprised, but was. "I mean, are you recalling more memories?"

"Oh yes," she responded, "many things."

"How was the baptism?"

Melissa withdrew her hand and leaned back in the booth, holding her papaya limeade in both hands.

"Jeffrey, it's the most remarkable thing. Well actually, a whole lot of remarkable things have happened; but I baptized more than three hundred voodooists."

"Voodooists?"

"Yes, that's what they call themselves. I feel like my hands spent the night doing God's work. Do you know how hard it is to get a voodooist to start believing in an invisible God and a man named Jesus? Think about it."

She sipped her limeade, then rubbed her finger around the rim of her glass.

"What new memories can you share?"

"I remember our divorce and how upsetting it was, especially to you. I feel so guilty that I put you and the girls through that. I'm not sure why I wanted a divorce, and you seem to be such a nice man. The way you stopped today and helped total strangers, risking your life for people you don't even know."

"Do you remember Rob Jeremias?" Jeff prodded.

"That doesn't ring a bell. Maybe I will remember later. Who is he?"

Jeff paused, thought about what to say and decided to say nothing, when Melissa spoke. She seemed more bubbly than last time, more like the real Melissa.

"Do you remember last time when you were here, over Mother's Day? I asked if you believed in God."

"Yes, I remember."

"You laughed like you thought I was joking."

"At first I thought you were, that you had recalled that I wasn't a ..."

"Believer," she finished. "I couldn't remember, but now I'm beginning to, little by little. You mentioned that if you could see a *sign* you would believe."

"I remember. Is that so bad, Melissa... to want to see proof of some kind?"

"You mean proof other than the eight hundred thousand words that were written about God in the Bible? Writing was very difficult to do when the Bible was written, and Moses wrote the first five books over three thousand years ago."

She smiled and rubbed the rim again.

"I've been having these dreams, strange dreams. And there's something else I remembered but don't know if it's a real memory, it's so odd."

"I wonder…" Jeff started but then stopped.

"You wonder what, Jeffrey?"

"I don't know, Melissa. I wonder how you forgot almost everything but remembered the Bible, and your faith. It's even stronger now than it was. That's just bizarre."

"It's God's doing."

"Maybe so," Jeff said. Then he thought it: *maybe so*.

"Some of my memories are coming back through these strange dreams. I dreamed of Audry and our adoption of her. Seeing the girls was good. Jeffrey, I do have a question I want to ask you, but I don't want to hurt you."

"Ask away. What is it?"

"You were very upset when we got divorced, I dreamed about it. It's the only time I think I ever saw you shed a tear. And for weeks you kept asking, 'Why did God do this to me?'

"Or you would say you just knew 'God had a plan for you, or he wouldn't have done it.' Did you say that, or was it just a dream?"

Jeff motioned the waitress, and she reggaeed her way to the table as Marley played in the background. Her dark blue shorts could've been shorter, but not much. He ordered two more drinks.

"I did say that, it's a real memory. Is that your question?"

"Why would you say that if you don't even believe in God? That makes no sense. My second question is, why were you blaming God for our divorce when it was your doing?"

"What do you mean?" Jeff asked. He didn't like the way this meeting was going. The drinks came, giving him a few seconds to gather his thoughts.

"Just what I said. You were blaming God, a God you don't believe exists, for a situation that you created yourself."

"I guess I don't understand what you're saying Melissa. I know I made comments about your beliefs; but other than that, I thought I was a good husband."

"Do good husbands have affairs?"

"What?" He was astounded.

"Do good husbands have affairs with girls named Mitzi Freeman? You never thought I knew about it; and maybe had I confronted you we would not have gotten divorced, but I kept it inside. It doesn't hurt at all now, but it did then."

"I don't know what to say. I guess I wiped it out of my mind, or tried. It was a bad mistake many years ago."

"But it was *your* mistake, not God's; unless you are telling me that God took Mitzi Freeman to your bedroom at the Las Vegas Hilton.

"Did I tell you about the strange light I saw?" she asked, changing the subject. "I saw it twice."

She knew she hadn't, because that memory had only recently been recalled. Jeff's pulse quickened. He had certainly seen a strange light, several times.

"No, you didn't." He tried to concentrate but suddenly found it difficult. He had forgotten about the affair, it had been so brief and so long ago.

"I only recently remembered it, and I'm still not sure that it happened."

"What kind of light?"

"The night of the wave was the first time. I think I might have died that night; but then I heard someone calling my name, shouting my name actually. My eyes were closed as I floated in the sea, but the light was so intense I could see the blood vessels in my eyelids. It was the strangest thing."

"What did the light say to you?"

"Are you making fun of me?"

"No. Something similar happened to me."

"When?" she asked.

"The same night. It called my name. It's happened before, but not since the night at Cayman."

"What did it say to you, Jeffrey?" She placed her hand on top of Jeff's again, and again he felt the warmth.

"It said my prayer had been answered, my prayer that you would come back." And here she was. The prayer had been answered. "I also had some strange dreams, I guess they were dreams, when I had my near-death experience. You wouldn't know about that, but in one of the dreams I was told that I would see you again. And here you are.

"So what did the light say to you?" Jeff asked.

"It told me to wake up, that God still had work for me to do. It sounded like a horn of some kind when it spoke. At first I was frightened, but then a calmness like I've never felt came over me. Last week I saw the light again, and that's what refreshed my memory. It appeared out of nowhere, right outside my cabin; but no one could see it except me."

"Did it say anything this last time?" he asked.

"Yes, it did."

She sipped her drink and appeared glassy-eyed, or maybe teary.

"It said my mission would soon be complete, and I would be going home. I think my mission was the voodoo people who saved me, to show them that God gave us the greatest sacrifice of all when he sacrificed his very own child, his only child, for us; to save us from ourselves."

Jeff and Melissa talked for another hour, walked through the small park behind the restaurant and held hands. They sat together on a porch swing, in comfortable silence.

"Jeff, I want you and Samarra to get married here in Jamaica. Bring the children so I can see them. I don't know when my mission will be complete, maybe when the witch doctor gets baptized; but I want so much for you to be happy, and I truly do hope you will seek out God. He will accept you if you just ask."

Jeff and Melissa said their goodbyes, and Jeff promised to discuss a Jamaican wedding with Samarra. The warmth was gone, replaced with a melancholy calmness.

The drive back to Geejam Resort was a soul-searching drive as Jeff thought about his one affair and the hurt Melissa must have felt over the years, the betrayal. He thought about blaming God for his divorce, which in retrospect was kind of humorous. She was right, God didn't create the situation, he did. His brief betrayal created heart-wrenching misery for Melissa, hurt for the kids; and then there was his own broken heart.

He gripped the steering wheel tightly as he hit yet another pothole, and he thought about some of the last things Melissa said.

"Pay close attention to the signs, Jeffrey," she told him, "because they are everywhere if one wishes to see. Get prepared because a time is coming on the world, a time of great despair and suffering like the world has never seen. Keep your faith when it comes, and don't bow to the Beast. It's coming like a whirlwind, so fast you will hardly believe it's happening. Google it."

Signs. His mom had warned him of signs, things to watch for just before this Tribulation was to start. He thought briefly about his niece, only twenty years old who had her second abortion last week. He remembered the funeral for Chad's brother, gunned down by a young street gang in Maryland while taking a neighbor to the hospital. He considered the new Supreme Court rulings legalizing polygamy, up to ten partners, and prostitution, ruling that the illegalities of such behavior were based on Judeo-Christian religion. Maybe these were signs that he failed to recognize.

"And speaking of signs," Melissa had told him, "You say you would believe in God if you only had a sign, some 'evidence'. Here's a sign for you: 78% nitrogen and 21% oxygen.

"Oh yeah, I almost forgot. I had a dream last night, it was so real. I was sitting in this small white church, and no one could see me. They were all talking about the rapture and why so many were left behind…"

"Was the church in a field of yellow daffodils?"

"Yes, it was," Melissa said. "Then a lady sat down beside me; and she could hear and see me fine, no problem at all. She seemed to know me, but stranger still she knew you. She said to tell you, 'Missy and Kipper said hello.' They said they will see you soon."

CHAPTER THIRTY-ONE

The Mother's Day Massacre had been a great success in Vinny's mind, not only the killings of the infidel maggots but also the fuel shortage. In the long run, the twelve-dollar-a-gallon gas proved crippling for the average American. Some of the fuel storage facilities still smoldered.

None of his warriors had been caught or lost his life, and the teams were gradually repositioned to other targets. The Great Satan tried to increase security at large events, so they concentrated on smaller congregations of infidels.

Vinny's jihadists were so *normal* looking, and acting. They fit in well, even perfecting regional accents. All were highly skilled, most with degrees in chemical or biological engineering. No one would know that though, because the warriors worked mostly as laborers, air conditioning and heating servicemen, water treatment plant janitors and painters. All had easy access to integral parts of the country's infrastructure.

Today was a special day for Vinny, and he could only laugh at the situation. Vinny had donated generously to Lukeville since the concrete plant was purchased by the anonymous Japanese financiers; free sidewalks throughout the small town, weekly fresh flowers for the Ladies of Lukeville luncheon and most recently, free leather-bound Bibles for the new Cub Scout troop.

The J. Blanton cement plant at the Lukeville border with Mexico had been a gift from Allah. New warriors came through the tunnel every day, and the three plutonium cores had been smuggled through Belize's new government with no problems. Now the cores were securely installed, and the thermonuclear weapons would surely lead the United States to surrender, Insha'Allah. The targets had been carefully selected.

Vinny pulled into Judy's driveway, one of the Blanton's who previously owned the cement plant. No one in Lukeville knew him as Vinny and considered him to be French. He rang the doorbell.

"Jean Philippe! You have a new car!" Judy answered the door too quickly, excited like a school girl. "Are you ready for your parade?"

Vinny was a little forlorn about the attention and was sure Allah wanted the glory; but Allah's glory would come soon. Like any American would do, Vinny did; and he hugged the beautiful Judy enthusiastically. He entered the small but elegant home to the sound of Condi Zimmerman and the news.

"...and eleven more bodies washed ashore in Florida yesterday morning. They are believed to be more victims of Hurricane Abby's rant down the east coast last January. That brings the death toll to almost eight thousand. Most of Florida's east coast was totally destroyed when the nearly two hundred-twenty mile per hour winds redesigned the Intracoastal Waterway and cut off escape routes. Many people died waiting in traffic."

Judy handed Jean a sweet iced tea, a slice of lemon neatly placed over the rim of the glass.

"Merci."

"You don't seem very excited, Jean Philippe. This is a huge deal for little Lukeville. We hardly ever have parades."

The parade in his honor felt a little awkward, plus it could bring unwanted attention. Lukeville had been chosen because of the small population. When he had approached the small town council of three about converting the plant hours temporarily to twenty-four seven, he knew the heavy cement trucks rolling in and out would be disturbing to the aging population. Judy had to be the youngest adult in the entire town.

The council, always courteous, wanted to please Jean Philippe; but the older people expressed their dismay about losing sleep. Jean bribed the people, though they didn't recognize it as a bribe, by promising to pave two streets in dire need and to open a small French restaurant for the town's citizens and the few tourists who stopped by at one of the T-shirt and novelty stands along Main Street.

"And now this from Doraville, Georgia."

"Could we turn this up, ma cherie, just a little."

Judy loved the accent but thought Jean Philippe seemed a little uptight, and why would he be interested in a story from Doraville, Georgia? She handed him the remote and listened.

Dejan the Bosnian had successfully completed the Mother's Day mission in Cushing, and it would be a long time before the Keystone pipeline or the Cushing Oil Fields would be back to normal, if ever. The mission was a huge success, and the results were as expected. Record high gas prices were collapsing the local economies.

He followed the Doraville Oil Storage service van, just as he had done for a week. The driver had a routine. Five-thirty in the morning, breakfast at Waffle House; six-thirty was check-in at the Doraville Bulk Oil storage facility and then a stop for a security check. The facility stored products from most major oil conglomerates, and large storage tanks were filled with millions of gallons of flammable liquid.

A weather siren broke the morning silence, and Dejan scanned the clear skies through the large windows of the Downwind Restaurant, looking for potential hailstorms. Then the siren went silent, another false alarm.

Dejan sipped his coffee and waited as business jets lined up below for takeoff. His iPad sat on the table beside him, and he tracked the service van through his GPS tracking app. The van proceeded through the first stop at check-in, and the tiny yellow tracking light stopped again, this time at security. He glanced at CNN as they covered the latest airliners shot down by *rogue* missiles. The yellow light moved again, this time toward the center of the oil facility, just a few thousand feet from Dekalb-Peachtree Airport where he waited.

Dejan gulped the last of his coffee, left a five-dollar bill on the table and walked out, unnoticed. He looked like everyone else at the small restaurant, just another working man. He walked down the stairs on the side of the building and took a deep breath of the crisp morning air. For a change, it wasn't so hot. That would soon change.

Outside the perimeter security fence of the oil facility, three school buses on a field trip stopped at the railroad tracks. The fifth graders were restless and waited anxiously for the train to come. In the distance the whistle sounded again, a warning.

Dejan exited the restaurant and turned left on Clairmont toward I-85. When he approached Buford Highway, the light turned green, perfectly planned by Allah; and he drove straight across. He dialed a number into his cell phone and on the first ring a connection was made. He listened.

The first explosion was hardly noticeable from the distance, but he heard it nonetheless. It was the second explosion he waited to hear, the one to set off all the others; and he was not disappointed.

Jean Philippe held Judy's hand and liked the softness of her skin as they both watched the screen in horror. Except Judy didn't see horror in Jean's face; more like obsession. Jean found himself unusually attracted to the young woman, she just seemed to be such a good and generous person; but he was sure she would never convert to the true religion.

Judy had an *influence* on him, a feeling of something… different. He couldn't quite put his toe on it, but he liked it. Judy squeezed his hand gently and watched him as he focused on the black smoke rising from the orange flames. The third explosion, much larger than the previous two, blew a wide, orange barrier fence completely away and the news helicopter video went dark.

"Did we lose him? Just a second, did we lose the helicopter?" Condi stared at her laptop. *"Folks, we'll be right back."*

The news helicopter pilot and cameraman struggled to stay conscious. The experienced pilot thought they were maintaining a safe distance; but now the aircraft was tumbling through the air, and the two men remained incoherent from the blast. The helicopter finally crash-landed upside down and was still recognizable, though it was much smaller than it had been a minute before.

The young cameraman was a graduate from the University of North Carolina, armed with a degree in journalism and a 4.0, straight-A average. His family later told the Channel 2 reporter that he had been so excited about his first day on the job.

"Now, we're planning a funeral," the father said and burst into tears. Smoke continued to rise on Judy's TV screen, and Jean was mesmerized.

"Are you ready to go? We need to get to the starting line."

"In a minute! Please!"

Jean Philippe hadn't actually yelled at Judy, but it was a stern command. She had met her share of control freaks and had no plans to go there again. She would pay closer attention to the man's actions rather than the French accent.

"The Doraville Oil Storage Depot is ablaze. We reported that a large, orange barrier fence was demolished; but... but, this is sad news folks, it wasn't an orange barrier, it was three school buses on a field trip. We have no casualty reports, but the buses seemed to just disappear. There has been no cause given for the disaster, but initial reports from security said it was 'accidental and not an act of terrorism' so stay tuned."

Of course there was "no cause" given. Vinny and his Jihad's Warriors buddies learned long ago to accept no responsibility for anything. Let them keep guessing.

"Are you ready, ma cherie?"

Judy and Jean Philippe spent the rest of the day together and rode in the white, 1999 Continental convertible at the front of the Lukeville parade. But something felt different, she thought. Jean's mood seemed elevated after the news, rather than dismal. He was almost jubilant. How could he not be dismal when he just saw three school buses full of kids get blown away?

The parade ended at 2:00, just as planned; and the Ladies of Lukeville Society, all five, gave Jean Philippe a round of applause as he strolled over to offer friendly hugs. Judy wasn't sure she had ever seen the Ladies so thrilled.

"Can we leave? I've developed a headache."

Though December, the early afternoon temperature already approached a hundred degrees; and Judy did have a headache. But it was more than that, and she hoped he wouldn't want to come in. In less than three minutes, they were back in Judy's driveway. She was polite, asked him if he would like to come in for tea but hoping he wouldn't.

"Merci but no, Miss Judy. I would love to, but I have to go meet Bubba."

"Bubba?"

Judy was sure she had never heard Jean Philippe mention that name, but this was the second time it had come up in two days. Yesterday at the Stop-n-Mart a government agent of some kind was questioning the owner about a man named *Bubba* and showing him a photo. The manager shook his head *no*, and the agent had shown the photograph to Judy. She studied the picture but didn't recognize the stranger.

"Pardon moi?"

"You said you were going to meet Bubba?"

"No, no… I said I was going to meet a buddy."

Jean walked Judy to her door when a sudden gust nearly blew her summer dress sky-high. She pulled it down around her legs, blushing all the while. Another gust-from-nowhere blew hard, and a trashcan flew down the street. That's when she saw a small piece of paper fly out of Jean's back pocket. She said nothing.

Jean gave her a friendly hug but found himself quite interested in the beautiful legs he had just seen. He would pursue this woman; he liked her.

Judy turned to close her front door but watched Jean through the small windows as he drove away in his minivan. After waiting to make sure he didn't turn around, she walked to the edge of the sidewalk; and there it was, stuck in the azalea bush.

The white piece of paper turned out to be a photograph of a man she thought looked vaguely familiar. She searched her memory and quickly recalled the photograph the government agent had shown her and the Stop-n-Mart owner, a man named Bubba. This looked like the same man. She turned the photo over, but the only word on the back was *Mahmud*.

CHAPTER THIRTY-TWO

"No attacks in three months. What do you attribute that to?"

Abe and Jeff waited on breakfast at *Family Restaurant*, watching the news and listening to Duluth's finest rush up-and- down Buford Highway. The restaurant was packed and the din of the mid-morning diners was constant. The aroma of 45 Main Street coffee permeated the air. No one even glanced out the windows anymore, screaming sirens had become the norm.

"Must be another robbery."

"They're waiting I think, Abe. Now that the ringleader broke out of prison, who knows? Bubba Haskins has been all over the news, so they will catch him. It's only a matter of time."

Jeff glanced out the large front windows and saw Marcus Johnson Wilhelm III, the town Romeo, hanging around outside by the newspaper stand and leaning against the wall.

The three thirty-something ladies who had been eating fruit salads in the back booth earlier, walked out the front door and across the newly-paved parking lot toward the burgundy Cadillac convertible. The wind was gusty as usual and blew their short dresses, teasingly.

Jeff found it hard to believe they could walk in the high-heels which seemed to get higher and higher every year, but they wore them well as other men in the dining area watched the three attractive women strut across the lot. They also got the attention of the town Romeo, no longer leaning against the wall for support but following the three toward the Cadillac.

"The American Legion's having another meeting tonight at the Red Clay Theater. They have two guest speakers, a couple of doctors who helped chase down a suspect in the Atlanta VA Hospital bombing. You want me to reserve you a spot?"

Jeff shook his head. "I've got too many things to do. I'm getting married you know!"

"Yep, and I will be there! I need to be there to pick you up if you fall down. Are you getting the wedding suite or the senior's suite?"

"We're getting the wedding suite, but I get the senior rate; the best of both worlds, smarty pants."

Jeff watched as one of the three women, the short one, took off her high-heels but kept walking.

"I read about the Legion in the *Gwinnett Daily Post*," Jeff continued. "Seems that the American Legion in Duluth and Alpharetta have formed a coalition to take back the streets. People are laughing, the folks are so old; but I'll tell you what… I went to a turkey shoot at the Legion last Christmas, and those guys can shoot. A sixty year old lady came in first. I don't think their Allah will be much help if they run into these war vets."

Abe laughed and buttered his grits. Another siren came their way, and a couple of people gathered at the window.

"Yeah, since the four rabbis were shot in Atlanta on Mother's Day, the groups have become more sympathetic to Israel, a backfire I would say. The VFW's also involved, as well as the Lake Lanier Bass Fisherman. Those guys are still ticked that the dam was blown up."

Abe glanced in the parking lot, more than inquisitive as the sirens moved closer.

"I think we're on the verge of martial law," Abe continued.

Jeff didn't mention that Wild Willy felt the same way.

"Do you know those three gals?" Jeff asked as the crowd grew at the front window, many laughing out loud.

"Yeah, they're on the way to the American Legion meeting, as soon as they get through with Mr. Wilhelm. Most people call them the Three Wild Women."

"Why do they call them that?" Jeff had heard of them before but couldn't place it.

"Uhhh, because they're wild? They are a little wild but in a good way. They win sharp-shooting awards, they all have a black belt in something and are always helping out the poor kids. Right now, they're probably holding Marcus for the police."

"Really?"

"Yep. Marcus gets drunk and thinks all the women fall in love with him. Sometimes he gets a little, shall we say, amorous."

A police car pulled into the parking lot, and before long Romeo was carted away with a bloody nose and an abrasion on his arm.

"Did you ever figure out what Melissa meant about the 78% nitrogen and 21% oxygen? Didn't she say it was a 'sign'?"

"Yeah, I think so. Did I tell you she saw our light in the sky?"

The two friends made their way to the cash register and past the attractive waitresses. Another set of sirens chased up Buford Highway, and Abe wondered how *Family Restaurant* got all the waitress babes.

"The waitresses look like movie stars."

"Yeah, Wild Willy would go crazy over the blonde," Abe chuckled, "or the redhead or brunette."

"Not anymore. Wild Willy has been in love since Labor Day. Says it's the real thing."

"Yeah," Abe laughed. "This time."

Jeff and Abe parted ways; and Jeff made his way toward Sugarloaf Country Club, hoping Samarra was as happy as she seemed. Tomorrow would come soon enough, and he had to pack for a wedding. New Year's Eve was less than a week away.

Jeff thought a lot about Melissa's "sign" and guessed it could be a sign, 21% oxygen and 78% nitrogen. It was certainly unique in the world, and he should've figured it out right away, considering his interest in astronomy. The world governments had spent billions looking for life on other planets but had found nothing remotely close to the atmospheric gasses that made life possible to sustain. It seemed that Earth was truly unique.

Entering his home, Samarra greeted him with a kiss and a smile that could melt any man's heart. He pulled her close.

"Whoa cowboy, we have company."

"Daddy, Mr. Hutz is on TV, come watch it with me."

Jeff walked outside to the Cabana by the pool. Audry was reclining in a lounge chair, sipping lemonade.

"He's talking about the rapture."

CHAPTER THIRTY-THREE

Vinny checked into the small motel in Newark. His meeting with Bubba "Mahmud" Haskins had mostly been for Mahmud's benefit, bringing him up to date on the planned New Year's Eve activities. It would be quite astounding if everything went as planned. Of course, hardly anything went off without a hatch, Vinny knew that for sure; but he also knew that Allah was on his side.

Bubba's escape from the high-security prison for terror suspects had been too simple. Once the EMP fried all the electronic circuits and the security guards had been killed, it was as simple as a small explosion outside the dormitories. With the walls breached, the thirty-two prisoners from Guantanamo were on their own to create more havoc.

The escape had been flawless as the men jumped into and sped away in the 1960 vintage pickup trucks, trucks built long before the days of electronic, solid-state circuits. There were none to fry, and the trucks ran flawlessly.

Vinny took a quick shower and applied the gray dye. After dressing, he walked out on the balcony of his third floor room and noticed the old man across the street standing at the front door of the huge non-denominational church. He wore a sandwich board advertising *The End Is Near* on both sides of his tall, lanky body. He held another sign in both hands and preached to the small gathering around the entrance.

"Come in if you *dare* to know the truth about the end of these days and the beginning of the new kingdom. Come in if you *dare* to hear the good news about Jesus and your escape from the coming wrath of the Lord. Pray hard so you won't have to endure the terrible Tribulation."

Vinny was a brilliant man, and with that came a certain curiosity. He combed his new head of salt and pepper hair, sprayed some cologne and headed across the street because he *dared.*

Entering the church and sitting in the back pew, Vinny looked *non-denominational* up on his iPhone. The church service hadn't started but would soon, according to three ladies talking loudly about the rapture. Vinny had never heard the term.

The women seemed to be arguing, something about a friend who disappeared "in thin air" while shopping at Walmart.

"She disappeared into thin air, that's what I'm talkin' about."

The huge flatscreen at the front of the church was tuned to a news program, and the mysterious Chuck Hutz was being interviewed. The church ladies didn't seem quite clear as to who or what Mr. Hutz might be; but they called for quiet, and the other members acquiesced. Condi Zimmerman asked Chuck why some people had disappeared but others who attended church regularly did not. The church was quiet as a church mouse.

"I'm not sure what it means, Condi. I guess I didn't make the first cut either." Chuck smiled an uneasy smile. "*Maybe there's a reason some are taken and some are left behind who feel they have a strong Christian faith. I haven't led a flawless life by any means. Some have been faithful their entire lives. I do believe that God has a purpose for all who love him, and don't deny him."*

"That means," someone shouted from across the large, open sanctuary, "That means that Chuck Hutz is full of donkey crap. That's what it means. There's a reason people call him *Hutz the Putz*. The man's a maniac!"

Self-proclaimed Bishop Jethro Moneyangel had no use for the likes of Chuck Hutz and his gloomy news about the fall of man. The bishop had grown his church from just a few members to several thousand in a short period of time; and the church members almost worshipped him. He loved the glory and attention he got from preaching what the flock wanted to hear.

Jethro Moneyangel was a prosperity preacher though he denied the recognition. He just preached the *Good* news about the Bible and God's tremendous love for all, especially those who tithed generously. No one wanted to hear all the doom and gloom the smaller churches preached. *God wants us all to be rich and happy* was his message with a common slant:

"The more you tithe to my church, the richer the blessings from God. If you want money, give God money. God Almighty asked for 10%! Think how happy He will be if you give twenty percent, or thirty percent! Praisssse Jessusss!"

It was a simple message; and the flock gave freely, though most couldn't pay their rent. Bishop Moneyangel wasn't used to being questioned about the rapture and had never spoken of the phenomenon. He wasn't even sure it was scriptural. The Book of Revelation was not in his repertoire, too scary for his flock. If the flock believed the end was near, they would stop tithing and hoard money for their families. That certainly wouldn't be Godly.

"What kind of purpose?" Condi asked.

"I don't know. Maybe some will be taken before others. Maybe some will be left here to help others become believers, so they don't have to experience the terror of all the last days.

Jesus told his own followers to pray they wouldn't have to go through the terror of those days. He had a way of always being right, know what I mean?

"When Jesus was explaining to his apostles what it would be like in the time of the end, he said that two people would be in a field and one would be taken, the other not. He didn't say the 'other' would have to endure the entire wrath of the last days. I can only believe that God has a purpose for me to be here talking to you, and to others. I hope I have God's blessings, that God has given me communication skills that will help others."

"Help others make the cut?" Condi asked with a smile.

Though Vinny had never heard of the rapture, he listened intently. There was nothing like it in the Quran. Still, he thought about the concept; and the possibility.

"Exactly. In the last days, it won't just be wars and people killing each other. The Bible describes all sorts of 'natural' disasters, but these will not be natural by any means. God will make it happen. He is fed up with His creation, and if..."

The OLNN satellite feed suddenly went dark, the listening flock now on the edge of their seats. The din rose in disappointment, but Bishop Moneyangel took it as a sign from God.

"The Lord has the final word," he shouted, and the ushers began to pass multiple gold, tithing plates. "There ain't nobody been raptured yet; or God knows, we wouldn't be here!"

The flock pulled out their cash, and Bishop Moneyangel seemed to glow as the bright theater lights shined down on him. His face beamed and he seemed to shimmer from head to toe. He saved his best smile for the new choir director, the slender, *gorgeous* choir director, as she led the congregation in a gospel song they sang every Sunday:

> *"He said He'd open up the windows of Heaven,*
> *Pour you out a blessing*
> *"He will supply you every need*
> *according to his riches in glory*
> *Give and you shall receive*
> *If you want to be blessed*
> *Give and you shall receive."*

CHAPTER THIRTY-FOUR

"There will be signs in the sun, moon and stars..."
Luke 21:25

"Cheers!"

The wedding crowd held their crystal champagne glasses in the air and saluted the newlyweds. It was approaching midnight, and the Jamaican sky was clear as a bell. A stream of meteorites flowed horizontally through the night sky, God's light show; and a new year would begin in less than an hour.

"Cheers right back atcha," Jeff toasted after his third glass of Dom Perignon. He was a merlot drinker; and champagne made him silly, or at least he had been told.

Melissa watched Jeffrey and Samarra as they walked toward the calm surf, just a few yards away. Suddenly memories of Samarra flooded her mind, her goodness and the turmoil she suffered at the kidnapping of her young son. She was happy, joyful actually, that Jeffrey and Samarra had become one. Her mission was completed yesterday when she baptized the witch doctor, and he accepted Christ as the world's savior.

Audry insisted that she be allowed to celebrate New Year's Eve with the wedding party; and Melissa cried softly, mostly in joy, as she recalled memories with her precious daughters. The twins were beautiful in the pink moonlight, and a small breeze ruffled their hair and sundresses.

The Admiral and Sheryl held hands on the beach, and Sheryl's flowing dress was beautifully tropical. Wild Willy laughed out loud as he told everyone over and over again about Aludra, his future bride, maybe. He really did seem to be in love, like Samarra and Jeff… Melissa's mind wandered and she felt almost like she was floating.

"You are gorgeous, Melissa. I know you may not remember me telling you that before, but… well, you look so happy."

Melissa vaguely remembered Abe the Bartender; but she really liked him a lot, everyone did. Though she had known him for only a few years, not like most of her friends who were long-term, she saw an inner beauty inside the man.

"I am happy, Abe. Love is in the air at this beach, and I am in love with God. I will be joining him soon."

Abe told her how distraught Jeff had been after the tsunami, thinking she had been killed. He told her about Jeff's Spanish Flu and near-death experience. But mostly they talked about the rapture, if it exists and the afterlife.

In the distance along the cove, The Admiral and Sheryl hugged in the night and stared at the beautiful Jamaican sky. Melissa studied the Moon and thought it was awesome. A pink moon with pink and white rings and a background of intermittent shooting stars crossing the horizon. She felt strange.

Chapter Thirty-Five

Vinny drove south along I-85 and was making great time. Interstates weren't nearly as busy as they had been, before Jihad's Warriors started their gradual takeover of the United States and European governments a few years earlier. He reminisced about the first attacks, the closure of the Lincoln Tunnel in New York was the best… except for the Buford Dam. He smiled at *that* explosion, like none he had ever seen; and the dam was destroyed in seconds.

His blue minivan looked *family;* and of course a family had been the previous owners before they took a swim. A decal on the rear window claimed an Honor Student at Lincoln High School, and a *Support the Ten Commandments* sticker was neatly placed on the back bumper and sanded to look a little worn. He had a long drive ahead of him as he entered North Carolina, two minutes 'til the midnight hour.

Their plan had been almost flawless; and the United States economy was close to collapse, even though the spinners kept telling everyone it was great and getting better. Not after *this* night, he thought and smiled at the coming destruction. He loved explosions.

Actually he would have preferred to be in Manhattan when the eight briefcase nukes went off, especially if they all went off as planned; but he was too valuable to the organization. Bubba had been a great leader, as covert as covert could be; but then he got caught. The organization was well-pleased with Vinny and his accomplishments since taking over for Bubba, especially Bubba's amazing prison-break from the so-called max-security prison. He would now be the man in charge. Off to the left of the interstate, the sky lit up with a premature fireworks display.

As the clock struck midnight and a New Year dawned, the Tiffany's crystal ball high above Times Square, complete with the latest LED lighting technology, began its final descent.

The record crowd of two million people roared; and the young girl held Momma's hand tightly, searching the sky for the large dark balloons she had just seen. The approaching sirens could no longer be heard above the crowds.

"Honey, watch the crystal ball. Look, you're not watching."

The child did turn and glance at the ball, but then her eyes diverted once again to search for the large balloons. She jumped as the fireworks began to display high overhead, each boom quite frightening as the huge crowd roared. That's when she noticed the helicopters in the distance, flying between the large New York skyscrapers, headed directly toward her.

Suddenly, as the crowd finally began to take note of the loud thump-thump-thump of the black helicopters, loaded to the gills with rockets, the intimidating flying machines made drastic climbs, turning almost vertically into the night sky.

Momma looked upward and pulled her young daughter close. Something was going on; but the record crowd partied on into the night.

CHAPTER THIRTY-SIX

Melissa and Abe meandered down to the white sandy beach where the wedding group stood on the shore, watching the nighttime display of glowing fireballs in the distance, God's own Fireworks Display. Less than a minute until the New Year dawns.

"I feel so… light-headed," Melissa said as she paused, the cool sand now between the toes of her bare feet. Bob Marley music played in the background.

"Are you okay?" Abe asked and held her by the arm.

"No… no, I feel great. I don't know if I've ever felt this great. It's so odd, and sudden."

"Are you alright, Melissa?" Samarra asked as she and Jeff approached. They weren't really concerned until they saw in the pink moonlight the look on Abe's face.

Melissa explained to the now growing crowd that she felt fantastic. They made their way toward the water's edge of the almost silent lapping of the sea, toward the twins and Audry.

Melissa's mind began to explore and like a movie, she recalled the events of the day. It seemed like it was in slow motion. She recalled nearly every word of her conversation with Jeff about the *sign*.

"Did you figure out what I meant by the 78% and 21% thing?"

"I think I did."

"I thought you would, Jeffrey; being the astronomy nerd." They had laughed. "So what did you figure out, Mr. Mensa?"

"You were talking about the atmosphere, the Earth's atmosphere, that it's made up of 78% nitrogen and 21% oxygen."

"Do you see why I said it is a sign that God exists?"

Jeff paused, thinking about how to answer.

"Melissa, it may be proof. I wish I didn't need proof, but it's the way I have always been."

"Jeff, if we had 77% nitrogen and 22% oxygen," Melissa continued, "we would all be dead, as would the plants. Just a single percent variation, and there would be no life as we know it. Isn't it odd that astronomers have never found anything… out there?" and she pointed toward the sky, "Somewhere that's even remotely like Earth and our atmosphere? I don't mean in our own solar system but out *there*, way out there. We've spent billions and billions looking for life *out there*, but we haven't seen even a slight glimpse of an atmosphere that could support it.

"You're right," Jeff agreed. "It is odd that in this huge realm of space that we can search, there hasn't been a single planet seen that is anything like Earth." Or even close, he thought silently.

"Mom, are you okay?" Jenni called out as the other two turned to face the approaching group. "You're glowing."

"What?" Melissa asked.

"Mom, you're glowing," Jami screamed, worried but at the same time in awe at the beauty of the sight. "Mom, you look like an angel."

The wedding crowd stared, and Melissa felt an overwhelming warmth of confidence.

CHAPTER THIRTY-SEVEN

With the screaming crowd and the screaming helicopters, the young girl covered her ears with her hands, clearly distressed.

High above the buildings of New York City, the helicopters searched frantically for the sets of balloons that had been detected by a radiation monitoring system on one of the unarmed surveillance drones flying over Times Square.

The bright crystal ball approached the ground slowly, the crowd shouted in glee and the young girl and her mother clung to each other as the helicopters began firing rockets just above the building tops. No one seemed to notice; and when the ball hit the ground, the night sky lit up like a thousand suns.

The first people blinded by the blast of the simultaneous nuclear explosions were the helicopter crews and a young girl and her mother, looking up into the night sky.

There were no screams among the Times Square crowds below as more than two million innocent revelers lost their sight, the retinas instantly seared beyond repair.

A conventional bombing would have brought screams and agony; but like the eyes, the vocal chords were instantly vaporized, along with the skin and lungs. Death was kind, because it was instantaneous.

A crowd of tourists that had been standing alongside the new Rockstar Café would be forever memorialized in the single, remaining marble wall of the building, their shadows seared into the wall as had been the case in Nagasaki and Hiroshima in 1945.

Like the crowds below, the helicopters weren't blown up but melted… evaporated actually under the intense heat of the nuclear-generated fireballs. Not a single piece made it to the ground as the carbon-fiber bodies simply ceased to exist.

When the blast wave subsided, there were no sirens; and far in the distance New York City's finest tried to reconcile what had just happened. The city had been down before, like after the destruction of the twin towers; but this time the police and fire department staff weren't so sure.

The new One World Trade Center no longer stood at 1776 feet, with the top two-thirds now lying in ruins on the streets below, a large pile of steel and concrete hiding the burning bodies of thousands. The terrorists had succeeded again, destroying the tallest building in America. The city was on fire.

With the loss of Wall Street and the financial capital of the world, nearly every ATM machine in the United States became inoperable in an instant.

CHAPTER THIRTY-EIGHT

Melissa enjoyed the cool sand squeezing between her toes; and the air seemed to have an extra dose of oxygen, the energy seeping through every pore in her soft skin.

She had never taken drugs, at least recreational drugs; but she guessed she must feel like someone high on *some* substance. She had certainly never felt this way in her life, and she started laughing out loud.

Jake the Bellman at the Geejam Resort ran toward the beach, shouting something in the native Patois; but none of the group understood the lyrical language. Something about news, it sounded like. The newly baptized witch doctor recognized Jake and glanced skyward in the direction Jake was pointing.

In the distant sky, a star appeared out of nowhere, unnoticed by the crowd but not by Jake and the witch doctor; and he continued pointing toward the heavens. He tried to scream as he pointed, but not a sound came out.

The star moved across the sky swiftly and stopped directly above the wedding crowd, not much brighter than any other star in the night sky; only it was moving. As Jake and the witch doctor stared open-mouthed, the light hovered over the crowd on the beach below and brightened. There was no sound.

Melissa turned and looked up at the strange light and knew she had seen it before. Jeff looked skyward, directly above him; and he too recognized the blip of light. He looked at Abe then back at the light he hadn't seen since the Cayman Islands tsunami. It brightened ever-so-slowly, something different from his other viewings where the light was as bright as a photographer's flash.

The wind began to blow, not steady like most Caribbean breezes but gusty and whimsical. The light continued to brighten high above, and it began to take shape of something; and this was also new.

Suddenly the crowd felt movement beneath their feet as the ground began to shift, and Jeff tried to recall if Jamaica had an earthquake history; but then the ground stopped moving as suddenly as it started. The witch doctor and Jake looked upward at the shape-forming light; and fear streaked across their faces, now plainly visible as the light intensity grew.

Melissa turned to face her children, but little Audry was the only one to speak.

"Goodbye, Mommy. I love you."

From what had been a small white light, high in the Jamaican sky, a downward spire of brightness began to lower and the wind became silent. Suddenly, there were no sounds, no night crickets singing love songs, just silence.

Melissa smiled at Audry, held her arms just above her head and focused on the light. Then she looked over at Jeff and Samarra standing next to her; and held Jeff's hand in her own.

"Listen to Abe," she said, "and you will know the truth. God is not mythology."

Melissa's face glowed, she kissed him softly on the lips and made a final statement in a language he had heard but didn't understand, Patois.

The blip of light transformed into the light Jeff had seen in the past, except this time it was shaped… like a cross, a crucifix-type cross. A loud voice descended out of heaven; but it wasn't God, Jeff knew that for sure, for it was Melissa's voice.

"Here's a Sign."

That was it, three little words. Then there was the bright flash, like the old Kodak Brownie flash cubes; and the light was gone. So was Melissa.

"Melissa!" Jeff shouted, but he knew she wasn't there. She was holding his hand, and then she disappeared.

"She's gone to be with God, Daddy."

Jeff ignored Audry's comment and continued to search for Melissa. Jake the Bellman, now a part of the crowd, saw Jeff glancing frantically, as was his new wife, up and down the cove.

"She be done disappeared, Mistuh Ross. I seen it wit my own eyeballs, I did."

"What did she say, Jake? She was speaking Patois."

Jake looked around the wedding crowd, mentally counting to see if anyone else disappeared.

"She be speakin' to you, Mistuh Ross. She pray God forgive you for not b'leivin' and she say…"

Jake's voice drifted to silence, and the witch doctor spoke.

"De Lady uh de Sea sayin t'ings goin' ta get riddy, riddy bad. Dat what she say."

The crowd meandered in silence, no longer searching for Melissa. They had seen her disappear with their own eyes. She hadn't ascended slowly up the spire of strange light. She simply vanished, clothes and all. Abe and Judi walked over to Jeff, and Abe looked him squarely in the eyes.

"Do you believe in the rapture now?"

CPSIA information can be obtained
at www.ICGtesting.com
Printed in the USA
BVHW070002050821
613450BV00004B/326